ASIAN ANTHOLOGY

NEW WRITING VOL. 1

EDITED BY

IVY NGEOW

First published in Great Britain in 2022 by Leopard Print

CONTENTS

INTRODUCTION

Asia. Four letters, three billion people.

These 23 shorts capture the paradox of richness, diversity and humour that is Asia.

Born and raised in Johor Bahru, I am now living in my fourth culture. Through my grandparents I lived my first culture, being Chinese. Through my parents, I enjoyed the abundance and distinctiveness (and food) of Malaysian culture, my second, then as an Australian student, my third (the culture of sun, sea, studies), and finally through myself, my fourth culture, British. I have found that humanity is more similar than not, which I'm sure you will also find apparent when you read the stories and meet the wonderful and engaging characters.

Asian Anthology: New Writing Vol. 1 is a unique first-of-its-kind project, whose objective is to give new voices from all over the world a chance as well as more established and prize-winning writers. It has always been my dream to read more of the kind of books that I was raised with — international stories with great storytelling on multiple themes.

Leopard Print is a digital first indie press established in 2019 in

London. Apart from the requirement for the writing to be set in Asia, writers of any nationality or gender were eligible to submit for this publication, in keeping with Leopard Print's inclusion and diversity policy. The contributors in this book have come from Malaysia, Singapore, India, Myanmar, Hong Kong, Serbia, Austria, France, the United Kingdom and the United States of America.

We brush with surrealism in *Riding the Killer Fish*, where a leprechaun in Japan warns about eating fugu. In *OBE in my Office*, the narrator enjoys an out of body experience (OBE) in his colleagues' presence. *Buaya Tembaga* focuses on a dive instructor on a symbolic self-discovery journey in Tioman who learns the legend of *Bujang Senang*, the killer crocodile.

From magical realism, we enjoy the wicked comicality of a satirical cozy paranormal mystery, *Night of the Seventh Month*. A psychic club meets in a faded Penang beach resort during the Chinese month of the Hungry Ghost. I'll say no more. Another story with strong characterisation and a supernatural element is the romantic suspense, *The Brooches*, told from the viewpoint of an Indonesian maid and the wealthy man who had employed her.

They say that in Asia, street food is never far from your front door or your heart. A favourite vendor, or hawker as they are known in Asia, gains a loyal fan in the coming-of-age story, *Laksa Uncle*, and in the *Mee Mamak* farce, food is a silent main character in the theatre of comedy.

What it means to be a modern woman in Asia is beautifully characterised and captured in both *Her Fluttering Womb* in which a Singaporean woman of child-bearing age starts to experience weird pangs, and *A Sparkle of Fireflies* where a young Japanese businesswoman has a hotel rendezvous with an older man. The irony of 'sparkling' and 'fluttering' would not be lost on readers: the modern Asian woman is confident, open-minded and independent, both financially and emotionally. But it did take us thousands of years and about forty minutes to get here.

The element of dark and psychological suspense is present in *The Dog Walker*, *Shark's Best Friend* and *Banu*. In *Shark's Best Friend*, the barbaric tradition of the shark's fin soup delicacy gives rise to chilling consequences while in *Banu*, the very real and pressing issue of ecological destruction is told through the themes of corruption and greed in the logging and deforestation industry. In *The Dog Walker* satire a gigantic dog is the silent main character connecting two worlds in KL, the super rich and the lower middle managerial class.

The socioeconomic divide is also told through stories of struggle. *Winter Solstice* takes us to Hong Kong, a smoky night of 'fire magic' or petrol bombs during its period of political unrest. In *The Deepest Heart*, a Burmese man reflects on his burning ambition to educate himself, while overcoming obstacles in an environment and family that is hostile to learning.

Struggles are not limited to those of an economic and sociocultural nature. Those pertaining to family were to be expected in this anthology, due to the significance and dominance of family life in Asia. The tension and guilt in Chinese family rifts are expressed explosively in *Treacherous Strand* and *Spring Onions*. Both from the viewpoint of young girls in conflict with the older generation, they raise the themes of 孝 or xiao (filial piety and duty). For thousands of years, the ideas which have stemmed from Confucius' teachings, have been passed down through the generations, such that with each decision, and each tier of education, young people struggle between doing what they want and doing the 'right thing', whatever the 'right thing' now means and by extension, do they even know what they want? Don't parents, with their experience and judgement, know better?

Similarly, we feel both parental and filial guilt and forgiveness, when a man questions his own role as a son and a father in *A Father's Son*; it is a moving account of a man who returns home to attend his abusive and estranged father's funeral in India, unsure if he will find reconciliation.

Writings with a sense of place, the unexpected encounter, the white-guy-in-Asia trope and the downright bizarre have always been popular. At once frightening, surprising and entertaining, they transport us. Someone once said that the most luxurious place in the world is in our mind.

Richly told and set in one of the most beautiful places on earth, a British middle-class couple scouting for a glamorous wedding venue are surprised to experience the ritual of Nyepi, the Balinese annual *Day of Silence*. In *Last Exit to Bugis Street*, a coming-of-age LOL story set in Singapore, a teenager and his brothers meet for street food dinner. The *Courier to Seoul* is an American man on a secret mission to deliver documents to Korea. *Full Moon Over Tawi-tawi*, a dark and humorous account of a not-exactly-ideal night, takes place in a not-exactly-ideal hotel with a grand name on a remote island in the Philippines. In Indonesia, a helicopter trip for a punctual and efficient businessman in *The Pocket Watch Expert of Kalimantan* leads to meeting a different kind of time-keeper.

Most readers in Asia are bilingual, if not trilingual. Those who can will enjoy reading the prize-winning *Diari Sepi Seorang Mudi* in its original Malay, which is followed by its English translation, *Secret Diary of an Outsider*. Lyrical, heartfelt and political, our final story is a lamentation in the Arabic tradition, from the viewpoint of a young Muslim woman, through whom we glimpse her oppressors.

As someone who grew up seeking and devouring Asian stories, I consider myself fortunate to be involved in this exciting project. It is in our collective interest, as readers and writers, to hear more diverse voices. It takes a village to raise a book.

I hope you enjoy these stories.

Ivy Ngeow
February 2022

Editor's note

The original language of the stories (British or American English) and the individual authors has been retained. Non-English words have not been italicised, just as croissant and spaghetti which are also non-English, are not, and just as palatable.

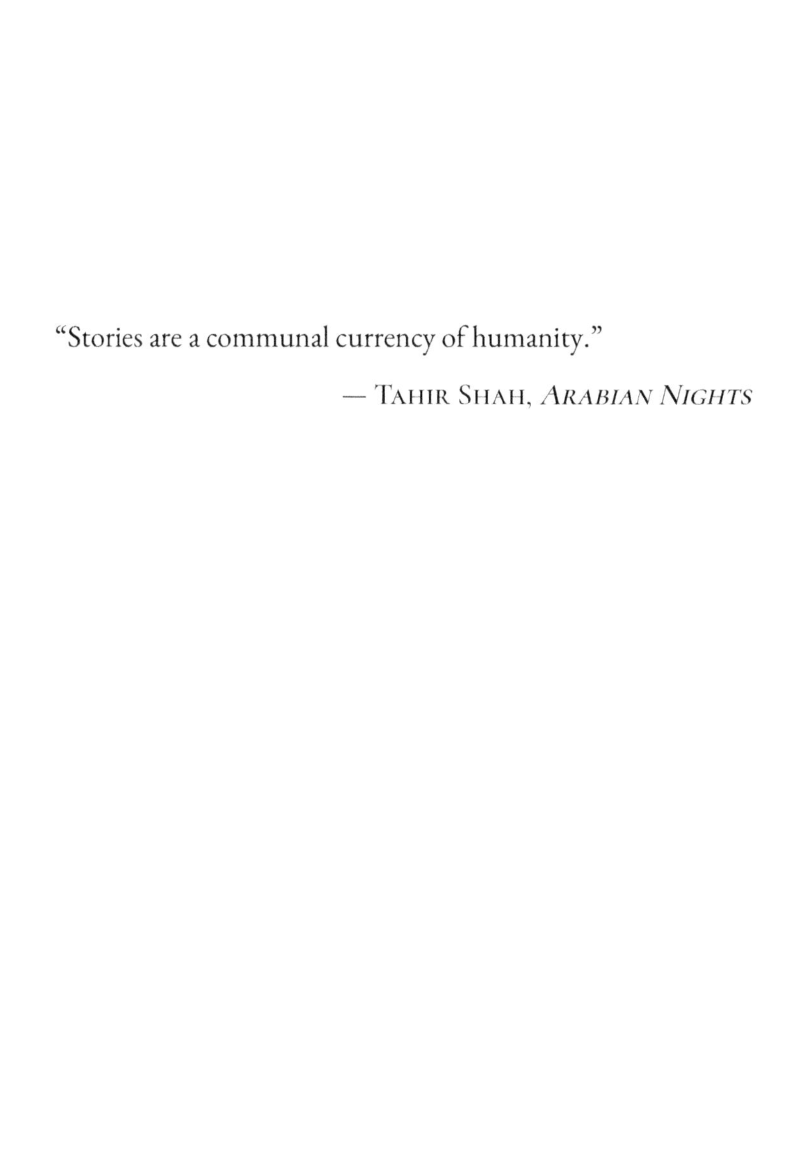

"Stories are a communal currency of humanity."

— Tahir Shah, *Arabian Nights*

Spring Onions

Yang Ming

Like most devotees, Ning's mother, Suyin, spent her Saturday afternoons visiting Singapore's Chinese temples. For the past year, she had meticulously listed them on a piece of neatly folded foolscap paper, and visited one each weekend after closing her steamed bun shop for the day. She arrived at the temple each week with two red plastic bags containing fruit. Ning stood next to her mother, hands clasped, observing her overturn the bags: apples and oranges tumbled out onto the table. Suyin assembled them on two paper plates in groups of five and placed them at the altar. It was done so mechanically that Ning swore her mother could have done it with her eyes closed.

That Saturday, Ning had accompanied her mother to Thian Hock Keng for prayers. Ning was a month away from an examination that had the potential to define her future. After learning about her daughter's dismal mid-year test results, Ning's mother had found it hard to sleep. Ning's older brother, Ren, on the other hand, had fared much better in his academic studies. A student highly regarded by his peers, Ning's mother did not need to worry about her son. Ning had never wanted to be part of this prayer nonsense but, at her mother's insistence, she dragged her feet to the temple. She considered it a waste of her time; she would rather film a series of life hack videos for TikTok than standing idly at the temple.

"Ma, why do you offer spring onions to Confucius?" Ning asked. Instead of fruit, Ning's mother had prepared a plate of spring onions and steamed buns as offerings to the Confucius statue. Outside, heavy rain fell on the ground like water gushing through a drain. Ning cast a glance at the temple's rooftop, its curved ridges and elongated eaves with upturned swallow-tail decoration blocking the grey skies. Fat raindrops began to whip Ning's legs, causing her to retreat further into the temple's statue shelter. Ning's mother had followed her usual practice of waiting for fifteen minutes for the gods to 'eat' the offerings before clearing them away. Ning wondered if they liked spring onions; she certainly did not.

"Spring onion is 聪 in Mandarin. Cong. It means intelligence. You will need it for your exams," Ning's mother replied, folding her arms across her chest.

The smell of the incense coil burning in the main hall spread through the air. Ning was surprised to find the smell soothing and she likened it to sandalwood incense sticks from her favourite aromatherapy shop.

"My friends say praying to Confucius will help you in your exams," Ning's mother said as she rummaged in her bag for her phone. She fished it out and began to tap away.

Ning wanted very much to tell her mother that she was going to fail her upcoming examinations, and no amount of prayers or offerings to any deities would work but she couldn't summon the courage.

"Time to clear the table," her mother said, walking towards the altar. Putting her hands together, her mother uttered a few inaudible sentences and bowed to the statue three times before shoving the offerings into the plastic bags. Ning followed suit, bowing grudgingly.

Under the minimal lighting, her mother had a pallid face; her yellow-stained nails and dark circles sagged under her eyes. She wondered why she hadn't noticed those hands and face marked with endless strife and pain.

On a one-way street, a solitary car lumbered past them. Ning side-stepped puddles of water scattered along the pavement while swinging the bag of spring onions recklessly.

"Stop that," her mother said, her voice echoing through the empty street.

"It's just spring onions!" Ning exclaimed in defiance.

Her mother slapped her daughter's head lightly. "I need to cook these tonight. You think what, I'm going to throw it away, is it?" her mother said, gripping a half-smoked cigarette between her forefinger and third finger. Ning heard her mother mumbling some words in Hokkien as she turned away. She rolled her eyes at the thought of eating a plate of stir-fry spring onions or any dish with spring onions in it.

If Ning could harness any power from a higher being, she would remove every stalk of spring onion from existence. Her mother's phone rang as they turned at the corner shophouse. Ning stepped back to give her some privacy. A group of young, giggling girls traipsed past them, enthusiastically discussing a hip coffee joint. Ning surreptitiously crept closer towards her mother, trying to listen in on the conversation. But she could only hear laconic replies that consisted of, "yes," "no" and "I understand." Her voice seemed restrained.

"Who was that?" Ning asked.

"Just somebody. Why so kaypoh?" Ning's mother asked, clicking her tongue.

Ning knew her mother deployed this snappy attitude to fob her off whenever Ning became too much of a busybody for her own good. The skies had finally cleared, releasing an earthy petrichor — a scent Ning secretly adored. The afternoon sun peeked out of the grey clouds, creating a golden halo with glorious rays of light around them.

Ning watched snippets of TikTok videos on the train home. Images of a mother and daughter duo swaying and jumping in one frame and morphing into each other in the next frame. A muscular man struggling to tear into an apple with his bare hands while a young man used a knife to cut an apple. A middle-aged woman synchronising her dance moves with a little girl. These entertaining yet addictive videos usually amused her, but Ning couldn't seem to shake that mysterious phone call off her mind. Why did her mother lower her voice? Or why did she sound so serious? The 'whys' inundated her mind throughout the entire journey, until her mother nudged her elbow to motion her to get off the train.

"Make sure you finish up all the spring onions later," Ning's mother remarked as they ambled through the housing blocks.

"I'm not going to eat any spring onions," said Ning. Those words had rolled out of her mouth faster than her mind could stop them.

Ning's mother glared at her with an expression as stiff as a starched uniform and Ning knew what came after this was going to be torture.

"Ma, I'm going to fail my exams next month. There's no point for me to eat those awful vegetables," Ning said, pursing her lips. She cast her eyes on the ground as though something incredible had just skipped across her feet. A group of boys ran past them, yelling, *Eh, where are we going ah? Let's go to the playground*. Their voices echoed through the communal void deck.

"And what are you going to do if you fail your exams?"

"Ma, I want to make buns, just like you."

Ning's mother closed her eyes and clenched her hands into fists. The last time Ning had witnessed this inscrutable face was three years ago when she returned home from grandma's place, and had seen her mother sitting on the kitchen stool, staring into nothingness. Ning had pushed open the door to her parents' room, only to find it in a chaotic mess — a smashed family photo frame was on the floor.

Before Ning could say anything else, her mother walked towards the lift lobby. She was surprised her mother hadn't rebuked her for speaking out.

In the kitchen, Ning quickly tore the omelette apart, only to discover an absence of spring onions. She grinned quietly to herself, thinking she had convinced her mother to exclude that awful vegetable.

Later that week, Ning parked herself at the side table in the bun shop, working on her Maths assignment. The afternoon news on the radio blared loudly in the background. She stared at the Pythagoras Theorem question and doodled aimlessly on the foolscap paper until her mind was drawn to her mobile phone. She tapped her TikTok app when, out of the corner of her eye, she saw Mrs Lim peering into the shop.

"Eh, ah girl, so hardworking! Where's your mummy?" Mrs Lim asked, raising her voice above the static crackling noises.

"Hi, Mrs Lim! She's in the kitchen making baos with Chen," Ning replied, pointing towards the back of their tiny shop, where their cramped kitchen was located. "Do you want your usual Char Siew Bao or Big Chicken Bao?"

Mrs Lim, a regular customer of Tan's Bun Shop for years, beamed upon hearing those words. Ning gave her a wide smile. Mrs Lim rarely hesitated to buy more steamed buns whenever she patronised the shop.

"Just give me five Char Siew Baos and five Big Chicken Baos," Mrs Lim said.

Ning pulled out the second tier of the bun steamer display cabinet and used a pair of silver tongs to pick those flavours. She enjoyed giving those soft and fluffy buns a little squeeze on the side as she placed them into the polystyrene boxes. She felt that was the least she could do as a daughter – assisting her mother and, at the same time, learning the trade. Halfway through, she heard a series of quick footsteps from behind her and before Ning could turn around, her mother was already standing next to her.

"Go and do your homework. I will help Mrs Lim with her order," Ning's mum said as she smoothed away a few strands of hair from her eyes. Ning gently placed the tongs on the table and nodded silently at Mrs Lim, whose face had already become annoyed. Ning grabbed her phone from the table and slunk away.

Inside the kitchen, a stack of large bamboo steamers formed a tower on an industrial stove. They were probably the last batch of assorted steamed buns that would be sold for the day, Ning thought. White steam swirled up in the clammy air.

On the other side, Chen, the ever-loyal shop assistant, was cleaning a dough mixer as he whistled and swayed to a catchy Chinese tune. Originally from Johor, Chen had been crossing the Causeway to work at the shop since Ning was born. Two small portions of left-over dough and a small bowl of barbecue pork were left on the table. Usually, these remnants would be thrown away at the end of the day, as Ning's mother believed in the freshness of ingredients.

Ning whipped out her phone and filmed the first part of a video, cut out a tiny piece of the dough, flattened it with a wooden rolling pin and filled it with a spoonful of barbecue pork. For the second part, she slowly gathered the pleat of the dough to seal up the filling, but the pleat looked odd. Chen glided towards Ning and commented, "Not bad. But still need a lot more practice."

Ning hushed him as the video was still recording.

"But you are getting better now. In the past, your baos looked so funny. If I have more time, I can teach you more things," Chen said, dousing the floor with warm water.

"I'm free on weekends or when Ma goes out to buy Toto," Ning said enthusiastically.

"No point. I'm going to look for a new job."

"Why? Has Ma found someone to replace you?" Ning asked, giving a quizzical look.

"She didn't tell you anything?" Chen asked. Ning shook her head. "Your ma is going to sell this shop."

Words became trapped in Ning's throat. The air grew cold. Sell the shop? Why would her mother even consider selling it? Those questions whirled in her mind like a gale barrelling through an open field. Ning's mother had barely scraped through her secondary school education. In her teens, she had repeatedly failed her exams and, like any hot-headed teenage girl with raging hormones, she got involved with boys and bad company. She eventually left school at the age of 15, much to her mother's chagrin. No amount of words could persuade her to return to school, until her grandma received a call from the police late one afternoon, informing her that her granddaughter had been involved in a gang fight which had led to the accidental death of an elderly passer-by.

Ning's mother was sent to a probation home for girls for two years. It was at that place where she had encountered a God-loving youth worker who persuaded her to think about her future and about the people who loved her. Upon her release from the girls' home, Ning's mother trudged home, only to discover her family wanted nothing to do with her. Out of kindness, they provided her a bed in which to sleep. Due to her bad record and a lack of qualifications, she worked several odd jobs to get by, until a kind elderly man who owned a steamed bun shop had taken her in and imparted his bun-making skills to her.

Those thoughts were interrupted when she heard a loud shriek floating from the shop front. Ning stepped out of the kitchen and caught Mrs Lim flinging her arms at her mother, remarking, "Crazy woman! You think your bao shop is the best in Singapore, is it?' If not for your daughter, I wouldn't even step into your shop." Mrs Lim spat on the ground before stomping off.

"She thinks she is a big shot! Everyone must kowtow to her," Ning's mother fumed, slapping the thick receipt book on the counter. It didn't come as a surprise to Ning, as Mrs Lim was probably one of those disgruntled customers her mother had offended on a regular basis. Ever since Ning's father had abandoned the family on the day her mother stared into nothingness, business had gone downhill. Multicoloured graffiti had repeatedly been sprayed across their shop's rolling shutter with words like, *OP* and *Go to hell!* Ning's mother had surmised the vandalism was the loan sharks' doing.

Already bestowed with the moribund steamed bun shop and heavily burdened with two young children, Ning's mother balanced her life between reviving the shop and paying off her good-for-nothing ex-husband's mounting debts. Ning witnessed the relentless spirit of those loan sharks sauntering into their shop on random sultry afternoons. The men, no younger than twenty-five years old, had blond hair and a uniformed phoenix tattoo on their forearms. They appeared harmless at first but what came out of their mouths was nothing but coarse language. This had led Ning's mother to a nervous breakdown, and she eventually became short-tempered.

As years went by, customers dwindled. Ning found herself greeted by bags of cold steamed buns at home every day. Ning's mother always shrugged it off with, "We made so many baos today. These were the leftovers."

"BUT MA, MRS LIM WAS JUST..." Ning protested, still holding on to her phone. Her mother quickly interjected.

"Stop playing with your phone. What's the point of doing all those videos? Can earn money or not? Ning, my friend just recommended me a tutor for you. She said he's a very good tutor. Can teach you Maths. I know it's too late but at least he can teach you what he can."

Ning gasped. Tutor? But how could her mother afford it?

Ning's head weighed a ton when her best friend, Farah, rambled on about her latest TikTok and Instagram videos during recess. She raved about the number of views she had garnered in a day. Farah's monologue suddenly changed subject, and she asked Ning if she'd like to study for their upcoming exams with her after school. Ning knew Farah was the more hardworking person of the two of them. Even her social media videos yielded more views and likes than hers. She forced a lop-sided smile. She wanted to tell her about the shop and the sudden change in her mother's behaviour, but she couldn't form the words in her mind. Before Ning could say anything, she saw their form teacher, Madam Nadia, walking towards them. Farah greeted her like any obedient child before slinking away.

Madam Nadia pulled Ning aside to a quiet section of the corridor. She interrogated Ning about the Maths assignment — Ning had completely forgotten about it. She sheepishly replied and said she left it in the shop but it was a lie. Madam Nadia raised her eyebrows sceptically, and with a straight face, she broke the news to Ning that, if she failed her upcoming exams, she would have to repeat another year. Ning acknowledged it with a nod and disappeared, but not before Madam Nadia requested to see Ning's mother, to which Ning lied that her mother was too busy.

At 8 that evening, Ning's mother returned to their modest three-room flat with a bag of assorted steamed buns. She was on the phone, speaking in a low voice. She didn't notice Ning sitting on the sofa watching a variety game show where contestants had to guess the price of household items. Ning quickly lowered the volume of the television, when she distinctively heard her mother saying, "The price is too low. I will consider selling it if the price is higher."

Ning was about to confront her mother when her brother, Ren, shouted at her for stealing his favourite blue gel pen. Ning glared at him, grabbed his pen from the coffee table and tossed it to him. Ning's mother untied the bag of buns and passed her improved steamed Pork bun to them to try. But Ren scrutinised the bag before settling on the lotus flavour bun instead and disappeared into his room. Ning obediently picked the lukewarm bun off her mother's hands.

She sank her teeth into the bun. The more she chewed, the more she felt a strange and bitter taste on her tongue. She spat out a morsel of the filling and discovered a slimy green vegetable — spring onions! Ning's mother scolded her for wasting the filling as she and Chen had spent the whole afternoon improving the flavours. A strange feeling inexplicably invaded Ning, and in one swift movement, she ripped the bun apart and threw it on the floor.

"Ning! Who teach you to do that?" Ning's mother yelled.

"What's the point of improving new flavours when you are going to sell the shop?" Ning shouted, matching her mother's screaming voice, the air between them turning hostile and cold.

"Who tell you? Is it Chen?" Ning's mother asked, turning away from her daughter.

"Ma, this shop is our life. What are you going to do without it?"

"Your brother needs money for his studies. His scholarship is not going to be enough to even cover his living expenses. And I need to save up for your university education," Ning's mother lamented, as she struggled with the lighter's spark wheel to ignite her cigarette.

"I'm not going to the university, Ma. You always think that going to university will guarantee you a good life. That's not true. There are people who are still out of work, you know," Ning exclaimed. She understood that good education did not equate with success in life. She had seen it in her cousin, Chee Kiong. Despite graduating from a top management university, he was retrenched from a bank after financial woes had swept across the globe.

"Okay, if you don't want to study, what you want to do?" Ning's mother asked, exhaling a white cloud of smoke.

"Ma, I already said I can help you at the shop—"

"This shop has no future—"

"I'm getting better at my wrapping skills. Even Chen said that. I can help you to rebrand your shop, reach out to a new generation," Ning said, anticipating every move her mother could make.

"What do you know about bun making? I wake up every morning at 4am to make fresh dough and finish work at 7pm. You think running a business is like playing masak-masak is it? Is this the kind of life you want to lead?"

"Yes!" Ning said in her crystal-clear voice. Inside her heart, she was whooping that she had finally been able to say her piece.

Ning's mother pressed the cigarette out on the ashtray. "I'm not going to let you follow my footsteps. From now on, I don't want you to come to the shop. You will come home and do your homework."

Ning was overcome by a sense of indignation. She had always been an obedient child; defying her mother was out of the question. She wanted to be the pillar of support, one who her mother could depend on when no one else would. But being denied permission even to step into the shop, the one place that determined her destiny? Those words fuelled her anger to the point her vision became blurred.

"I hate you!" Ning exclaimed, rubbing the tears from her eyes as she ran towards the bedroom she shared with her mother.

THE NEXT DAY, Suyin was making her steamed buns when her phone rang incessantly. When she was finally able to answer, it was Madam Nadia calling to show her concern about Ning, citing reasons her daughter had given for not turning up for school. They also had a brief chat about Ning's future. Her anger soon gave way to anxiety when Ning failed to return home in the evening. She called Ning's phone repeatedly but it went straight to an automated message.

As the evening drew to a close, Suyin ordered Ren to contact all of Ning's classmates but, knowing none of them, he decided to post a message on his Facebook with a recent photo of her.

When the glowing embers of her last cigarette faded away, Suyin stubbed out the cigarette and raced towards the nearest police post to file a missing person report. The officer on duty kindly offered her a cup of water and took down the statement as much as he could, in the midst of her incoherent speech. There was nothing she could do except to return home and wait for news.

Suyin trembled as she prayed to Guan Yin, asking the divine being to bring her daughter safely home. She stopped her mind from thinking all the worst scenarios – kidnapped by the loan sharks or seeing a dead body at the foot of another block. The more those thoughts penetrated her mind, the more fiercely she prayed.

When the bones in her body could no longer support her, she lay on her bed, stiff and helpless. Ning's last words amplified in her head, like a constant reminder of her failure as a mother. She believed karma had bitten her back. Those screaming matches she had with her mother in her teens were coming back to haunt her. She considered this as the folly of a youth who thought she knew everything.

A dream kept replaying in her mind – she was walking along the train track with little Ning, holding her hands tightly. But the young child wriggled out of her tight grip and ran towards an oncoming train. She ran towards her daughter. Her movements became heavier with each stride and her screams were hidden in the wind. The train passed so close to little Ning that her mother imagined she could feel blood squirting out and onto her face.

Suyin woke up, her heart thumping.

The first sunlight leaked through the curtains into her tiny and cramped bedroom. She scrambled for her phone. Two missed calls from Chen. She returned the call, hoping to inform him to close the shop for the day, when Chen informed her that he had found Ning hiding in the shop.

CHEN SILENTLY POINTED Ning's mother in the direction to the kitchen. She found Ning sitting on the plastic stool sobbing quietly. She lightly squeezed her daughter's shoulder. Ning turned around and noticed the ashen look on her mother's face.

"It's ruined," Ning's voice quavered, pointing at some oddly shaped steamed buns on the table. Ning's mother noticed there was a half-eaten steamed bun. She picked another bun and took a bite.

"It tastes fine," Ning mother said, reassuringly.

"I didn't put spring onions in the bun. It tastes nothing like you make. I thought without the spring onions, it would taste better. But it doesn't," Ning said, wiping the tears from her face with the back of her hand. She stood up and retrieved a plastic bag to collect the ruined steamed buns. Ning's mother stopped her.

"Ning, I didn't finish school. And I don't want you to follow me. I'm scared. I know you hate spring onions and school. But spring onions give a different flavour. It's the most important ingredient in our steamed buns. If this is what you really want to do, you must prepare to go through hardship," Ning's mother explained.

She went to the cupboard and retrieved a mixing bowl. She poured the Hong Kong flour, wheat starch and powdered sugar onto the weighing scale, and then sifted it into the bowl. She made a well in the middle of the flour mixture and added yeast and lukewarm water before kneading the dough with her hands. She instructed Ning to cover the bowl with a damp cloth.

While they waited for the dough to rise, Ning chopped the meat into tiny pieces. Her mother heated up the pan with oil then threw in the meat and a handful of spring onions. She added different spices and the secret family sauce into the meat mixture to elevate the taste.

When the dough had risen, mother and daughter stood side by side, gathering the pleats of the dough with their nimble hands – master and disciple making buns that would bind them together.

Night of the Seventh Moon

Winston Lim

The Greater Throgging-on-Tyne Psychic Club checked in at the Whitesands Beach Resort appropriately at midnight, on the first day of the Chinese Hungry Ghost Festival, and surprised the hotel's night staff. Every one of them was clutching a copy of Raymond Flower's *View Over The Bay*.

As the book had been out of print for some time already, the following morning's shift was asked to investigate the matter. They needn't have bothered.

Apparently, Ms Commings, one of the Whitesands' regulars, had read Mr Flower's accounts of the ghostly goings-on at some of Penang's less well-known tourist attractions and convinced the other members of the Psychic Club that a thorough investigation was called for. A nice holiday in the tropics was an added incentive that nobody cared to mention.

Ms Commings had actually purchased and taken to Greater Throgging-on-Tyne thirty-seven copies of *View Over The Bay* and these she had distributed to the more prominent members of the Psychic Club immediately upon her return.

It soon turned out that the only member of the group who did not seem to be interested in those particular spirits was Major

Beauchamp. Unlike his wife, his interest lay in the kind that came safely sealed in bottles.

He never once joined his better half and the other members of the Club on their excursions to the island's haunted buildings that the travel agent had arranged, preferring instead to spend his afternoons scanning the bay for lost mermaids. Or so he said.

It must have been a particularly arduous task as he was frequently found resting from his labors in the shade of the resort's largest coconut tree, the scattered remnants of his particular research into spirits lined up neatly beside his gently snoring form.

As the Psychic Club was booked for three weeks at the Whitesands, it was only a matter of time before he quickly became friends with Pat and Bert Lawton, two of the Whitesands' perennial returnees. And after that, it was only a matter of time before the Major joined the other regulars at Wira's sundry shop and informal beer club, just a little farther up the road from the Whitesands Beach Resort. He didn't seem to mind particularly that his presence at Wira's caused him to miss the Club's nightly séance in the Dahlia Room at the resort.

These séances had been instituted when Mr Feathergill noticed the embroidered hangings over a large antique bed which the resort kept on display in the Dahlia Room, stirring mysteriously. He insisted that he also felt an eerie chill descend on him before the hangings fluttered in the windowless room.

It was Bert who informed the Major that the hangings always fluttered whenever someone stood at a particular spot near it as the hidden air-conditioning in the room caused a draft which deflected off whomever happened to be standing there. Being a retired engineer, Bert's word should have been enough but it was going to take much more than that to convince the Club's members that they had not experienced their first genuine haunting. After all, the resort staff delighted in detailing a variety of inexplicable happenings that had occurred since the resort opened.

Mrs Beauchamp and Ms Commings flounced off in a huff when

Bert attempted to explain the *thing* and Mr Feathergill rolled his eyes and declared that there would always be those who would never be sensitive to the promptings of the other world.

NEARLY A WEEK into the Psychic Club's adventures in Penang, the Major was woken from his rest by his wife's declaration that the Gates of Hell would be opened the following night and that he must absolutely join them at a little séance they had arranged.

Cracking open one bleary eye, he regarded his excited spouse and her equally twittery companions with less than spiritual sensitivity.

Apparently, the Club had taken the trouble to verify the actual dates of the Chinese seventh month and then timed their holiday to coincide with it. The seventh day of the Chinese seventh month being the time when the souls of the departed would be released on holiday from the Nether Regions, the hotel had been asked to arrange for an evening with the supernatural accordingly.

Prudence Blenkinsop, the Club secretary, personally interviewed her room maid and the waitresses at Las Palmas, the Whitesands' twenty-four hour coffeehouse; she verified that the resort was built on the very spot where the Japanese had delighted in murder and rapine during the Second World War. In fact, she was informed that the Whitesands had been built over the foundations of the very same mansion that the Japanese soldiers used for their unorthodox recreational fun.

The hotel's Chinese staff always conducted prayers and sacrifices for the souls of the unhappy maidens who had suffered at the hands of the lecherous Japanese soldiers on that particular day. Therefore, Ms Blenkinsop, Mr Feathergill and Mr Glossop, another Club stalwart, had determined that that particular night was the most opportune time to contact the spirits of the murdered maidens.

LOCAL LEGEND HAD it that the maidens were a pitiful sight, being blood-spattered and tear-stained after being ravished by whole companies of soldiery. The Club members were told that more than one local lad, staggering home after a night out drinking, had been accosted by a beautiful young lady begging to be taken home. The story always ended the same way. Upon arrival, the young man would find that "home" was an unmarked grave on the hill side.

As the local Chinese cemetery was located not three hundred yards from the Whitesands, behind a small hillock, the Club would split its intrepid ghost-hunting reserves into two parties that night.

One group, mainly male, would camp at the cemetery and try to contact the beautiful ghosts while the other, almost all women, would repair to the Dahlia Room and conduct a séance to determine the identity of whatever had made the silk hangings flutter in the day.

As the Major had been posted to Penang during the war, it was hoped that he would accompany the first group to the cemetery and keep the snakes and other creepy crawlies away from the investigators.

The Major was not particularly pleased at the prospect of having to watch for scorpions, wild cats and king cobras when he could have been enjoying the pleasant conversation and cheap beer at Wira"s with Pat and Bert Lawton, so it had taken Mrs Beauchamp more than six hours to wear him down.

Although she missed the resort's ceremonial prayers to the wandering ghosts, Mrs Beauchamp considered it well worth it as the Major had finally agreed, albeit very grumpily, to keep watch at the cemetery. She was sure that Prudence Blenkinsop, with her brand new camera, would take enough photographs of the whole thing to fill an entire art gallery. Besides, all that incense the Chinese staffers insisted on burning was bad for the lungs, she suspected.

The Whitesands had been asked to provide boxed snacks for the gallant ghost hunters at the cemetery while the ladies in the Dahlia Room would be served more refined refreshments in the form of tea and French pastries by the Banqueting boys. At a quarter to seven, sundown being exactly seven-thirty that evening, the Las Palmas waiter sent the boxes to Mr Feathergill's room.

These, Mr Feathergill distributed with military precision to the members of the Club who had volunteered for the expedition to the cemetery. Mrs Axington, the only lady member of the Club joining the men that night, received her box, grimly dressed in her ghost-hunting outfit, a thick sweater, brown khaki slacks and the thickest pair of boots she could buy from the Greater Throgging army surplus store.

When it came time for the expeditionary force to venture forth however, their guide and protector could not be found. A frantic search for the Major failed to locate him and one of the resort's security staff was persuaded to accompany them instead.

Mrs Beauchamp, swallowing her mortification at her husband's shameful disappearance, quietly went off to join the other ladies at the Dahlia Room.

It was a dispirited little group that met up again in the Whitesands' garden after midnight, that night.

For one thing, the only thing that the male members of the Club encountered was a startled frog which Mr Feathergill nearly stepped on. That it had hopped on to Mrs Axington's hand and caused her to scream bloody murder at the cold contact was what probably scared the unhappy ghosts away.

The séance had produced no more tangible proof of ghosts than the men's graveyard vigil. Unless you counted their designated medium, Prudence Blenkinsop's moaning and writhing about as proof of possession, although by what, nobody cared to explain since she had been observed over-indulging on lobster and cheap white wine at the buffet.

The Major was greeted with stony silence when he went up to the Dahlia Room to look for his wife. He wanted to explain that he had been helping a fellow guest look for her wedding ring in the resort's seven-acre garden that entire evening.

As the lady had been not only most upset, but also insisted on wading into the night-black sea to look for her ring, being clad only in a bikini and very thin sarung, he had volunteered to do so and had been so thoroughly dunked that he feared coming down with a cold.

It was at that moment that Bert Lawton, who had come upon the disconsolate Club members, asked Major Beauchamp a queer question. "Did she have a small egg-shaped birthmark on her left wrist?"

The Major was brought up short by Bert's inquiry but dutifully screwed up his brow and thought for a minute before replying, "I do believe she did. I remember thinking that she had a cut on her wrist at first."

Bert Lawton had the full attention of every person in the Dahlia Room by this time, "Mavis Jones lost her wedding ring and thought that it had dropped off either in the garden or when she went swimming in the sea. We all helped her to look for it right up until sundown when we all thought that she had given up searching. Nobody knew that she went back into the water to look for it again later."

The Greater Throgging-on-Tyne Psychic Club never forgave Major Beauchamp. Bert's last words that night were, "Mavis Jones drowned right in front of the hotel exactly a year ago today."

Winter Solstice

Cheung Louie

He took a deep breath, pushed the door, and stepped inside. Plastic slippers shuffled across tiled floors. In a moment Mrs Lau popped out from the kitchen doorway staring at him, lost for words.

"Ma," he said.

"C'mon in," she broke into a smile. "Sit for a while, dinner's almost ready."

He found his slippers tucked neatly in the shoe-rack. In the toilet, he saw his gaunt reflection stare back as he washed his face. His cut an odd figure, lanky in this baby-blue hoodie too baggy for him. Besides, blue was never his colour.

But it did its job. When he was about to leave Central earlier, he saw a message on the Telegram app: *1718 Tsim Sha Tsui pier dogs picking up arrivals.* But he had to take the ferry. He'd vowed never to take the MTR again – 'CCP subway' as he called it – and cross-harbour buses cost HK$7.1 more. So he slid the hoodie over his black shirt, and on arrival slipped out of the pier without trouble.

These days he always carried a spare shirt. He went into his room and, as the fluorescent lamp flickered on with a buzz, saw that the sheets had been changed but his table remained messy as he'd left it.

From one drawer under his bed he picked several shirts. From another he rummaged through the tangled mess of wires and anime figurines until he pulled out a square toffee tin. He was prying it open when his mother called out from the kitchen.

"Ka-Ming, dinner's almost ready! Come help set the table."

He quickly took its contents, a small stash of red packets from the previous Chinese New Year, and stuffed them into his backpack with the shirts. Outside, he went about setting a foldable table and three stools on their metal legs, taking up much of the living room. From under a coffee table he stooped to take some old newspaper. The one at the top of the pile showed a waving Xi Jinping framed by the headlines: *Flair of a Powerful Country Cannot be Challenged*. He snorted and drew out another. *Rioters Destroy, Everyone Foots the Bill, 2.1 Billion At Least*, it read. He frowned. He squatted and went through the stack of *Oriental Daily News* until he found one that did not get on his nerves: *Four Knife-bearing Burglars, Robbed Watches Worth Millions*. He laid its pages on the table.

"You're back," a gruff voice behind him said, a half-statement, half-question. Mr Lau, without looking at Ka-Ming, carefully lowered himself onto a stool. He smelled of ointment.

Mrs Lau appeared from the kitchen bearing crispy garlic shrimps. "I made your favourite, Ka-Ming."

Ka-Ming started coughing.

"Been eating hot-air food again?" Mrs Lau glanced at him as she sat herself down. "Lucky I made double-boiled soup. Watercress with pig's lungs. Best for bringing down inner heat!" she said, filling his bowl.

Ka-Ming knew his cough had less to do with McDonald's fries than the chemicals in his lungs, but said nothing and took a sip. It was sweet. He'd missed soup. Home-made soup. Not the soup in restaurants which was just water with MSG.

As he munched on apricot kernels floating in his soup, he wondered if his mother actually knew. After all, she believed in the folk wisdom of 以形補形, 'like nourishes like' or 'you are what you eat' and often made pig's brain soup before his school exams.

Mr Lau nonchalantly switched on the TV and wolfed down some rice. A familiar news jingle came on. Ka-Ming braced himself. *Brainwashing crap,* he thought.

"Welcome to news at six-thirty," a female voice said. "A rally was held in Edinburgh Square in Central, during which a protester took down a nearby national flag..."

"Ka-Ming, come, eat while it's hot." Mrs Lau dropped off a glistening piece of salt-baked drumstick in his bowl. "This chicken I got from Sister Ling's, HK$85 a catty. Not bad! I'd thought wet-markets would all raise prices today."

The TV screen was a flurry of banners, batons, pepper sprays, cameras, shoving, shouting and pointed gun.

"Huh," Mr Lau grunted.

Mrs Lau shot him a look.

The newsreader, in the same matter-of-fact tone, went on: "Financial Secretary Paul Chan said illegal acts like destroying shops not only harm law and order, but also smash the rice-bowls of working folks..."

"Huh," Mr Lau grunted again, louder this time.

Mrs Lau laid down a piece of pak-choi cabbage on her mound of rice. "Let's watch something else. It's not every day we have a festive family dinner," she said, reaching for the remote.

For a while they ate in silence, save for a voice on TV, now on another channel, excitedly announcing one supermarket deal after another against a merry jingle.

Suddenly, through the windows came the distant wails of police sirens. Ka-Ming's instinct was to bolt upright, but he kept his head down and strained his ears as he stared at a heap of shrimp shells on the newspaper. He discerned which direction the van was heading and guessed from which police station it'd set off. He made a mental note of the time. 18:38.

"Almond Roca, HK$99 for two, only HK$99 for two," gushed the voice on TV.

"That's a good deal!" said Mrs Lau.

Relax, Ka-Ming told himself. *It's all right. Other Scouts have this covered.*

"What's the use of so much candy?" asked Mr Lau.

"What's the use? We can buy it early for Chinese New Year!" Mrs Lau replied.

Ka-Ming was vaguely startled. Chinese New Year? For weeks, if not months, he'd been living day by day, not knowing what tomorrow would bring or whether there was a tomorrow at all, as the situation spiralled from bad to worse to even worse. There were moments he feared he would not live to see 2020. Yet here was his mother, merrily planning candy for relatives' visit next February. As though everything will be fine.

If only everything will be fine.

Just then he heard sirens again, this time closer. *What if the dogs bit someone?* he thought suddenly.

"I need the loo." He put down his chopsticks. While peeing, he quickly flicked through the 107 new messages on Telegram. Scouts were diligently reporting the whereabouts of police vans in various districts, but save for *1832 Dundas St auntie in black shirt short pants arrested*, nothing much seemed to be happening in his area.

He was about to flush, when he sensed that his parents were talking in muffled tones. Funny how they always thought they spoke softly, when little could escape earshot in this little flat. Ka-Ming crouched beside the louvred half of the toilet door.

"Black-shirts stirring up trouble again, you think? But it's winter solstice," Mrs Lau whispered.

"Cockroaches just want to ruin Hong Kong; you think they care what day it is?" Mr Lau said, not so quietly.

Ka-Ming sprang up. In a few seconds he'd flushed, washed his hands, opened the door and his parents fell silent.

"I'm full," he said curtly. "I'll sit for a while in my room."

As he was closing his bedroom door, he saw his mother shoot his father an angry look. "Told you to be quiet," she murmured.

Instinctively, he turned the lock but the lock was jammed. *Dammit,* he thought. Of course it was jammed. He broke it that day. That day when he woke up with a headache because he'd cried himself to bed, sobbing as his heart was breaking over the comrade he'd never met — that boy lying cold in a desolate carpark now pronounced dead.

HE WENT OUT to the streets that day when the swelling crowds chanted "Hong Kongers add oil" and "Hong Kongers resist" no more but "Hong Kongers avenge."

"Hong Kongers avenge!" he cried at the top of his lungs with all his heart, all his strength until his voice went hoarse. He was wishing death – no, worse than death – to all those he had no doubt in his mind were raping, killing and destroying this city which was the only home he'd ever known.

As night fell the situation grew tense, and he channelled his fury into the only useful thing he knew how to do.

1833 Nathan Rd / Nelson St 50 riot police setting defence line. He went from street to street, sometimes stopping, texting the admin of a Scouts channel on Telegram every few minutes.

1907 Nathan Rd / Shantung St fire magic at roadblocks.

2035 Nathan Rd / Argyle St water cannons fired.

2151 Nathan Rd / Argyle St teargas buffet.

2319 1 man fell, gun type not yet known, first-aiders here.

0057 Nathan Rd / Fife St 40-50 riot police pushing forth.

火魔法. 'Fire magic.' *Petrol bombs,* he thought. "Raptors outflanking! Run!" a boy nearby cried suddenly. Ka-Ming took one backward glance at the police popping out of nowhere and he ran down one side-street then another, goggles fogging up and seeing only light and shade and pink halos of neon-light. Suddenly, by instinct, he turned into a building without doors and leapt up the narrow staircase two steps at a time, not stopping until he reached the third floor.

I'm safe, I'm safe, I'm safe, he panted heavily through his respirator.

When he'd finally caught his breath on the landing, he stuffed his gear into his backpack and turned the key as quietly as he could. Surely, his parents must be asleep by now.

He was creeping towards his room when the lights came on. He froze. "Where've you been?" He turned and came face-to-face with his father.

"My... study group ended late." Ka-Ming looked down.

"You need all this to study? What's this?" His father yanked at his bulging bag and the zippers slid, revealing its contents. "Helmet, goggles, pig snout, think you're playing war games? Having fun now?" He grabbed and flung them to the ground.

"Why so noisy?" Mrs Lau emerged from her bedroom, sleepy-eyed.

"Look at your son. We've a black-shirt cockroach in the family now. How did you teach your son?"

"What 'my son'? Don't you have a part?"

"Who taught you to betray China, ruin Hong Kong?" Mr Lau turned to Ka-Ming.

"We're fighting for freedom and democracy!" said Ka-Ming, finding his voice.

"Freedom, democracy! Think you can eat them like rice? And that means you can set fire everywhere now, does it? It was exactly yellow-ribbon scums like you who beat the shit out of Ah Keung. Smashed his van. It's Cultural Revolution now!"

"He deserved it; he could've killed someone ramming into the crowd of hands-feet like that!" Ka-Ming said, 手足 hands feet being the word for comrades. "You and your generation, you're not only not stopping CCP, you're helping them destroy young people today. Or being Hong Kong pigs doing nothing!" He glanced at his mother.

"My generation, you say?" Mr Lau bellowed. "I tell you, my generation worked day and night to bring you up. Now Hong Kong is so prosperous, so stable. And you good-for-nothings dare to complain? What've you ever done for this home?" He pointed at the gear scattered on the floor. "Who gave you that?"

"I bought them with my own pocket money!"

"Your money? You think you open your hands and money will appear? Sit and someone will feed you? You know what, my hard-earned money, not a penny will go into ruining Hong Kong. If you like war games so much, go ask your foreign forces for money!"

"You think with your morsel of money good for a chicken you can lord over me like that?" Ka-Ming stormed into his room and banged the door, locking it behind him.

"Go find your own money if you're so smart," his father shouted outside. "And don't you think you can still go out to stir up trouble!"

Ka-Ming flung a pillow with all his might against the wall, then slumped into his bed. He was outflanked now, besieged in his own home. His helplessness turned into panic when he heard the click of a padlock on the latch outside his door, which he'd quite forgotten about.

That night, Ka-Ming rattled the door and for an hour tried prying it open with a screwdriver. The rusty latch, left by previous occupants who'd used his room for storage, was stronger than it looked. All he managed to do was break his own lock in the door. When he'd tired himself out, he curled up in bed, still in his T-shirt reeking of sweat and teargas, and sobbed softly as he drifted off to sleep.

HE WOKE up the next morning and peed into a bottle. He tried the door again but to no avail. He looked down from his window but, even if he had removed the grilles, there were no canopy or pipe to cling onto. Rallies across the city were starting soon, including one nearby, but now he sat down and did the only useful thing he could: he monitored the live news on his computer and reported minute-by-minute developments to the Scouts channel.

The next day was a Monday and, as Ka-Ming had expected, he woke up to find the padlock removed. *Nothing beats good grades, even if the world is falling apart,* he thought. When he'd finally showered and was returning to his room, his father, sipping milk tea and reading *Oriental Daily News* on the sofa, said without looking at him: "Be back by 5 pm." Ka-Ming soon re-emerged from his room in school uniform, with his schoolbag and sports duffle_bag, and left without a word.

That night, Ka-Ming did not go home. He'd packed some clothes and cash, but not enough to splash on hotels. He found a 24-hour McDonald's, where several middle-aged 'McRefugees' were settling down for the night. He found a quiet spot and ate some soggy fries left on a tray. He slept little that night.

The next day, he posted on the LIHKG online forum under the name MaryHadALittleDick: "Argued with blue-ribbon dad, ran away from home." Replies poured in. "Bro or sis? If pretty sis, come stay with me [grin]," someone wrote, which was promptly down-voted by 261 users. Some helped look up cheap hostels. A few offered their couch, or to transfer him HK$200.

Thus began a month of drifting about, going to school in the day, selling buns at a shop in the evening, and sleeping on different couches, beds or benches in the night. On some days he skipped school, whether to join protests or out of sheer exhaustion, especially when two universities became besieged and smoke rose from the campuses and the world seemed coming to an end. He felt weary, as though the bitterness of adulthood had landed on his shoulders overnight. But somehow he kept going.

A classmate introduced him to his cousin. Shing was a chubby 38-year-old financial analyst with plastic-rimmed glasses and a brightly lit apartment. After hearing his plight, he offered Ka-Ming his couch for as long as he needed.

"Old folks like me, even if we wanted to run around at the frontlines, we'd be out of breath and drag down the entire village," he laughed. "I don't know how else to thank young hands-feet like you."

Shing was also a volunteer tutor for students too busy protesting to study for their DSE public exams. "I don't even know if Hong Kong still exists next year," said Ka-Ming. "Exams you can always retake. But there's only one Hong Kong. It's now or never."

"Do you really think the end is near?" asked Shing. "We've been fighting for five months now. This is protracted warfare, attrition warfare. If you want 'if we burn, you burn with us,' you need to take good care of yourself to keep going. Besides," he added, "what if Hong Kong became independent? CCP might not have imploded. If you want help on the international front, you need the skills, you need good English. You need to study hard."

When Ka-Ming received a text from his mother imploring him to come home for winter solstice dinner, it was Shing who persuaded him to go. "Some things, once they're lost, they're lost forever. Besides," he laughed, "you look like a malnourished child in my clothes. Go fetch some shirts for yourself!"

IN THE DARKNESS of his room, Ka-Ming checked Telegram, partly to distract himself. A petition asking Germany to impose sanctions on the CCP was circulating. There was a list of court hearings of arrested protesters the next day. Several channels listed upcoming rallies.

There was an image of Pepe the Frog clad in a yellow helmet, and the words:

The longest night is here, the dawn will be near.

Then Ka-Ming stopped at another image: protesters at the top, a prison in the middle, and the smiling faces of two students believed to be killed at the bottom. The words superimposed on each segment read:

They
cannot celebrate winter solstice with their family.
They
cannot choose who to celebrate winter solstice with.
They
can never ever celebrate winter solstice again.

At this moment his mother knocked on his door. "Ka-Ming, come have some 湯圓?"

Ka-Ming took a deep breath, put down his phone and went outside. A bowl of ginger soup with the four tong yuen rice balls had already been set at his place.

He was biting into one when Mrs Lau said to Mr Lau, "Haven't you got something for Ka-Ming?"

"Huh," he grunted. He drew from his pocket a red packet and pushed it towards Ka-Ming.

Ka-Ming looked at it hesitantly. He did not remember red packets being given out on winter solstice. "Thanks...?" he said.

"It's for your birthday," his mother explained.

His birthday was two weeks ago. That evening, during a calm moment in the streets, his comrades bought him a paper-wrapped chiffon cake with HONG KONG stamped on top, which looked like 'add oil' if you rotate it to one side. They even managed to find a candle.

"I got a lighter," one of them said. "I'm so smart! If not, we'd have needed help from Johnny." Johnny was a 'fire magician.'

"No thanks," Ka-Ming laughed, "he'd petrol bomb my cake to the ground."

Then they sang *Glory to Hong Kong* in lieu of the birthday song, and Ka-Ming blew out the little candle and wished with his heart of hearts that glory will come to Hong Kong, one day.

"These tong yuens, aren't they delicious? They were on sale, usually they're very expensive!" said Mrs Lau.

Ka-Ming bit into the perfectly round ball and black sesame paste oozed out. *Funny they still have something black in the house,* he thought.

"Ka-Ming," his mother said, "it's Christmas in a few days. Will you stay? I've already changed your sheets."

Ka-Ming stared into the heart of the rice ball.

Her Fluttering Womb

E. P. Chiew

Wan's gynaecologist peers at her over his bifocals and says, "Let's get that smear over with and then we shall see."

She puts away the magazine she's brought in from the waiting room. In it she'd stumbled across an article about the three laws of randomness. It intrigues her. The gynaecologist asks Wan when her last menstruation was. He asks her if she'd had any interim spotting. He snaps on his gloves, puts her legs up in stirrups and swabs her vagina. He inserts a finger and palpates her uterus. While he's doing this, Wan stares up at the ceiling. A quote from Germaine Greer pops into her mind. Something about the very first gynaecologist in the 17th century. Also male. Rhapsodising about female secretions. Fine liquor, he called it.

"Everything feels fine," he assures.

"It doesn't feel fine," Wan says. "My womb is fluttering. I can't control it."

The doctor blinks. "When does it seem to happen?"

"I don't know. When a man is present?"

"Is it fluttering now?"

She says no, then realises he's teasing her, but not in a nice way.

His smirk, the arched eyebrow. He thinks she's making it up. Drama seeker. Primadonna. He turns his back to her, the white expanse of his back as osteoporotic as a bent cane. "Well, we get the results back in three days. If anything is abnormal, you'll hear from me. Otherwise, just carry on as usual."

She could feel a flutter about to begin. Her annoyance mapped onto a white back.

As reflex, Wan slips the magazine into her handbag.

It's taken a lot of courage even to tell her gynaecologist about it. Wan isn't just embarrassed by her womb, she's mortified. The fluttering makes her feel abnormal. She can't pinpoint when the gentle flapping began. It rose into her consciousness one day when she was sitting in a meeting with her boss and their biggest clients in a glass-panelled office, with panoramic views of Marina Bay Sands.

They were on couches around a coffee table and Wan, lower in the office hierarchy, had to take the office swivel chair, which ironically placed her slightly above their sitting level. The trembling had escalated, became almost a juddering, and she'd crossed one leg over the other in embarrassment and then uncrossed it. All the men in the meeting had looked at her. Specifically, her legs.

Her skirt had ridden up more than usual and a fair expanse of thigh was showing. She saw several pairs of eyes wander to the little aperture where the rim of her skirt didn't quite meet the curvature of her thighs.

Later, in the lunch queue, her boss had called Wan over, "Hey Legs, we need to talk about that Nordbank account." She'd barely heard anything he said about the trade he wanted to promote to them, the call she'd have to make. In her five years on the sales trading desk, Wan had been called a lot of worse things. But this appellation, even with its jocular undertone, had brought a twist of unwelcome shame.

The butterfly feeling in her abdomen is a lot more noticeable. It comes and goes, but she somehow knows that the feeling isn't originating from her intestinal tract or her bowels or kidneys or bladder. It's solidly from her uterus. A subdued quivering at times, a violent trembling at others.

The doctor doesn't call. It must mean everything's all right, mustn't it?

Even so, she's worried enough to take a pregnancy test. Five months since her last sexual intercourse. Five months since Neil. A girlfriend of hers had been five months pregnant and not known it. These things happen if your period is irregular. Luckily, there's only one pink line.

The fluttering brings social grief. In a drinks get-together with her colleagues, John, whom she's been attracted to for months, starts a flirty banter. Instead of feeling gratified, she suddenly feels this incredible need to empty her bladder and barely makes it to the loo.

The pattern continues. A sudden trembling followed by the desperate urge to pee. Sometimes she doesn't make it in time and has to take emergency measures, running out without pants to the shopping centre to buy another pair. Humiliating. A grown woman of 34 in need of toilet training.

The results from Wan's pap smear comes back. "Everything is fine," says the gynaecologist. "Relax, try to have fun with it," he adds. Have fun with a juddering vagina? He probably didn't mean to patronise. Still, an image of a man trying to penetrate while her uterus is juddering like a pneumatic drill hits her funny bone. She guffaws. On top of histrionism, see, there's now female mental instability.

Wan tells her sister, Moon, about her vagina. Moon has four

strapping boys and lives in a big spanking mansion within a few minutes' walk to Goodman Arts Centre. Seldom a good idea to confide in Moon, especially not by phone. But giving voice to it makes it real and acts as a counterweight to her disbelieving gynaecologist.

Moon's tone is dry. "You know what you need? Pay heed to your mothering instincts. A woman's pregnancy risks increase dramatically after 35." Wan can hear Moon chomping on toast. The crispy crackle of the bite, the grinding of it in her mouth to dust.

Wan says, "Just because it's my uterus, it's automatically linked to procreation and the biological imperative?" One of Moon's boys is yelling in the background. Patrick, probably, cramming his brother's head into the freezer and trying to shut the door. Moon says, "S'cuse me, I've gotta go be Wonder Woman now."

Truth is, Wan hasn't had fun with her vagina since the break-up with Neil. That last session of post break-up desperate sex: desperate because of the valuation gap between her emotions and her mind, and if they are at war, the gap is filled with numb ambivalence, frozen indifference, guilty anger, unexpected shame. There are so many complex combinations of emotions that aren't love.

She'd met Neil during training. Like her, he was another sales analyst who had just graduated from a top business school. Their class went carousing in pubs afterwards, and she'd found herself in close quarters with Neil. Amidst an atmosphere where another female trainee literally ripped the sleeve off a guy's shirt, and another did a lap dance, Neil and Wan had exchanged a glance that said the same thing – we all recognise desperation on the ladder to success and we all leap first to judge it. Nothing more serious developed until that evening at Raspail, an office dinner, and she'd been caught out afterwards in the rain, unable to find a taxi. Serendipitous moments. He came out of the restaurant with a brolly and it was yellow. They sailed down the street.

Cindy, her friend, says that love should be like any organic matter. When it dies, it needs to decompose, have its molecules gradually break down. Cindy advises her to throw away the stuff that reminds her of Neil. But what does one do with love's residue, once it has shed its treasured glimmer and become a worn thing? Her mind spirals far into the future, coming up with scenarios where certain objects from their shared existence might still have their uses. A garden fork and terracotta pots. What if she wanted to have a terrarium some day, plant freesia in terracotta pots along her window-sill like a gung-ho hausfrau, stewing prunes and canning fruits? How Neil used to love burying his nose in her hair with its freesia fragrance. Her womb goes on fluttering, maybe sending her a desperate Morse code of its own divining.

It flutters when she has to pass a construction site on her way to work. The men in hard-hats stop whatever it is they are doing—drilling holes in the pavement, supervising the loading of plywood —to stare at her, to deliver those gender-defining wolf-whistles. She places a hand on her stomach and blows them kisses. They stop, their mouths still puckered in mid-whistle.

It flutters when her boss looks at her in the cafeteria. She looks down at the lone baked potato sitting on her plate like a brown rock. She wants to tell him to stop calling her 'Legs'. Then she remembers Neil's face in the morning, the beginnings of a stubble, his tousled hair, his pale chest. How he'd tried to pick up a tune on his guitar from something he'd heard on the radio. The messiness that came with having a guy you were dating spend the night twice weekly – toast crumbs on the kitchen counter, empty Coke cans next to the couch, sports magazines lying open next to the toilet, the toilet seat always up. She was planning to keep the music and books he'd left and the T-shirt that still holds the smell of his body outdoors. Although if he knew he had left them behind, he would likely ask for them back, wouldn't he? But what about the toothbrush? What about the old daily contact lenses swimming around in their case? The half-empty bottle of shaving foam, with the foam all congealed around the spout?

Her womb was one of those gawky, late-bloomer types. When every girl she knew had started menstruating, her womb had pussy-footed month after month, well into her fifteenth year. It hadn't sent the necessary messages to her chest; the buds remained tight-woven kernels amidst the pan-like flatness of her chest. Had there been muscular spasms in her womb and ovaries then, when she spotted a boy kissing a girl next to her locker or when a boy jogged past the bleachers and she glimpsed the jouncing sacs against the fabric of thin polyester shorts? She was a loner, awkward and gauche. With the braces she'd had to wear, no boy ever asked her to school dances. No boy tried to cop a feel during group movies. No boy ever slipped her a secret note. Remembering these things gives her a sticky feeling, an unaccountable feeling of being pegged and found wanting. *I'm not worthy of my womb*, she'd caught herself thinking. But Neil. Neil had put his finger behind the whorl of her ear the afternoon of the yellow brolly. He'd whispered: "Hello, most beautiful earlobe in the world."

The article she finally gets round to reading says: First law: *randomness exists.* It might even pose as coincidence and serendipity. Second law: *some events are impossible to predict.* Present data cannot predict future outcome with any accuracy at all. Hence, is the future just not completely knowable, or is it that it's not knowable at all? Why then did people persist in believing in fate or love if it were so random? Why did they govern their hopes and expectations of happiness based on the continuance of dates? The fact that you've had 58 dates with one person didn't mean that Date No. 59 would surely happen, or that you would be more likely to marry or have children with this person. But why does most of the dating world act as if you would? If Jean Francois Lyotard was right that political economy was libidinal, is libidinal economy a priori political?

Hello, gorgeous kneecap.

The third law gives her pause. It posits that random events behave predictably in the aggregate even if they're not predictable individually. It's called The Law of Averages.

When she tells Cindy about these laws, her friend laughs. "Just like you to resort to numbers and theorems to analyse dating behaviour. The objective and masculine cannot quantify that which is subjective and unknowable. Reject those binaries!"

Those tropes, those clichés. Hadn't they sprung from binaries to begin with? The one about there being only two kinds of men in the world — the 'marrying kind' versus the 'commitment phobic'. The "it's not you, it's me" excuse.

Neil had called and said those things about breaking up. He had surprised her. Shattered a subconscious illusion she had about him, that he was somehow different. They'd argued. He came over. They argued some more. Had passionate break-up sex. Another cliché. Life riddles you with them, and you let them happen. Then he told her that all this time he'd actually had a girlfriend. A girlfriend! The humiliation had attacked her like a school of barracudas. Was he trying Wan out? To see if another uterus might suit better? Between them, shouldn't he be the one feeling the shame; how had it transpired that he redistributed his shame to her? She was so angry she threw her alarm clock at him. He closed the front door just in time. Then had the nerve to call her two days later. But the call undid her. Her heart tugged.

Hello, frail, veiny eyelid.

Hello, cute tidy elbow.

Hello, subtle toes that I love to suck.

Hello, lovely Nubian mole. Hello, gorgeous pink nub. Hello sublime.

Cindy says it takes only a singularity to knock all the risk and return graphs out of whack.

Wan starts timing her flutters, jotting down the frequency of occurrences and duration, the intensity on a scale of 1 to 5. Over a period of weeks, by charting the raw data of occurrence, duration and intensity, she sees that she's been completely mistaken.

Her womb doesn't flutter when she's in the presence of men. It flutters most intensely and long when others see nothing of her but her womb and she has failed to register this. She had loved how Neil compartmentalised her – thought it the language of love, a sexual antiphony of call and response, but in the end, he had only compartmentalised her. What is a woman who behaves like a man at work, shouting out trades on a trading floor, but who wants to be adored like a woman in bed? What is a woman estranged from her uterus, a woman no longer the sum of her parts? Between her mind and her uterus, her uterus has been wiser.

She spotted Neil with a new woman on his arm coming out of Starbucks. A gusty wind blowing through Cecil Street, but what sieved through her wasn't the wind and its hot speckling of dirt, but the glimpse of the yellow brolly dangling from the new woman's arm.

The Law of Averages supports the idea that the biological imperative governs all courting behaviour. Men pursue, women surrender. Procreation happens. Wan steals another magazine, this time from the dentist. She reads an article about stem cells and incubated babies. A Chinese research scientist is penalised, but Wan wonders, why? Take marriage and procreation out of the social calculation of romance and what are you left with? Is it nothing, or can we finally begin afresh?

She attends a book launch by an interior designer, friend of a friend. The house is a wedding cake. Five floors, joined by a circular staircase with black iron railing. One of the bathrooms is the size of a bedroom, with an antique lace doll collection and fascinators pinned all along the wallpaper, in a kind of hybrid caper. A pair of stockings full of holes and a pair of old biker boots, carefully tarnished, hang from the wall as an aesthetic statement. *A uterus could be one of these things*, Wan thinks, *antiquated and Victorian once decoupled from its function.*

The house has too many overwhelming accusatory objects. Everywhere her eyes track down something that causes blood to pound feelingly through her veins, her heart to swell and race. She feels the beginnings of a gentle flutter, a butterfly tickling. Escapes into the bedroom/bathroom and sits by the sink, texting. Random friends text back about their partying GPS. She has too many choices and nowhere to go.

A man comes in, looks around. Roguish in his tuxedo. Wavy brown hair. He asks if there's a toilet anywhere in the commodious bathroom, tone wry. There is. A fancy toilet complete with bidet and gold fittings, enclosed in its own cubicle behind an enormous sanshui painting, all flowing hills and the lone peregrine etched onto glass.

He laughs. "You don't mind then?" She shakes her head, listens to the sound of unzipping, the peal and sprinkle of his urine. The offhand intimacy. He comes back into the room. Looks at her. Her womb starts fluttering again.The brownness of his eyes. She places the palm of her hand against her belly and listens to what he does for a living. He's some kind of spin doctor; right now he's busy spinning an entire culture campaign on the glorified history of a banana republic for a Latin American economic-politico.

Wan says she's a stock trader.

His eyes make contact. A movement within his retinas. Twin reflections of herself in his irises. Wan's palm cradles her womb; the fluttering in it intensifies.

"I love an aggressive Asian woman," he says.

"I'm more about persuading," Wan says.

"I bet you're a helluva persuader." American lexicon, British pronunciation, Latin American looks. The global sheen. The muscular ranginess, the boyish charm. The machinery going to work.

She says, "This is what The Law of Averages overlook. The singular event. The one that has the potential to change everything. The risk is extremely low, but its magnitude enormous. The law of cold averages does not account for all the moments in between numbers."

The expression in the man's eyes changes. His pupils are dilated, his gaze direct, a sign of someone being attracted to you. He shifts closer (yet another sign). "I have no idea what you just said, but you're beautiful and I want to kiss you." He's very close now. She can smell his aftershave. He has a beautiful throat, revealed by a white collar.

"Come on then."

He leans in; she samples. On a scale of one to five, he's definitely a four. Maybe even a 4.5. He touches her wrist. When she doesn't resist, he circles her wrist with his hand, still kissing her.

Just then, three or four other men come in. "Oh hey, sorry. Oh, it's you, Martin." They whistle. Trilling male laughter. "Scoring so soon," Wan hears. They melt back out the door. The man called Martin jerks his head away. His hand still a cuff on her wrist. Even though her limbs feel numb, lethargic, Wan abruptly gets up and pulls away. Only the flutter in her womb escalating, escalating; her heart has raced an orbit and won, returns to an even beat.

"Where are you going?" he whispers.

"It's not you," she says. "It's me."

"Hey!" she hears behind her as she leaves.

One man. Four, five. It's *libidinal economy* and her womb is saying no.

"Her Fluttering Womb" was long-listed in Short Fiction Competition and Fish Short Story Competition.

BANU

MARC DE FAOITE

Banu watched the logging camp from the forest's edge. In the shadows of the giant trees, she was almost invisible. Cicadas screeched their whining song. The men were washing and cooking after their day's work, the air filled with the woodsmoke that rose from a small cooking fire. Most of the men were shirtless. Thin but muscular. Visibly tired. Banu could hear their voices but could not make out their words. A langur they had shot was skewered on a stick and roasting over the embers. To Banu, the peeled unmoving body looked just like a human baby and made her hate the men even more. But she took some consolation that they would be plagued that night by the monkey's fleas. Eat and be eaten. Banu knew all about fleas, how their bites were more painful and itched for longer than mosquito bites.

This wasn't the first time she had come here to watch the loggers. When they were away during the day, she walked through their shelter and rifled through their things, but beyond the thin sweat-stained foam mattresses and a few clothes and bars of soap, they didn't seem to own much. She should have been at school, but being here was better than enduring the beatings the teacher gave her and her classmates. Sometimes he made them hold their ears and squat as punishment for unknown transgressions. Other days he made them stand out in the hot sun without anything to drink, showing that he had power over them and could do whatever he wanted and get away with it. The day he slid his greasy hand inside Banu's t-shirt, she decided that she would no longer go to school, not even if her mother scolded her. She learned nothing from this teacher. Well, that wasn't entirely true. She learned that men can be as cruel and dangerous as any of the spirits who lived in the forest.

But it wasn't that Banu didn't want to learn. The arrival of the loggers opened a door to another world she could only dimly imagine. She observed while staying hidden, the loggers never knowing or suspecting that they were being spied upon by a curious eleven-year-old girl.

They had appeared a few months earlier. First they made a track, cutting a wide line through the forest. She remembered the sight of the smouldering stumps, how the smoke had filled the air for days. Even when she went back to the settlement where her family lived, the smell stayed in her nostrils, while the whine of the chainsaws still rang in her ears. Then the loggers brought big groaning machines to dig up what was left of the charred stumps, huge tangles of blackened broken roots that were pushed to one side, leaving the bare earth exposed, a pinkish clay that looked like a wound.

When the rains came, the water gathered in murky puddles that mirrored the empty sky when the rainfall stopped, reflecting clouds where once were treetops. The clay that had lain hidden beneath the forest floor now turned to sticky mud and the water in the stream that ran through the exposed patch of ground no longer ran clear downstream.

Despite having everything they needed to build a shelter at hand, the loggers used heavy big-wheeled trucks to bring the flat sheets of wood and ribbed sheets of corrugated iron that they nailed to a frame made of pre-cut beams of timber. Her father and uncles had laughed.

Were these loggers too simple to understand that a roof of nipah palm would have been quicker and much easier to build? That it would protect them from the heat of the sun, instead of amplifying it. These newcomers clearly knew nothing about living in the forest, but everything about destroying it.

Banu watched the men until the light started to fade, the screech of the cicadas slowing with the cooling air. She tried to understand how the loggers could spend their days ravaging all the beauty around them. Most of the birds had fled the area, frightened away by the noise of the machines. When they returned to their roosts at night, they circled in confusion, the once familiar trees strangely missing.

As the trees began to fall, the animals had run away too, which pleased her father and uncles for a while. Straying into unfamiliar territory, the disorientated boar and deer were easier to track and hunt, and Banu and her extended family had eaten and shared more meat than usual, at first. But the animals that escaped the blowpipe darts soon learned the unfamiliar terrain and became more wary prey, and the family's hunting grounds were disappearing every day the loggers worked.

Banu watched the men sharing the monkey they had cooked, tearing the limbs from the tiny body. Then she turned from the raw wound of the logger's encampment and made her way through the familiar forest, her bare feet moving silently as she made her way between the giant columns of trees. She wondered whether they would be spared and survive the onslaught of the loggers' noisy chainsaws.

THIRTY YEARS HAD CHANGED the town, but Pastor John still recognised it as the place where he had once grown up. Beneath the plastic banners and hoardings, the old shop facades were the same, even if many of the original retailers had long gone out of business.

Now the five-foot-way was flanked with vape shops and places selling cheap and colourful phone cases. A few of the old businesses were boarded up, but Mister Tan's hardware shop was still there, as was Mister Tan himself. The two men expressed surprise at seeing one another after such a long interval and chatted with an easy familiarity they had never shared as younger men.

"Just back for visit?" asked Mister Tan.

"No, we decided to come back home to retire. My pension can stretch a lot further here and besides, there's no place like home."

"Where you were? Australia? Canada? Some place like that?"

"The UK. But it has changed so much. It's no longer the place we moved to. So expensive these days. And it's getting harder to be a foreigner."

"Brexit?"

"Yes, the usual story. You people coming here to steal our jobs they say, as if anyone could steal a job. If they want to be angry about foreigners working in their country, they should blame their fellow countrymen for giving foreigners jobs. Nasty. Brexit made things worse for us. It didn't feel safe there anymore. It was time to go. Time to come back home. And how about you?"

"Still here. But everything else is also changing. People only want to shop in the aircon mall outside the town now. Business here is no good anymore."

"And your children?"

"All overseas. Melbourne. Toronto. Even got one daughter in Dusseldorf, the youngest girl. I tell them go make life somewhere else. Nothing here. I think this also may be my last year. See which daughter will let us live with them. Spend time with our grandchildren. Grandfather started this shop before the Japanese war. Busy then. Now, some days not even one customer, or only Bangladeshi workers from the plantations. But what can they buy? A new pair of rubber boots? A fishing net? A rat trap? A parang? Best business now is spare parts for chainsaws. Without that, I close already."

"Chainsaws?"

"Loggers. You travel up the hills you will for sure no longer recognise. All the forest gone already. Even the rubber plantations finish. Palm oil, palm oil, palm oil. Plantation after plantation. They say it is good business, but only for a special few. Not to anyone in town anyway. Nearly everyone gone now, retired or overseas. Like I say, things have changed."

"But I thought the town was doing well in general? That huge new road is very nice, with all that grass and those palm trees. The shopping mall. Very modern. And the new golf course is already very famous. Designed by Rimau Kayu, or one of those celebrity golf chaps, isn't it? There was even an article about it in the in-flight magazine."

"You know who all owns that golf course? You know who owns the logging companies?"

"No, who?"

"Members of the royal family."

"I thought the plantations were private businesses."

"Another kind of royalty. But they all help each other. Politicians too. All like a club. Get up on a stage and say, 'You help me, I help you.' Don't even have the shame to hide their corruption and their wealth. Here I will take the timber, make lots of money, then I sell the land, make even more money, then negotiate a percentage on palm oil profits, more money. Like that also can. Buy big boats and build new palaces. These flers got so much money they don't know what to do with it. That big road, they use to race their Ferraris and Porsches and don't know what all else."

"You sound angry."

"Of course I'm angry. They steal my children's future. Even scoring Seven A in SPM they still cannot go into their universities. We are always second-class citizens here, and always will be. Maybe you away too long you forget already. And then their own people. How many of them in poverty? Marrying their children to old men for money for rice. What kind of life is that?"

"I know it's still a work in progress, but there have been many improvements. There's electricity. Better WiFi than the UK."

"These flers use this internet for their propaganda. That's the only reason it is so important for them. Cybertroopers spreading lies. But someone tell the truth cannot. Can go direct to lokap only. What to say? I think you make a mistake to come back here. Holiday can. Very nice. Proper food. But full-time lah? What to say? I only hope you don't regret."

Pastor John left the hardware shop feeling disheartened, not so much about material things Mister Tan had talked about, though he hadn't quite seen things from that perspective before, and wasn't entirely sure if everything the shopkeeper was entirely objective or factual. No, what troubled Pastor John more was the fact that he had left the old man clearly more agitated and upset than he had been before he had decided to call in and say hello. As a pastor, surely his role was to make a positive difference in people's lives, but by allowing their conversation to take such an unexpected turn, he had clearly failed in this instance.

Instead of leaving the hardware shop empty-handed, he had bought a pair of rubber boots, not really needing them but not knowing what else to buy, feeling a duty towards the shopkeeper, ceding to the suggestion made about the Bangladeshi workers' shopping habits, while reassuring himself that a good pair of rubber boots always came in handy. And even if they didn't, he could always give them away to someone who might have more use for them.

"BUT I WAS BORN HERE on the island," said Pastor John, trying not to let his frustration show. "I grew up here."

He had sat for more than three hours in the crowded hall waiting to hear his number called so that he could speak to the immigration officer through the tiny gap at the bottom of the glass window.

"I understand sir, but you cannot have it both ways. When you were here, you wanted to leave but after you left, you wanted to come back. When you left the island, you gave up your citizenship. You made that decision not us. All we are doing is respecting your decision. The maximum period you can stay here is one year. After that, you can apply again."

"So if I apply again in one year, I can continue living here?"

"We cannot guarantee. Come back in one year and apply again. Only then you will get the answer."

Pastor John rubbed his face with his hands.

"All right. So in one year's time, what documents will I need?"

"We cannot say, sir. It changes all the time. But each application will be treated as the first."

"This is very frustrating. Very disappointing."

"I understand sir but please understand that we are only doing our jobs here. We do not make the rules, we just apply them."

"I understand. And there's really no other solution possible?"

"No other official solution, no."

"Meaning there might be an unofficial solution?"

"You say you were born and raised here. You know how things work."

"I see. I think I understand what you are saying. If I wanted to have a coffee or something, is there a place nearby you would recommend?"

"Personally, I like the Ocean Sun restaurant. Do you know it? It is quiet and discreet and they do good seafood, fresh from the sea."

"I don't know it, but I can find it. What time would be the best time to eat there?"

"Seven o'clock is usually a good time. You can enjoy the sunset."

PASTOR JOHN TRIED to remember the immigration officer's face and wondered if he would recognise the man out of uniform. But that didn't matter. The immigration officer found him and sat down beside him, facing out towards the advertised ocean view and a suitably stunning sunset. They ordered food, Pastor John's treat of course, then when they finished eating, the man named a figure. Pastor John countered with a much lower number. Eventually they agreed on a price lower than the initial figure, but still what must have been equivalent to at least one month of the immigration officer's salary. In return, within the week, Pastor John had a stamp in his passport that would allow him to live and work on the island for a period of five years. He would have preferred something more permanent, but five years gave him room to breathe.

DESPITE BEING FROM THE MAINLAND, the preacher had a huge following on the island. He had a weekly television show, a podcast, with new episodes whenever he found the time to record and upload them. But most importantly, he had his own brand of permitted foods and cosmetics, so that his followers could be sure not to pollute their bodies while purifying their minds. Running the company took up more time than preaching, but both were two sides of the same coin. A cynical observer might have pointed out that his sermons were little more than glorified advertisements for his food and cosmetics business, but invariably that cynical observer would then be hounded on social media by the preacher's devotees, some of them going as far as issuing death threats to anyone who dared call into question the integrity of the preacher's brand.

With that sort of customer fidelity, the preacher was well on his way to buying a second yacht and seriously considering a new range of clothing that would be both reassuringly expensive while covering and hiding any hint of the real shape of his female devotees' bodies. He made a note to ask one of his P.A.s if there was anyone in the devotee database who was a fashion designer or who might happen to own a sweatshop where the garments could be cheaply made.

But all these were worldly concerns. He had to work hard to maintain his focus on the important business of saving souls. To this end, he was working with a firm of architects to design an easy to build prayer hall that could be mass produced and flat-packed and shipped on trucks, ready to be assembled and placed all over the island, and perhaps, if it was successful, even on the mainland. Each prayer hall would have a small shop attached, where all the products from his brand could be sold as well, because it would be stupid to miss out on the opportunity to make more sales and revenue.

But he insisted that the architects make the shops discreet, that they shouldn't distract devotees from his sermons; though, now that he thought of it, if he followed through with this clothing idea, and why shouldn't he, the shops might need to be slightly larger than they were on the latest draft blueprints.

As for the sermons, they would be beamed live by satellite internet connections into every prayer hall, so that all his devotees could hear the same thing at the same time, giving them the reassurance that they would always benefit from the same standardised level of excellence regardless of where on the island they happened to be attending. At least that was the plan.

It was ambitious, certainly, and wouldn't necessarily be simple to achieve, but the preacher didn't get to where he was without dreaming big or knowing whose palms needed to be greased for things to happen on the island.

PASTOR JOHN'S four-wheel drive was parked in the clearing beside the logger's hut. Apart from two clear intersecting arcs on the windshield, the car was covered in mud, though Banu knew that the colour of the hidden paintwork was originally grey. She also knew Pastor John, everyone did, but he had never driven here before. In the past he parked much further downhill, on the tarred roadside beside the near invisible trailhead, close to the simple hut where her mother sometimes sold bottled honey and bundles of petai to visitors from the towns and cities on the mainland. He would make the long walk to the settlement where he would be shyly welcomed. Then he would sit and rest while various family members followed the trail back to his car, curious to see what Pastor John might have brought this time.

Sometimes there were bundles of old clothes with words written on them in English. Sweets that were shared among everyone or cooking utensils. However, Banu preferred the flavour of food cooked in lengths of bamboo. Always there were heavy bags of rice, salt and sugar, and more often than not, cans of condensed milk. They didn't need the food, the forest provided all they needed, but it was easier than digging out tubers and the sweetened milk made a change.

Pastor John usually stayed a day or two, talking with the elders, checking on the health of the children and any new babies. He was a thin old man with wrinkled skin. When Banu was very young, Pastor John used to come with a woman who might have been his wife. Or maybe they were just friends. But whoever the old woman was, she was no longer able or willing to make the steep climb to the settlement. Maybe she had died. Banu wondered about these things, but not enough that she would ever voice her questions aloud.

Before they ate, Pastor John said a few prayers to his god and the adults nodded seriously, waiting patiently for him to finish. Banu's people had their own beliefs, but Pastor John was just one of many who wanted to believe in something else. Instead of speaking to the spirits of the forest, Pastor John spoke to a god who lived in the sky, far above the clouds in a place where he promised they would all go to when they died, if they agreed to believe in his god. Banu had long understood that when things died, they didn't go to the sky — they went into the ground, feeding the forest as it had fed them. But Pastor John was a kind man and one of the few people who ever came to visit.

The preacher looked up from his spreadsheet, allowing a satisfied smile to linger on his lips. This year's figures were good. In fact, they had exceeded his targets and by no small amount. When trying to understand why his projections had been so much lower than the actual results, it soon became clear that it was simply because he had underestimated the number of new converts and the exponential growth they brought, mostly thanks to the heavy discounts given for any devotees who could bring two or more new souls into the fold. In turn these new converts, eager to gain access to the preacher's branded products at bargain prices, each brought in new converts, who in turn further spread his reach.

So far, five prototype prayer halls had been successfully assembled, all of them equipped with fibre-optic broadband connections. The locations had been chosen on that basis, his technical manager arguing that wireless satellite connections would really only be necessary and more suited to the remotest of locations.

As it happened, one such remote location had recently become a little more accessible, thanks to a new logging road that cut deep into some of the remotest parts of the island's forests. Better yet there were people living there, simple people who knew little of the outside world or of God's plans for them. It would be the perfect location to test run a completely off-grid prayer hall, one with solar panels on the roof and perhaps a little wind turbine generator if there happened to be a crosswind.

There was just one snag. The preacher's sources had informed him that a pastor from a different franchise had been observed paying regular visits to the people there. But the righteous path is beset with obstacles, and it wouldn't be the first time the preacher faced competition. He believed fervently in the strength of his brand, bolstered by the enthusiasm of his increasingly engaged devotees. Their fervour could be harnessed to his advantage. No, there was no way a meddling soul-stealing pastor was going to stand in the way of the preacher's dreams of total market domination.

BANU ACCOMPANIED Pastor John back to his car, along with several other people from the settlement. They waved goodbye, not knowing when they would see him again, though the old man had promised to return with more supplies before the next rains; these would include textbooks, pens and paper, and hopefully, with luck, a young dynamic teacher who would revive the abandoned school.

He already had the perfect candidate in mind: a young woman from a good family who regularly attended prayer meetings in the town. Her fiancé had recently jilted her and left for overseas, like so many of the young people, or anyone who could afford too. While prayer and the support of the small community helped, it was through the path of action that she would find herself again. Yes, running the school would be the perfect project to give meaning to the young woman's life and help mend her broken heart.

Banu cut across the hairpin bends, moving swiftly downhill through the ugly clearings that had so recently been part of this great forest that once covered the entire island. Each time she caught sight of Pastor John's car she waved, smiling, and saw the old man smile in return, though his hands were clutching the steering wheel too tightly on the bumpy track for him to risk a wave in return.

From the clearing, Banu plunged into the stretch of forest that still grew along the tarred road. The loggers had spared a stretch wide enough that any passing motorists would never even begin to suspect the devastated landscape that lay just a few hundred metres from the roadside: vast clearings that exposed hills and valleys and bare earth where once had been a sea of trees. Though the huge tree trunks chained to the beds of trucks that regularly made their way down the tarred road might have alerted anyone even half-observant to the extent of the deforestation.

Banu squatted in the trees by the roadside, hidden in the shadows, ready to spring out and wave goodbye to Pastor John one last time, the smell of sun-baked tar hot in her nostrils. But she didn't move from her hiding place.

Instead, she watched as two big black cars with tinted windows blocked the road in front of Pastor John's car, while another two cars pulled up behind him. Doors were opened and men dressed in black quickly emerged, holding what could only have been guns, though they were very different guns to the one her grandfather kept wrapped in an oily cloth.

They wore black masks that covered their faces, and goggles that covered their eyes, so that they all looked the same, all moving quickly as if controlled by one mind. Pastor John was roughly pulled from his car and bundled into the back of one of the black cars, while one of the men took Pastor John's place behind his steering wheel. Then they were gone, leaving just the smell of their exhaust fumes.

The entire operation had taken less than a minute, happening so fast that Banu wondered if she had imagined the whole scene. She was trembling now and noticed that she was squatting over a patch of ground soaked with her own pee. Her mother had once told her of being this afraid the time she had come face to face with a tiger in the forest while picking fern-heads when she was a girl only Banu's age.

Banu would have to tell her family what she had seen. They would believe her because they knew that she only told the truth. She was not a storyteller, she didn't have that skill, and even if she did, what she had witnessed was far beyond anything her imagination was capable of conjuring up. She would have to tell what had happened to Pastor John, but what was there to tell? Who were these men who had taken him? There was so much about the world beyond the forest that Banu still did not understand, perhaps would never understand.

THE CLOUDS BLOCKED the stars on a moonless night as the men rolled the blue plastic barrel down the loose planks that connected the boat to the jetty's edge. It was a straightforward job, but it wouldn't do for the barrel to fall into the water, at least not yet. The barrel was heavy, half-filled with the concrete they had poured over the old man's folded body. He had hardly weighed a thing and was easy to fit into the barrel, not like some of the others the men had dealt with before, who needed to be cut into pieces first.

The barrel safely aboard, the planks were withdrawn. Three men stayed in the boat while the others returned to the black vehicles. The little boat's outboard motor chugged to life, a quieter engine than the noisy long-tailed boats the local fishermen liked to use. The man at the stern let the motor run at a low speed. There was no hurry, no lights visible on this quiet side of the island, though in the distance on the horizon the lights of towns and villages twinkled from the mainland, so near, yet a world away. It was a still night, with no wind. The boat drew a small wake behind it in the water, the liquid path soon erased.

They left the coast of the island far behind, until they were close to midway to the mainland, a place where the men knew that the water was deepest; a place where a weighted barrel could rest undisturbed and undiscovered, as if it had never even existed. Over time, shellfish and seaweeds would make their homes on the smooth blue plastic, slowly colonising it until it was covered, absorbed and camouflaged, just another part of the seabed.

The helmsman cut the motor and allowed the boat to drift to a silent stop. When they heaved the barrel overboard, the boat rocked violently. One of the men laughed nervously as he staggered to keep his balance, but the barrel had hardly made a splash and sank instantly beneath the inky dark surface of the sea.

Then the outboard chugged again, the propellers gurgling and spluttering as they were lowered into the water. None of the men spoke on the return journey, though the helmsman lit a cigarette, the red tip glowing intermittently in the darkness as he drew upon it. Another of the men let his fingers trail in the water, feeling the day's absorbed warmth still present in its surface, allowing water to trickle through his fingers, momentarily immersing himself in the gentle resistant tug. Then he withdrew his hand and wiped it dry on his trouser leg, thinking about how this was the easiest, best paid job he had ever had.

Banu awoke to an unfamiliar noise. Since Pastor John had been taken, she no longer slept as deeply as she once had. Even when she did sleep, her dreams were disturbed by the images of what she had seen. The sound was getting louder, distant still, but closer, almost like the sound of a strong wind blowing through the treetops, yet different. Besides, the trees were gone. Perhaps it was the ghosts of the trees calling out, asking not to be forgotten, or maybe seeking their revenge.

She crawled out from the little nipah shelter where she had made her bed. No one else had been awoken by the sound. A small amount of smoke still rose from the remaining embers of the evening's fire. Though it was dark, Banu's eyes were keen. If she climbed a tree, she might be able to see what was causing the approaching sound, or hide from the angry tree ghosts, if that's what the source of the sound was. She sensed a new coolness in the air around her, and the unmistakable smell of mud.

She shouted, hoping to wake the others in time, climbing now, not because it was something she had chosen to do, but because it was something her body had decided without asking her opinion, her bare legs gripping the rough bark of the tree as she climbed, heart pounding. The damp earthy smell drew all around her, the hissing roar almost deafening. She reached a crook in the tree and held tightly to the trunk as the loud glistening torrent flooded through the encampment, sweeping her sleeping family away, carried off in an impossible river of water and mud.

BANU STAYED in the tree until the sun came up. The unexpected river had only flowed for a few minutes, yet she couldn't bring herself to leave the safety of the tree until first light.

The encampment was gone, erased as surely as if it had never existed. She searched for any members of her family, but they were gone too, returned to the earth as she had predicted, not above the clouds as Pastor John had promised. The logger's cabin was gone as well, the loggers nowhere to be seen, the huge machines toppled on their sides, half-buried in the mud. She stayed, not knowing what else to do.

Then the machine appeared. At first she thought it was a bird, though it buzzed like an insect, hovering over the clearing, moving sharply away, then hovering again, as if surveying the wreckage. This machine had clearly come from the world beyond the forest, the world that had brought its destruction to this place, the world that had caused nature to turn against itself, taking everyone Banu had ever known and loved with it.

The first pebble missed, but Banu was a good shot. She loaded the sling again and the second pebble squarely hit its target. The machine jerked and tilted, then fell from the sky. She smashed it with a rock, not even taking the time to examine it or try to understand what it was or how it worked, but she took one of the blades from the tiny wreckage. It was hard and sharp enough to be a useful tool, while serving as a reminder.

Banu turned and left the wasteland, making her way to the forest's edge, taking the barely discernible trails that led deeper into its heart, following tracks mostly made by animals, knowing that sooner or later they would lead to water, whether a stream or a pond or a spring. She recognised familiar trees and plants along the way, instinctively noting their locations, knowing what was useful, what was edible, what was to be avoided.

She walked for three days, stopping only at night to sleep in the safety of trees, after checking them for snakes, putting distance between her and the past, between her and the world beyond the forest, the world of men.

Laksa Uncle

Jenny Hor

At eleven sharp in the morning, the sound of ringing bells would alert the neighbourhood. Then came the sour-spicy smell of assam and lemongrass, aromatic enough to activate the olfactory receptors. The stimulating combination was powerful enough to push anyone out of their houses.

An old man in his seventies stepped on the pedals of his bicycle while pulling a heavy food cart behind him. As he moved forward, the white *Good Morning* towel around his neck absorbed the sweat falling from his forehead and temples. The cart was a normal roadside stall, with two embedded pots containing the steaming broth and boiling water each. It was a miracle that the utensils and containers stayed still despite the jostling of the cart as it traversed across uneven asphalt road and rolling gravel.

We called him Laksa Uncle, like the delicacy he sold.

Laksa Uncle would stop his bike when he saw that someone had halted him at the roadside. He only knew Hokkien, although some people claimed he could understand simple Mandarin. I always made my order in Hokkien, despite my terrible fluency.

"Uncle, laksa, nor-bao," I told him, while handing over my three-layered stainless-steel container.

"Okay."

Laksa Uncle began by simmering a handful of thick vermicelli noodles in the boiling water for a few seconds. While his right hand scooped the hot orange-red broth, his left fingers threw the veggies and condiments into the container. Aligning the containers vertically, Laksa Uncle secured them tight.

In exchange, I gave him a green five ringgit note. The price was not much, but it made Laksa Uncle show off his crooked teeth.

At the dining table at home, I divided the noodles and broth for two people. One for me, and one for my Ma.

For a bowl of laksa from the streets, the broth had a rich combination of ingredients. The addition of thin mackerel and sardine flakes in the broth enhanced the sweetness and chewy texture. Laksa Uncle had mastered the technique of cooking perfect noodles, smooth to slurp and breakable when gnawed. The evenly sliced onions, cucumber, chili and pineapple gave the laksa colour. A glaze of the black belachan paste elevated the laksa's earthy tang.

"Twenty years already, Uncle still makes good laksa," Ma indulged in another sip on the broth. "He knows where to get good ingredients."

Laksa Uncle's immovable reputation had gained admirers around the neighbourhood. He received the admiration of the pasar aunties with the freshly delivered fish and veggies. The boss lady from the spice shop would reserve the best spices for his broth. These gifts propelled his customers to lick their bowls spotless.

This was my Saturday's brief moment of bliss. As the weekday weariness wore off, I forgot about my responsibilities as a Form Five student. Screw revisions, laksa was more important.

Sometimes I would be lucky enough to encounter Laksa Uncle on my way back home from school. By then he was done for the day, because there were no more laksa noodles or broth to sell. The content smile on his face was enough to motivate himself for the next day.

ANOTHER SATURDAY CAME. In the living room, I had my notes and the stainless-steel container ready. I just needed the clear signal to run out of the gate to stop Laksa Uncle's bike.

I waited, and waited. But there was no sound of ringing bells.

My cochlea detected the sound of deafening sirens, getting closer and closer to our neighbourhood. Like a true busybody Malaysian, I carefully walked out of the house to understand the situation. A group of aunties and uncles had huddled together around the street corner in rowdy discussion. I blended into the crowd, eager to find out what the commotion was about.

There was Laksa Uncle, lying unconscious on the ground.

The whole scene looked like a screenshot from a Cantonese crime investigation show. The poor man had blood gushing out of his head, and his limbs were bruised a nasty shade of black and blue. The cart had flipped over, causing the broth and ingredients to splatter across the street. Police had barricaded the area with the long Do-Not-Cross tapes, while the victim was carried into the white ambulance.

"Aiyoo, these Ah Longs," an auntie murmured. "So ridiculous."

"Blame his son, lah," another cried. "Nothing to do after meal, borrow money from the Ah Longs."

"I'm sure the sohai son will get his karma one day."

It was no secret that Laksa Uncle's unemployed only son had a huge reputation as a gambler. People had seen him in 4D lottery shops and Genting's casino. While the son was worrying about the winning numbers of the day, his father was selling laksa in hot weather.

"What are you doing here?" Ma somehow found me among the crowd. Grabbing my arm, she dragged me back into the house.

"But Laksa Uncle—"

"Stay here," she closed the metal gate, locking me indoors. "Go back to your room."

I could only observe the situation from my room's window. It was two hours before the mob scattered. Ma returned, her complexion pale. I knew she was shocked, so I did not implore her for more details.

The morning became deadly quiet since. We had been waiting for Laksa Uncle to make his glorious comeback with his fresh batch of laksa. I had torn two calendar sheets, but he had yet to come to our neighbourhood.

On the day before my final paper, the bike returned. It had the same ringing sound, and the same cart with immovable containers. The only difference was the broth's smell, which was not as pungent as before.

"Uncle," I called when the bike went past my house. "Laksa Uncle."

The bike stopped. A younger-looking man got off the seat and glared at me. He had a cigarette stuck in between his lips, with ashes falling to the ground like smoky snow.

"Uncle," I nervously called. "Laksa, jit-bao."

The man slowly made his way to the cart. Grabbing the noodles, he coarsely dumped it into the boiling water. The splattered broth did not bother the careless fella when filling it into the plastic bag. He only remembered about the condiments when he was about to tie the plastic bags.

I had given him a five ringgit note, expecting him to give me a change. Instead, he kept the money in his pocket.

"You forgot my change."

"One laksa five ringgit."

"Last time it was two and a half ringgit for one laksa."

He clicked his tongue, flashing the whites of his eyes. "Price increase already."

I was too tired to argue. Heading back to the kitchen, I poured out the noodles and the broth into a bowl. The veggies were cut into ugly, disproportioned slices, and the man forgot to add the belachan paste. More importantly... why did the broth taste like water?

After one big slurp on the noodles, the vermicelli soon melted in the mouth. There was something hard moving in my mouth, grazing through the inner cheeks and tongue. Spitting out, it was a silver wire gauze. It seemed to be mingled together with the noodles.

Blegh.

I told my Ma about the extra-special laksa. She took a glance at the noodles and stirred the broth to check the ingredients.

"Did you buy this laksa from Laksa Uncle?"

"Yeah, it tastes funny."

"Oh no," Ma groaned. "That's Laksa Uncle's son."

So that was the good-for-nothing son? Talk about drastic difference.

According to the gossip Ma heard from the pasar aunties, the poor man broke his legs from the incident. His frail legs had lost their strength to step on the pedals and standing still was challenging to him. Losing their only source of income, his reluctant son had to take over Laksa Uncle's job.

"The bastard has downgraded the laksa," Ma cried. "Doing everything so half-bucket."

From what I had seen, he did not look like he had a change of heart to take over his father's job. It could be temporary. Laksa Uncle might return once he was feeling better.

As expected, the bike did not return after weeks of operation. Some said the family had moved because the Ah Longs threw red paints at their house, while some speculated Laksa Uncle had passed away.

It was the end of the best laksa in the area.

Not long after, I moved to the metropolis on Penang Island for college. I met my flatmate, Nathan, a local foodie. Our first encounter was him dragging me to the campus' nearby food court that harboured the world's finest cuisine, from local delicacies to international delights.

Nathan bought me laksa, which he claimed was the champion of the food court.

"Come, come," he shoved a small bowl of laksa. "You must try this."

The size of the blue plastic bowl was big enough for a sparrow's appetite, but the content was rich with flaked fish, veggies, and noodles. A layer of glossy black belachan paste covered the white soup spoon, a smart hawker's trick to ease the condiment blending process.

"Wah," my lips widen in delight. "Looks pretty."

"One of the best," Nathan stirred his spoon into the broth. "You should eat, brother."

Imitating my friend, I stirred the paste into the orange-red broth. The noodles were cooked to perfection, not too hard and not too soft. I could taste the broth's finest combination of sour and spiciness, with the flakes and veggies enhanced the texture.

It was the exact taste I had been yearning for months.

"This laksa," I gave a thumbs up. "Ho liao."

"I know, right? This laksa only open for two months and it already become so famous," Nathan pointed to the other side of the food court. "I heard the uncle is from Mainland."

Somehow, my legs sprang up from the seat and headed in the direction Nathan mentioned. There was a sense of familiarity that was calling to me, forcing me to have a look.

"Where are you going, brother?"

"Da bao."

The other food stalls might look tempting, but I could instantly smell the assam aroma coming from the end of the stalls. Getting closer, the gentle ringing sound of a bell became clearer. My sensory stimuli summoned my arrival to the food court's laksa stall.

Among the clutter of cooking utensils, I found a familiar face sitting on a red plastic stool. His hands were busy grabbing the fresh ingredients and scooping the broth into a line of plastic bowls. He still had the same white towel around his neck, except this time his head was not as damp as before.

"Laksa Uncle?"

Laksa Uncle paused his tasks. The wrinkles and age spots on his face had increased, making him look older than I remembered. His bony legs were lacking muscle definition, and red scars from the horrifying accident remained visible. His condition made him unable to stand up too much, so a cardboard sign had been set up to remind his patrons to be patient.

"Ah boy, lu ai ha mi?" Laksa Uncle asked with a smile. He seemed to have forgotten about the tragedy he had experienced. Cooking under the roof was definitely better for him than riding his bike under the sun. There was no trace of his bastard son, who'd probably ditched his father behind while escaping from the Ah Longs.

Just like every Saturday morning, I said:

"Uncle, laksa, jit-bao."

Day of Silence

Yvonne Lyon

Ava leant against the high wall enclosing their villa and looked down at the hard packed earthen road. She caught a mix of smells: exhaust fumes, and oleander from the garden just out of sight. The little street was quiet enough though the metallic hum and thrum of traffic noise could be heard in the distance. John was on the alert and nudged his fiancée when a car nosed its way around the corner.

"This is it, then," he said. "No going back. I reckon it'll take about twenty to thirty minutes to drive to Denpasar."

The driver, Wayan, leapt out of his seat and welcomed them like old friends though it was only their third day on Bali. They both liked his open face and smart appearance. Yesterday's successful trip, to see the area's most famous temples and restaurants recommended in *Lonely Planet,* meant he was booked for the rest of their holiday. "Can you drive us to the capital, Wayan?" John asked. "We've got an appointment with a Wedding Planner," and he read out the address.

SUZI BANNISTER OPENED her current client folder and scanned the details for the couple who would be knocking on her door in half an hour. Ava Morton and John Carne, aged twenty-six, from Leeds in England had written that they'd like an initial consultation, a fact-gathering mission for possible wedding venues while they were on holiday in Bali.

Suzi had been to Leeds once when she was a student. She remembered a Victorian town hall with two stone seated lions. Even then she'd recognised it as a symbol for a city that was sure of itself. She glanced at the couple's address, Roundhay, and quickly typed the name into her laptop. *An affluent suburb with a 700-acre park.* She thought she might pay Leeds another visit on her next trip back to see her father. Her eyes drifted over John and Ava's words then focussed when she came to the photographs each had individually selected. Suzi sent all prospective clients an image questionnaire. It was the quickest method of learning about people. Words could be deceptive: image choice, rarely. In the seven years since she'd taken over the business from her aunt, it had caught out many who'd wanted to hide behind their prose.

John clearly favoured traditional architecture. Houses with nooks. Gothic churches. Victorian theatres. Strange, when his own profession was the building trade. Presumably Carne and Son's clients wanted contemporary homes? Ava had chosen natural objects and scenery: mountains, hydrangeas, a batik sarong and, unlike John who'd gone for more Western depictions, a Balinese house. A picture was beginning to emerge. Suzi got up, made herself a strong coffee, then returned to her desk to send a few emails and waited for the buzzer to sound. It was unlike her to be nervous before meeting new clients, but she recognised the signs.

ARRIVING IN DENPASAR, Wayan nonchalantly pointed out the sights as he wove through narrow streets and avoided overtaking cars.

Ava craned her neck to look at a huge market area where fruit, cooking pots and clothes spilled onto the pavements. Then there was the state museum with its stone frontage and the Pura Jagatnatha temple soaring craggily skywards.

They said goodbye to Wayan who would return in two hours' time and looked up at the tall, modern building they were about to enter. They agreed that the city felt stifling compared to their village, surrounded by rice fields.

Now alone in the lift, the couple fell silent. As the door slid open, Ava put a hand on John's arm. "Let's take our time over this, eh?"

"Sure. But give it serious thought otherwise it's half a day wasted."

Ava twitched her shoulders back and raised her head as the door opened to reveal a petite, beautiful woman of about thirty wearing Western office clothes. Suzi Bannister greeted them warmly and ushered them inside.

"What a view!" John said, walking over to the panoramic window overlooking the city. Ava, only an inch or so taller than Suzi, looked up to examine a wall of wedding photographs.

She saw they were from the Wedding Planner's website: blondes in bouffant white dresses standing next to grooms under flower-covered arches in front of a sparkling sea or gazing down a ravine. Ava knew her friends would be mad on having that kind of wedding, but something about the images niggled her.

Suzi waited a moment before inviting Ava to sit in the other armchair facing her desk. She waved a hand in the direction of the photo-wall. "There's many ways to get married in Bali; in traditional buildings for example, though the ones shown on the wall are the most popular."

Ava smiled, grateful for her perception. "I'm afraid I don't have any set thoughts about themes... locations. We've decided to visit a few places that you recommend, take home some ideas, then..." She finished in a rush. "You'll think us disorganised, but we haven't even set a wedding date. The main point of coming to Bali was to explore it. See as much as possible."

John turned in his seat. "It is, love, but we can do both, can't we? Bali would be a really cool place to get married."

"Where have you been since you arrived?" Suzi asked, noticing a flicker of friction.

"We watched a temple dance ceremony yesterday." Ava lifted her hands to her face before dropping them to her lap as if mirroring the dancers' movements. "It was..." She looked at John. "Unbelievable, wasn't it? Tiny girls, so elegant and yet powerful."

John stretched out his arm and clasped Ava's hand in his. "Absolutely. Though I think I'll enjoy the mask workshop even more. Our driver's taking us to one this afternoon."

"That's interesting." Suzi looked at him more closely. John was a good-looking guy with smooth cheeks which gave his face a kind of polished appearance. "I remember you chose a mask in your questionnaire. Do you have an interest in them?"

"I've worn them once or twice, on stage. Ava and I are members of an amateur dramatic society. The reason I chose that one was because I've always wanted to go to Venice for New Year's Eve and wear one of those masks with the embroidered head-dress. You know, white face, and the black outlined eyes. You'd never be able to guess who it was under it."

"I can see the attraction," Suzi agreed.

"And tomorrow we hope to go snorkelling. Fortunately, our villa's quite close to a beach."

The couple chatted to her about their plans while Suzi tried not to show the consternation she was feeling. She knew their type: well-off young people with promising careers who holidayed in exotic locations. They said they'd come to Bali to explore it, so how could they not know about Nyepi?

"I'm afraid snorkelling or any kind of outing is impossible for tomorrow. Didn't you know that it's Bali's Day of Silence? It's our biggest purification festival. No one, not even tourists, can go outside. And there'll be no transport, electricity or phone coverage for twenty-four hours. The traditional view is that evil spirits are fooled into thinking Bali has been abandoned so they will go elsewhere. For us, even talking to each other is forbidden. You'll be fine in your villa, but many tourists book into a hotel for twenty-four hours because they can use the swimming pool and there's always prepared food available."

John and Ava looked at each other, wide-eyed. "I thought you said you'd gone through the guidebook cover to cover?'" Ava spoke first.

"I did read something about it, but I thought tourists would be exempt. Sorry, love. Look, why don't we do as Suzi suggests, go to a hotel as we don't have a pool?"

Suzi was on edge as she waited for the young woman's reply, but Ava threw her another question.

"What do people do instead when they can't work or go outside?"

Suzi had often given explanations to tourists about the spirituality of the island, but she tried hard not to sound glib or use the same words. Each person needed an individual response. "Those who take Nyepi seriously, whether they are tourists or islanders, truly benefit. Many people use it to meditate and think about their lives. They prepare offerings to the gods. It's a very special time. I'm half Balinese, half English. I grew up in England, my father's country, but came on holiday to Bali for the first time when I was twenty-two. I returned long-term and after a few years took over the family business. I take inspiration from the beliefs of my mother's people. I will use Nyepi to think about what I want to do next. Nyepi is for the big things in life."

The couple were silent. She saw them in their own heads, mulling over how to use tomorrow.

Ava came to a decision. She squeezed her fiancé's hand. "John, love. I want to fully embrace Nyepi, as Suzi suggests. I know you'd rather be in a hotel but I want to stay at the villa. Would you mind if we spent it apart?"

John's jaw tightened and he stared at the wall of photos. "Not be together on holiday? We haven't spent a night alone since God's knows when."

Ava understood why he was upset but how to explain her reasons? She didn't fully know why she wanted to observe Nyepi but it was vital she make this less awful than it was.

"We both said we wanted to experience Bali, love, and this is the best way of doing it. As we can't go exploring tomorrow, why don't you take advantage of the hotel? Find out if it's the kind of place where we might have our reception." She held her breath. Would he go for it?

John made some acquiescing noises and appearing mollified, agreed to Ava's proposal. He took charge of arranging another meeting with Suzi and slipped the hotel business card she gave him into his pocket.

AFTER A LATE LUNCH of babi guling, spit-roasted pig, in an airy restaurant, Wayan took them to a traditional village where they found the mask-making workshop. Despite the fascination of seeing a master carver at work, Ava was ready to leave after an hour. She found the static, often grotesque faces staring down at her from a wall, disquieting. But it was difficult to drag John away. He spent a long time examining each one. After some cajoling, she persuaded him not to buy a mask to take home.

"It'll hardly go with our Ikea furniture and the Orla Kiely curtains, will it?"

"I guess not," he agreed. But he couldn't help imagining a non-existent den at the back of their house with a blank wall crying out for something to hang upon it.

The last stop of the day was in a town close to their villa to view a traditional procession. Wayan explained its nature; that the papier mâché figures they would see, called ogoh ogoh, represented gods and deities which cast a strong influence over island life. "The deities have both positive or negative energies," he said, "as well as godly or malicious ones. Our festivals aim to keep harmony between both types of energies. This one always takes place the day before Nyepi, our New Year." He told them to come and find him in a restaurant, in the main street, when they were ready to leave.

The crowd was already thick with tourists and locals spilling off the pavements. Side by side they sauntered along enjoying the rising pitch of excitement surrounding them until separately, each realised the other had disappeared.

Ava stretched to her full height, a hand to her eyes to shade them from the evening sun. Could it have happened when she'd paused to look in a shop window, or when John turned sideways to let someone squeeze by? He was somewhere in the mêlée, had to be.

Then the monsters appeared.

On the creatures came: ten, twenty feet high. Limbs contorting in a fiendish street-dance, snarling at bystanders, fangs on display. Ava stared, amazed at the ingenuity of their makers. One monster had breasts as large as pumpkins. They were attached to bamboo rafts carried by dozens of boys in white tee-shirts and checked sarongs. As the glowering figures moved slowly up the street, she was pushed forwards; the only option to follow them. When the parade reached the end of a line of shops, the ogoh ogoh began to sway, buck and rear like ships in distress as the boys manipulated the rafts more vigorously. If possible, the noise increased.

Ava knew John would be searching for her. He would be more worried than she was herself at being alone. She imagined his eyes darting here and there, his arms working like oars, chest pushed forwards as he attempted to free himself of people, unable to make a passage through the teeming street. Surrounded by boisterous youngsters, excited, jostling, and happy, she had no more volition than a wind-up toy. She gave up trying to escape and sank into the cheers and whistles; allowed herself to thrum in time to the incessant drumming on brass and wood. One of them would spot the other. Bound to.

In a matter of moments darkness fell, blotting out the last streaks of red sky. More monsters swayed past, followed by girls carrying banners with Indonesian writing. Flames on the end of sticks appeared and shadows leapt high. When at last she spotted John ahead of her, his height and pale skin marking him out, a flare lit up a dark patch of sweat on the back of his shirt. She worried that he might not have enjoyed the experience as much as she had. A certainty about the rightness of things, doing this, taking part, pervaded her. John loved the masks for sale in the workshop this afternoon but was it the exoticism that drew him rather than what they symbolised? As for the ogoh ogoh procession, she had no idea what he'd say. It disturbed her how unsure she'd become about his reaction to things these last few days.

THE NOISE and disarray of the ogoh ogoh evening had given John a headache. After exchanging opinions about how they could ever have lost each other, they checked on Instagram for a place to eat, far from the chaotic street. "I was scared I'd lost you," John said, letting go of Ava's hand as he opened the restaurant door.

Later, Wayan drove them back to the villa and waited while John packed an overnight bag, kissed Ava goodbye, then took him to Suzi's recommended hotel.

After they left, Ava felt the emptiness of the villa surround her. Its unfamiliarity wasn't threatening, just unknowable. As she wandered into the lounge area, she questioned how often she was ever alone. Only when she went to the bathroom, she supposed. She went across to the kitchen and from the fridge took out a bottle of wine and poured herself a glass before going outside to sit on the verandah. She'd learnt from the maid who came every day to clean and cook for them that the Balinese used different areas of their houses and grounds for different activities. So, cooking and washing areas might be across the garden from the sleeping and relaxing spaces, as they were in this villa. In more traditional homes the spaces weren't glassed in but open, like pavilions.

Ava took a sip of wine, an imported Chardonnay. The garden was pitch black now with a new moon. Strange-shaped trees bent towards her. She heard rustling amongst the leaves. A bird or possibly a bat swooped across the sky. She experienced a moment she could only describe as weird: part terror, part joy. She was alone in a strange country and after midnight there'd be no phone connection. Her Nyepi was starting two hours before the official time. She went indoors to the area the maid had said to use for relaxation and sat down. Did anyone on Bali have a pavilion just for thinking?

At home, people were everywhere: shoppers and dawdlers in the street, gym-bunnies and swimmers at their health club, colleagues, and frenemies at work. Not to mention weekends with John's or her friends and both sets of parents. She stood up to close the large windows and turned on a light. When would she ever get the chance to do this again? She moved amongst the dark wood furniture, touched chair arms, straightened a picture on a wall then saw her rucksack on the tiled floor.

She bent to rummage through it, thinking she'd look at the wedding brochures Suzi had given them before the lights went off at midnight. There was her water bottle, purse, and comb but no wedding literature. John must have taken the brochures to his hotel. The images lingered in her mind from their time in the office. He had been like a big kid flicking from one fancy venue to another.

"Which should it be? Marrying in a jungle or on top of a volcano?"

He wasn't joking either. In her opinion, the photographs verged on the schmaltzy. A word she didn't think she'd ever used before. Couples gazed into each other's eyes over precipices. Waterfalls glistened in the background. She hoped John wasn't being sucked in by the fairy-tale commercialism. At least Suzi had steered him away, pointing out other venues: churches even, or traditional Balinese buildings.

AVA WOKE around seven-thirty still thinking about the photos, aware that last night had been a practice run and her true Nyepi was about to start. She threw off the bed sheet and padded across the garden to the kitchen. The maid had left boxes of prepared food, enough for two, and she took a bowl of fresh fruit, biscuits, and yoghurt, into the garden. Lush was a word she'd heard frequently in reference to Bali: green, verdant, blossoming. Barefoot, she followed winding paths, stopped to dip her hand into a trickling basin of water. At her feet was a carpet of fragrant flowers, fallen from a frangipani tree. Other plants sprung up in random profusion: hibiscus, bougainvillea, oleander, and jasmine. Their fragrance was delicious.

John often used the word lush at home, though not about gardens. She realised now that it was an interpretation she disliked. Such and such an actor was lush. So were his dad's meals and the golf club-house décor. He was probably flicking through the brochures right now, circling the lushest wedding venues with a red pen.

Ava found a sun-lounger and stretched out on it. It was still early enough not to need any shade. A jade-coloured butterfly alighted near her feet, fooled by her stillness into thinking she was part of the furniture. Sparrow-like birds perched in branches then flew down close to where she lay. One, with a bright red head, joined them. Insects and birds: they fluttered, twirled, changed direction. Her very own Balinese dancers.

And there it was. Those dancers at the temple two days ago. Like the wildlife now, not performances at all. Tourists were welcome to watch of course but those young girls had danced with a purpose, to cast out spirits. And last night's procession with the ogoh ogoh, months of careful sculpting, painting, painstaking craft, all because their makers and procession revellers believed in something. And what lay ahead for her? A photo album filled with tawdry myths for plastic versions of themselves?

Her eyes pricked with unexpected tears, and she lifted a hand to dash them away causing the birds to fly into the trees and pause their singing. Silence. No traffic from the road beyond the villa's wall. She remembered their first morning, waking early with the *put putter* of dozens of motor bikes heading out of the village.

Suddenly she was aware that she had something important to do. Suzi had suggested she meditate but Ava didn't know how. She and her friends didn't go in for that kind of thing. But there were other ways to contemplate life. She knew about visualisation. Watched TV programmes where shopping addicts lay out all their possessions to begin decluttering their homes. With a mix of the two, Ava emptied her life, as many aspects as she could think of, onto the pristine lawn at her feet.

She started small: minor irritations with work colleagues. Her sister's sniping comments about how much she spent on holidays. She went through her days cataloguing regrets, surprises, delights. Then came the big stuff.

John's last birthday present to her, a bag with a full set of golf clubs, lay on the lawn in a patch of its own. On her birthday, she'd been unsure how to respond. *Wonderful darling*, with a big kiss on the cheek. *How did you come up with that idea?*

He'd told her that playing together would mean they'd see more of each other. "You won't be a golf widow before you're a wife, now."

Ava lay back and threw another memory onto the lawn. Something she'd said to him later that day. "I chose a man who is like my father."

He'd touched his neck before replying, as if feeling for an incipient double chin. "You mean I look old?"

"No, idiot! A kind man. Someone who listens. Asks me how I am. Does jobs around the house without me nagging him to. Who wants to spend time with me. The trouble is..." She'd unzipped the bag and touched the cold steel of a club. "I've never played golf."

"You soon will."

AFTER LUNCH, Ava walked across the courtyard to the house temple; a high structure topped by a miniature open pavilion in which sat a small, blue statue of a god. She saw that an offering had been left on a flat shelf, perhaps by the maid or gardener the day before. The flower petals were curling, and the fruit had gone, probably eaten by mice. She left it there and sat on a cushion close by and placed a notebook on her knee. On a sheet she drew two columns and began an exercise she'd done in school years ago in a careers lesson when the students were asked to think about their futures. Aged sixteen, half a dozen words showed the limit of her horizons.

This time she gave herself more space to write.

The last 10 years has been...
The next 10 years will be...?

She added scenarios: **Work, Place, Self,** and began...

AROUND FIVE O'CLOCK and feeling hungry, she ate one of the prepared rice and vegetable dishes and more fruit. After rinsing the plates and cutlery in the sink she went back outside. The light had changed. Leaves and stems were a softer green. Riotous scarlet and yellow flowers were less harsh on the eye. The garden felt hushed and secret, no longer forbidding as it had the night before. It was familiar now, like a den from childhood. But there was more to think about before Nyepi was over: particularly the way she and John had met and how quickly they'd come together as a couple. Back then, she'd loved the fact that they'd bonded so easily without all the embarrassment that early dates normally entailed.

The first time she saw him was amongst a group of other amateur actors, all serious about their work, newly gathered from different parts of Leeds to rehearse *An Inspector Calls*. Some were drama teachers, most, like Ava who was a fashion buyer, weren't and John worked for his father's building firm. A woman called Roz had sat next to her. She knew John from an earlier production.

"He's great. Everyone loves him," Roz enthused as she went through the merits of each cast member. "A joy to act with. Gets deep into whatever role he's playing."

Over time, Ava saw this was true. Off stage he was kind, thoughtful and steady. If he were older, he'd have been a dead cert for a Tom Hanks' movie character. A year ago, before their engagement, she'd played Desdemona to his Iago. *John Carne gave an outstanding performance*, a reviewer wrote in the local paper.

Ava's thoughts swirled. Her mind flitted around *Othello*...and John's role; the way he'd portrayed the character's duplicity, pretending to be everyone's friend when he was nothing of the sort. Of course, he wasn't an Iago and yet, didn't everyone pretend to some extent?

She remembered her dream from the night before. The setting was back home in Leeds. John had secretly purchased a wooden mask and surprised her with it. It hung on their lounge wall, a demon with a red tongue and fiery eyes. She'd taken it down and fitted it over her head.

On stage, people wore masks pretending to be someone else. At the workshop, the owner had told her that when a sacred mask was worn in Bali, the wearer *becomes* someone else.

As the light in the garden changed, a dream memory rushed back, as vivid as when she lay asleep. Whilst wearing the mask, she'd felt powerful. It had given her knowledge...

A BALI SUNSET WAS STARTING, seeming more like an outdoor cinema experience than a natural phenomenon. Ava went indoors to make a soft fruit drink. Alcohol didn't seem appropriate for Nyepi. There was still more food to get through. She looked in John's guidebook for the rules about tipping and how to say thank you in Balinese, thinking of the trouble the maid had gone to so Ava wouldn't go hungry.

Before she went to bed, she took up her notebook knowing she needed to add to the columns. She read what she'd written in the garden:

The last 10 years have been fun, prosperous, challenging, romantic.

Now she added two new words:

Self-indulgent. Unaware.

In the work column, she put a line through **Fashion business** and inserted a question mark. She did same for **Place** and **Leeds.**

The next 10 years I will be: an adventurer? / Bali? / John???

The writing and thinking wasn't over, but it was enough for now.

IN THE MORNING, the motorbikes were back. Ava woke to the sound of their stuttering and roaring. She dressed in loose trousers and a linen top then went to the wardrobe where she took one of John's shirts off its hanger. Using a pair of nail scissors, she snipped off the bottom button. Next, she searched her make-up bag where she knew there were earrings he'd given her last year. From a pocket in her suitcase, she extracted a ticket for a charity dinner dance in May, to be hosted by *Carne and Son*. John had presented it to her on the flight to Bali as a surprise. She put the items in her pockets, scooped up some fruit, cut a few garden flowers and took them over to the house temple and lay everything out on the offering stone. Beyond the inner gates and outer wall came the sound of a horn honking as a scooter passed the villa. Ava stepped away from the temple as if reversing from royalty.

On her return, her phone was ringing in the bedroom and John's photo flashed up on the screen. "How was your Nyepi?" he asked.

"More than good." She paused. "John, there's something I need to say to you." A twinge of guilt clouded her decision. Could she say it? "I hate playing golf."

Her heart pounded while she waited in turn. John was rarely lost for words. Neither did he get angry. Perhaps he should, sometimes. She heard a faint crackle, like static, on the line.

"Me too. I just play because dad thinks it will be good for my career and he can introduce me to people," he said eventually.

"Is there anything else you're *just* doing?" She was full of concern. She hoped he could hear it.

His voice was shaky. "I think there might be."

She imagined him sinking down into a chair in his hotel room, anxious but relieved she'd started the process.

AVA HAD the fridge door open and a bowl of fruit in her left hand when the phone rang for a second time. The screen lit up with an unknown number and a woman's voice bid her good morning.

"It's Suzi Bannister from the agency. Do you have a moment to talk?"

Ava sat down. Suzi's manner seemed different. A little on edge perhaps. Two days ago, she'd been friendly, business-like, but no way pushy. Someone Ava would be happy to see again. "Yes, I'm not busy and John's still at the hotel."

"How was your Nyepi? Mine was quite revealing."

Ava gripped her phone. She felt a surge of apprehension. Had no idea where this conversation was going.

"It led me to consider making a huge change in my life. I wondered if you could come over to the office before you fly home? I have a business idea I'd like to share with you. I understand you have a degree in Marketing and you're a fashion buyer. I think we'd work well together."

Ava thought of the different aspects of her life that she'd placed on the lawn. She pictured her question marks in the notebook.

She took a deep breath. "I'd like that."

She looked at the garden which awaited her return and the offering she'd just placed on the temple; something from both of them. "But there's one thing I need to do first; take John back to the workshop. Two days ago, I dissuaded him from buying a mask and that was wrong of me. And I will ask him to come with me when you and I meet."

The Brooches

Krishnaveni K. K. Panikker

Tanty

The Indonesian maid was waiting for Datin to join the rest of the family for breakfast. They ate and discussed family matters as usual. Everyone was at the table except Datin, and she was never late for breakfast or any other function for the matter.

Tanty had been working for the wealthy Datuk Johari's family the past three years. His wife, Datin Jasmine, was wheelchair-bound. Tanty had to keep an eye on her hyperactive boss who also had epilepsy. Datin ran a few boutiques which sold expensive baju kebayas and batik sarongs. Rumour had it that Datin was much richer and older than her younger handsome husband. They had three children; the eldest, a son named Imran and two daughters, Aimi and Mimi.

Tanty decided to check on Datin's whereabouts. As she knocked and opened Datin's bedroom door, she heard water splashing out of the faucet. Tanty rushed into the attached bathroom which was ajar and was numb with shock. She found Datin's wheelchair nearby the bathtub and Datin face down in the bathtub which was full of water.

Tanty assumed that Datin must have had an attack of fits while she was brushing her teeth as there was a toothbrush floating in the bathtub. The tube of an uncapped toothpaste was still at the sink with her facial cleanser.

Datin was never allowed to be alone in the bathroom in the mornings. She was always accompanied by either her husband or one of her daughters but, unfortunately, that morning the entire family was busy preparing for the opening of a new boutique.

"Datin.... Datin!"

The maid's screams brought the family to her room. Datuk Johari's knuckles were white as he held on to his wife's wheelchair. Young Imran was in a daze, still half-asleep after last night's partying. Aimi ran in with the quotations and invoices that her mother gave her the night before. Mimi, the youngest, screamed when she saw her mother in the bathtub, "Ibu! Ibu! What happened to Ibu?"

Datuk called the family doctor. "Dr Chong, can you please come over to the bungalow? I think my wife had her usual fits and had fallen into the bathtub." With that, he walked down the stairs to wait for the family doctor.

Imran was busy making calls. "No... no... Rajen, we have not removed mother from the tub. Ya... ya... I understand the procedure. No, no, she was alone in the bathroom. Please come fast."

"Was that Inspector Rajen you called, Abang?" asked his sister Aimi.

"Yes, he is coming with his team. Told us not to touch anything," reminded her brother.

Mimi hugged Tanty and sobbed, "Is Ibu dead, Kak?"

Tanty watched. Did Datin fall into the bathtub accidentally; did she have her fits or did someone push her into the bathtub? The confused maid closed her mouth in horror and stifled a cry. Poor Datin was such a lovable person, so full of life even though she was wheelchair-bound. Tanty was treated very well by Datin, who never raised her voice when Tanty made mistakes.

Datin was a very soft-spoken and kind-hearted woman; she loved helping single mothers. Her beautiful smile was something Tanty will never forget. She loved to dress up even though she was in a wheelchair. She wore beautiful tudungs that matched her pretty kebayas. Tanty's favourite accessories were Datin's exquisite brooches, whose valuable stones sparkled like her eyes which would light up when she narrated tales to Tanty about her adventures overseas during her younger days. Datin loved brooches and it was during her younger days that she bought many expensive brooches which were embedded with precious stones.

TANTY REMEMBERED one rainy night when she walked past the Datin's room. She heard Datin crying. Tanty knocked on her door and the crying stopped.

"Who is it?" asked Datin softly.

"It's me, Tanty, Datin. Can I come in? Are you ok?" asked the maid with concern.

After a short while, Datin opened her bedroom door. She was in her wheelchair, dressed in a beautiful batik kaftan. She had removed her tudung and her hair was long and shiny. She must have cried for awhile as her eyes looked misty and puffed. Tanty walked into a brightly-lit bedroom and noticed Datuk was not in the room. The king-sized bed had only one pillow and Datuk's bed clothes were also not on the bed.

"Datuk sleeps upstairs in his office; he gets lots of phone calls and he doesn't want to disturb my sleep," explained Datin when she saw her maid looking around suspiciously.

Tanty noticed there were rows and rows of brooches on the bed. The precious stones on the brooches shone like stars. There was music in her room. Datin loved music and she played the piano well.

Datin stroke the brooches gently and whispered, "These brooches are my life and soul. I love them very much. I have been collecting them since I was a young girl. I was the only child and also the only granddaughter. My grandmother was an avid collector of expensive brooches and she left them to me. I am very proud of my collections but sad to say my family will only think of their value and nothing else. I don't want them to be sold off. I want them in the family; I want to pass them down to one of the children, but I think none of them will ever value and love them the way I do. I only wish there was a child like that. My family had not seen the entire collection of the brooches and I hope you can keep this a secret."

Tanty helped her to place them in their individual tiny boxes which had soft velvety cushions. Datin hid them in one of her antique cupboards that had many secret compartments. The cupboard was her wedding gift from her late grandmother. She brought it along with her when she married Datuk Johari.

WHEN THE FAMILY DOCTOR ARRIVED, he pronounced Datin dead. He confirmed that she had a bout of fits, fell into the bathtub and drowned. Police saw no foul play since the doctor, who produced the death certificate, was aware of Datin's frequent attacks. Tanty knelt beside Datin's casket and whispered a soft farewell to her. Finally, she was laid to rest at the nearby cemetery.

It was late evening and everyone who came to pay their respect for Datin had left the bungalow. The house was very quiet as everyone had retired to their rooms. Tanty was feeling exhausted and miserable. She was going to miss Datin very much and wondered if she would still be employed, now that Datin was no longer around. The thought of living with Datin's family made her very sad. She loved working for this family, and she was not ready to leave yet. With a heavy heart, Tanty went to her bedroom. She had a splitting headache. She slept the minute her head touched her pillow.

Suddenly, Tanty woke up with a start to the sound of someone's pitiful crying. The neighbour's dogs were howling. She sprang out of bed and listened to the strange spine-chilling sound. Her room was filled with blackness. The eerie sound was coming from inside the house. Tanty looked pale and frightened. She walked slowly to her window. Darkness had fallen and everything was still in the garden except for a slow breeze. She took a deep breath and looked across the garden. There were some movements among the trees, and she thought she saw a flash of white between the flowerpots. Maybe it was their pet cat, Putera, who loved to wander out at night to look for his girlfriends. Whatever it was, it was lurking in the shadowy clumps of bushes. The dogs had not stopped howling and someone's window was rattling. Suddenly, there were loud knocks on her bedroom door.

Tanty screamed and covered her ears. She did not open her door but bolted it securely. The quick and loud knocks carried on, becoming louder. With trembling hands, Tanty switched on her room light.

"Who is it?" Tanty shrieked. The knocks continued. "Who is it, please?" she murmured hoarsely.

"Open the door Tanty, it's Datuk," bellowed Datuk Johari.

Tanty opened the door nervously. Datuk and his children were staring at her, all of them looked sleepy.

"What was all the noise about Tanty?" questioned Datuk.

"Ya, Kakak, we heard someone crying from your room," explained the youngest girl.

"I heard the noise too, but it was not from my room. Datuk, I think there is someone in the garden," whispered Tanty softly.

Datuk looked at his maid strangely. Tanty glanced behind him uneasily. Datin's wheelchair was at the stairway. She remembered pushing the wheelchair into her room before retiring to bed.

"Why is Datin's wheelchair outside?" asked Tanty with a frown.

"Ibu's wheelchair was at her doorstep when we came up looking for you," remarked Imran in an irritated tone. Imran never liked her simply because she was very close to his mother. Tanty remembered Datin had joked that their maid was prettier than his girlfriend.

"Were you in Ibu's room?" asked Imran.

"No...no, I was sound asleep until the eerie crying woke me up," answered Tanty.

"Ibu's tudung and brooch collections were scattered on her bed. It could only be you, Tanty. You are the only one who knew where Mama kept her things. What were you looking for?" questioned Datin's eldest daughter in a hostile voice.

"Please don't shout at Kak Tanty. I think she is telling the truth. Why are all of you treating her like a thief?" asked Mimi in a pitiful voice.

"Mimi, you stay out of this. Just because she was close to Mama doesn't mean she is a good girl. She is an actress. You go to your room now," chided her brother.

Nobody spoke for a while. The eerie moans had stopped. Datuk Johari was watching his wife's maid. Tears were brimming in her eyes, and she was fidgeting with her buttons on her house coat. He looked long and hard at her, walked off and the others followed.

Tanty could not sleep and in a while, it would be dawn. She heard the nearby surau's azan and decided to start her household chores. Too many doubtful thoughts were going on in Tanty's mind as she walked out of her room. No one had bothered to push Datin's wheelchair into her room. As she entered the room with the wheelchair, Tanty was shocked to see Datin's beautiful tudungs and brooches thrown all over the bed and some were even on the floor.

Tears ran down Tanty's cheeks as she picked each of them up and placed them in their pretty, coloured cushioned boxes. She hugged and inhaled the perfumed smell of Datin's tudungs. She loved the soft material that only the rich could afford, not forgetting the kebayas with the elegant workmanship. Datin loved flowers and birds with unique patterns which no one else wore. These elegant costumes clung to her figure.

Tanty remembered that before the accident, when Datuk and Datin hosted many dinners for their friends, Datin would walk down the stairs dressed in her best fitting kebayas and sarongs and Datuk Johari could hardly take his eyes off her. Tanty overheard Datin's friends joke that she was trying to keep up with her husband's youth.

After her accident, Datin moved to the room downstairs where everything was made convenient for her. Datuk chose to stay in his huge office upstairs, hardly visiting her in her new bedroom. All discussions pertaining to business as well as household matters were discussed in the mornings at the breakfast table.

Datuk's morning farewell peck on Datin's cheek became a mere pat on her back. Tanty noticed that the couple lacked their usual loving touch; it was now a regular duty for them, just like brushing their teeth. Datuk's eyes used to roam when Datin's friends dropped in to visit her. Tanty could see his yearnings; after all, he was an attractive and virile young man.

Tanty heaved a sigh and mumbled to herself that the rich and famous life was a tough one. She had been instructed by Datuk to take Datin's kebayas and sarongs for dry cleaning. She had to follow the driver and instruct the dry cleaners accordingly.

Breakfast was ready as usual, and everyone was seated at the table. Some serious discussion was going on and Tanty wondered if it involved her.

"Tanty, can you come here for a while," called Datuk Johari.

Tanty walked slowly to the breakfast table, "Yes, Datuk."

"Ok. Now. It's like this. Since Datin is no longer around, we have decided we don't really need you. I am sorry to inform you at such short notice but not to worry, I will compensate you accordingly," assured Datuk Johari.

"Moreover, there is nothing much for you to do in the house, now that Ibu is gone," continued Imran.

"I am sorry you have to leave early, Tanty," consoled Datuk.

"Ayah, no need to sorry-sorry her. She has nothing to do here, so she better leave. We keep her further she will slowly roll you round her thumb like she did to Ibu. Must be some Indonesian black magic. I know these women; they come with great plans to our country," Aimi told her father.

Datuk just nodded his head as he sipped his hot tea with a faraway look on his face.

"Hey, Tanty, you still don't want to admit that you took Ibu's brooches? Bang, call Inspector Rajen or shall we take her to the police station?" asked Aimi.

Datuk banged his cup of tea on the table. It rolled and fell on the floor into pieces. It was one of Datin's favourite cups.

"Will all of you stop this, please. No need to take her to the police station. She looked after your mother very well. I will not deny that, and I am sure you agree too. You have checked her room thoroughly and you have found nothing there. Keep on searching, I am sure you will find them. I wonder where your mother had kept them. By the way, I will speak to the agent first before I ask my secretary to book a flight for Tanty. This discussion is over. Tanty, make sure you leave Datin's kebayas at the dry cleaners. Do you understand what I am telling you?"

"Yes, Datuk," the maid replied.

"The faster she is out of the house, the better it will be for all of us. Good riddance to bad rubbish. Ayah, please don't ask me to take her to her airport," said Aimi.

"Count me out too, I don't want any thieves in my car," said Imran.

"Kak Tanty, don't worry I will get you a Grab," assured the youngest girl.

The maid gave a smile to Mimi. She was like Datin, beautiful, soft-spoken and gentle. Tanty loved this child and one day, if she had a daughter, she would want one like Mimi.

Datuk

Years passed. The huge bungalow felt very quiet and empty. His children never had breakfast with him and hardly visited him since they had families of their own. The little one, Mimi, had left for studies overseas. She wanted to be a fashion designer, just like her mother. Before she left, she received a parcel with her mother's brooches, not from Indonesia as Aimi had claimed. It merely stated,

> *To the most beautiful and soft-spoken girl. Your mother would have wanted you to have these. Please treasure them.*

There was no sender's name nor address. Datuk could see that his daughter was very happy to receive her mother's missing brooches.

Datuk was tired of working and he had enough savings to last him a lifetime. His greedy son and daughter were too busy with the rat race; they had no time for him. He decided to go on a holiday to somewhere far and where no one knew him.

The airport was congested. It was the end of the year, and everyone was travelling. Datuk joined the crowd and moved with them. He watched the crowd, many with families and others alone, just like him. He wondered if they were travelling alone or waiting for someone.

Every head turned to watch a woman passing by. She had a confident gait but if you watched her closely, you might notice that she was a woman who had gone through a lot in life.

Her eyes shone; her lips heavy with a dark lipstick. Her hair was loose and falling on her shoulders. She was wearing a tight-fitting baju kebaya with a beautiful batik sarong, clingy as her second skin.

He had arrived promptly as he promised. He was dressed casually and there was a touch of grey at his temples that gave him a distinguished look.

HE HAD NOT WANTED her to take a Grab as Mimi'd suggested.

He remembered driving her to the drycleaners, then to the airport. He gave most of his wife's kebayas and sarongs to her; he knew she liked the attire. She thanked him with tears in her eyes and left without looking back. That was the last time he saw her.

He looked at her, and gave her a slow, intimate smile, the smile that never left his face as they had made love when the Datin was sedated on some nights. The adjourning door to Datin's room made it all too convenient for the young maid to leave and visit Datuk without being noticed.

"You look so beautiful, Tanty," he complimented, his voice a husky whisper.

She looked at him and gave him a smile. They were both in a new place and they wanted to start afresh. She wanted to know him better, not as a boss but a partner and lover.

"I am sorry you had to go through hell with my children," he said.

"No, I had my faults. I took advantage of Datin's kindness. She was very good to me."

"But you returned the brooches. You did not keep them for yourself," he said.

"Stealing her husband was bad enough," she said. "I have to confess something to you. I kept one brooch with me. I promised myself that if ever I have a child like Datin, I will carry on her tradition with the brooches," she explained with tears in her eyes.

"What do you mean?" asked Datuk.

Tanty turned around and a little girl with bright eyes and the most beautiful smile came running towards them. On her dress there was a brooch with two swans dancing; beautifully and delicately designed many years ago.

"Mama, you told me you will come and get me; you almost forgot me," complained the little girl.

Johari looked at the young cheeky girl. Tanty must have been pregnant when she left his house. She had kept the child a secret.

"Why didn't you tell me, Tanty? Why?" inquired Datuk.

"I didn't want my child to be treated the same way as I've been," said Tanty.

"I am so sorry you had to bear it yourself, Tanty," said Datuk.

"Hello, young lady. It was my fault. By the way, I am Datuk. What is your name?" He spoke gently.

"Hi, my name is Jasmine," the little girl replied.

He looked at Tanty. He saw sorrow in her beautiful eyes. It was the same with him; he had lived in guilt. The morning that his wife passed away, he had gone to help her as usual. Datin told him that she would not be needing his assistance for long and to look after Tanty if ever she was not around.

When he'd tried to interrupt, she raised her hand and told him to leave the room. "Johari, she is a good girl, and I don't blame you for falling in love with her. Don't feel bad for me. Please leave." That was the last time he'd spoken to his wife.

"Come on, I am hungry, Jasmine's hungry, Jasmine's hungry," the girl sang.

A Sparkle of Fireflies

Doc Krinberg

The blur of the landscape framed in the window made Hotaru's eyes heavy. There was a ground cover of fresh snow from the first day of February that in the train's high speed viewing made it shimmer as summer beach sand. With an hour until her travel terminated at Shinigawa Station, she stared sleepily out her tinted window and again wondered if she'd done the right thing.

Although the idea of fresh snow gave her hope, she took one last look outside and then pulled down the blinds and settled in as the sleek bullet train was hitting maximum speed after the last stop at Hamamatsu.

She awoke as they decelerated into Shin Fuji Station. Fuji-san, visible from the station stood high in its winter glory; a postcard dressing of white wrapped around it. Yawning and stretching, the vision of Fuji renewed her feelings. Was not Fuji-yama the symbol of beauty and perfection? After taking refreshments, she again reflected on why she was *en route* to Tokyo.

Him.

He was in his early fifties, fit, and his suit didn't hang on him. Being in retail clothing for the last ten years, it was the first thing of which she took notice and could spot off the rack a kilometer away. There was an arrogant casualness in how well he looked in his clothes; the subtlety of this act again not lost on her. Turning her smile down at the corners of her mouth, she recalled it was the first flag of attraction when he entered the Miyako Hotel bar alone, her sister Sora placing a discreet elbow into her ribs as they enjoyed their weekly after work cocktail.

"Hmm, that *one*," her sister said poking her. "He walks as if he has a set unlike some milquetoast salary man. Executive material."

"Hush," Hotaru whispered. And by then they had locked eyes.

Sora was right, she thought. After he slowly walked up to the seated women, he smiled and immediately broke the ice asking if they were *The Makioka Sisters* making Sora, her younger sister and already married, laugh and stated they weren't seeking a husband for their *other* sister. They invited him to sit and ordering fresh drinks were relieved he was so very confident, humorous and easy going, not the usually stuttering and nervous wrecks who attempted their company on cocktail nights. He was indeed an executive with a huge shipping corporation in Tokyo and down in Kyoto purely on business, staying at the Westin and hearing of the prowess of the Miyako's barman, decided to try his famous Moscow Mules. Hotaru looked into her sister's eyes and sent the message that it was time to cut bait, and seeing the *look,* Sora knew it was time to retire and leave the field to her sister.

"My husband will be surprised I have cut short cocktail night with my sister, but I must go." Giving Hotaru a kiss on each cheek, with a whispered 'be good', she stood. He, already on his feet, gave each other small courteous bows.

And it had been a good night. The spark ignited at the Miyako became a small bonfire at the Westin. After a leisurely in-suite early breakfast and exchange of business cards, they embraced. Hotaru got changed at home and arriving at work, pulled Sora to the side, giving her a quick debrief and both giggled.

Two days later, the card, first class train tickets and hotel reservations with instructions arrived at their business.

"Well?" Sora inquired. "Do you feel like a Kyoto geisha of old meeting a benefactor?" Her teasing was not lost on Hotaru.

Hotaru sighed, "I'm not getting any younger. I told him I was thirty-three and it didn't seem to bother him. Then again, I don't think this one is fishing for a spouse. I could feel a widow hovering overhead."

Her sister looked at her warmly.

The mention of age reminded Hotaru of her last suitor who had in public, while intoxicated, called her his "Christmas Cake" and said how lucky she was to find him, to the group's embarrassment. Hotaru was twenty-six at the time and the insult of nobody wanting that *cake* after the 25th hit hard. The engagement had been broken off at her sister's request the next day.

"If you go, be open minded, have fun and if at the very least, it's an expense paid trip to Tokyo," Sora encouraged her, smiling wanly.

And so Hotaru was traveling at over 300 km/h across Japan.

SHINAGAWA WAS busy and crowded with the Shinkasen passengers disembarking amid usual daily traffic. She found the short, stone-faced man holding the card with the shipping corporation logo and her name under it at the end of the long platform. Close-shaven and serious, he gave a curt bow, tipping the bill of his cap with two fingers to Hotaru when she acknowledged him. Dressed in sharp grey livery, he walked in front of her, the luggage roller out in front of him, parting the waves of passengers. They quit the station. Arriving at a Mercedes the same color as his uniform, he opened her door and placed the roller in the boot. Sitting in plush leather seats, she knew conversation with this one would be more akin to dentistry and so enjoyed the ride listening to the classical music played on a CD. Not once, but twice she caught his eyes looking at her in the mirror.

Smiling each time she noticed, his eyes darting away quickly. *Well,* she thought, *my little stone man is human after all.*

They arrived at the Park Prince Tower in Roppongi. Her driver jumped out and opened her door before the parking attendant could. Retrieving her bag, he escorted her and assisted in her check-in, only speaking to the concierge. The shipping corporation kept a small row of rooms, he informed her, and asked if she needed him to accompany her upstairs. Bending slowly and rising, she again gave him a smile.

"Thank you so much for your help. It is very much appreciated but I can manage." Her driver's face reddening, he returned her bow, then curtly handed her a card, informing her he was at her disposal and would return promptly at six to drive her to dinner. She moved to the elevators, and then turning, she stopped and looked back at him and said in her sweetest tone:

"And what is your name, please?" The card had only a mobile number. His face reddened even deeper as he cleared his throat.

"Iwao."

"Iwao...the stone. How very fitting!" She smiled again and taking her stroller bag, went to the elevator.

The room was spacious and the bed was what she figured was a Western-style king size. Sitting down on the edge, she looked the room over and seeing the fruit basket and bouquet of white roses on the table in the sitting room of the suite bounced her eyebrows in interest. Inside the bouquet and just visible was a small envelope. Taking it, she walked to the window, checking her view as she helped herself to a small pear. Tokyo Towers loomed closely. The note read:

Welcome!

Dinner will be at 6:30, and your driver will be there at six. I remember you saying you liked Italian food and so be it.

Until then, relax. You have an hour spa appointment scheduled (my small gift)

And he signed his name. This isn't a bad start, she decided.

At four, she entered the spa and giving her name to the uniformed young woman at reception, discerned a discreet eye roll when the reservation was found.

"Oh yes, Miss. We have you here. Your technician will be out in a moment. "

Hotaru sat, but only for a moment before the tech came out to greet and escort her to the changing room and baskets with spa attire. Bowing graciously, she entered and while changing, she could hear two whispering voices.

"Yes, *another* one for S— Corp. They always book them in this time." Then a giggle followed.

"Hmm, they like to tune them up before the dinner dates."

"I wouldn't care but the gratuity is always so poor, and the women never think of us or our work."

"Hai!" the other voice agreed enthusiastically. Then the technician came to get her.

"This way, Miss." Her smile was fixed and wide.

Hotaru felt the spa service was excellent and she felt amazing afterwards: refreshed and 'tuned' up. She finished dressing and found the girl who was her technician.

"That was very good, thank you. You made this a very fine experience," she said, her smile as wide as the technician's. The girl blushed and bowing, thanked Hotaru profusely.

Then, Hotaru in her executive voice, asked, "What is the standard amount of the gratuity that S— Corp allows for its 'girls?'"

The younger girl's eyes widened in horror, knowing her indiscretion was being challenged and she was probably going to lose her job.

"Come on," Hotaru demanded.

Red-faced, the girl told her and began a stream of apologies. Hotaru held up a hand to make her stop. She did.

"Don't apologize for telling the truth," she said and handed the younger woman a small envelope that held a ¥5,000 note. "And I'm not *another* one." She turned and walked out of the spa, the girl's mouth open.

Back in her room, she took out the black dress she brought for dinner.

"I plan on getting some mileage out of you," she said to it softly. "Or will you be getting mileage from me?"

Iwao was waiting in the lobby as she exited the elevator, bowing from the neck in affirming her presence. She smiled inward at his name. *Stone.*

"Greetings, Iwao-san," she said, knowing that probably irritated him.

Grunting, he gestured to the door as she walked by him.

While Kyoto lay under a soft blanket of snow, Tokyo barely saw a dusting. As she peered out the Mercedes' window, she noticed the city had that clean, hard frozen sheen; the air creating a cold, hard focus. It was barely over 1 degree C and she shivered even in the relative comfort of the car. Luckily, the restaurant in Hiroo was close. Pulling up to the curb, she could see the brightly lit entrance with *Trattoria* over the door.

Iwao opened her door and touching his bill said gruffly, "Enjoy your dinner, Miss Hotaru."

"Thank you," she said, surprised he said anything, and feeling the cold quickly entered the restaurant.

It was busy on that Friday night in the lower entry area. She could see that beyond the maître-de desk the bar area was lively and clamorous; cigarette smoke heavy above the bar like a low, heated cloud so very different from the cracked glass cold of outdoors. She dropped his name at the desk and was met with a brisk "hai!" before being directed to follow the man dressed in a dinner jacket upstairs where the restaurant proper was.

He was at a corner table with two men, younger but just as nattily attired. Before them were ashtrays, empty and half-filled cocktail glasses, and a bottle of red wine open and breathing. Seeing her, he rose and taking the cue, the younger men stood as well. The maître-de pulled her chair out, took her coat and seated her. The men stood as he greeted her and introduced the two men as junior associates, smiling at them. They bowed before taking their seats. The formalities seemed unnecessary to Hotaru but obviously were vital to him.

The younger men, draining their glasses, then excused themselves and said they would be in the lounge downstairs. Hotaru bade them farewell and it wasn't lost on her that they were there to see her on display, taking her into account. She felt herself blushing, feeling somewhat objectified and following the indiscretion of the spa attendants in regards to being labeled *another,* she wondered how many times this scene had been replicated.

He reached across the table and, taking her hand, said he thought of her all week, and was so very glad she accepted his invitation. She thanked him for the beautiful bouquet. Their small talk circled around her trip from Kyoto, the snow and if she received a good spa experience, the quality of the room. He complimented her on her dress and how she wore her hair; swept up on one side, her pendant earring of subtle white metal in her one exposed ear.

"You certainly know how to dress," he said in approval. Blushing again, she thanked him.

He'd ordered their meals before she arrived, as they were quickly served antipasto and lightly grilled calamari. "I hope you like manicotti," he smiled. She was relieved, as she did like that dish, but still. He had the eggplant parmesan, explaining to her how exquisite it was at the Trattoria. The waiter poured the wine for him and, awaiting approval, was granted permission to fill her glass. In lifting his to make a toast, she noticed for the first time that he was showing signs of being inebriated.

The cool and composed man from a week ago was now somewhat grandiose and louder; his voice, which before was calm and pragmatic, now seemed stretched with threads of narcissism woven in as he displayed his prowess in understanding and ordering Italian food and wine. He had, of course, visited Italy several times, for pleasure and on business. During the meal, she was mostly silent.

Dessert was offered along with a list of aperitifs, cordials, coffees, teas, and post dining liqueurs. He wanted cognac while she desired Amaretto with her tiramisu, to which he offered a windy lecture on after dinner drinks. Looking to change the subject, she mentioned Iwao and how committed he seemed to be in his job, hoping to break off the now boring soliloquy.

"Ahh, Iwao. Yes, he is akin to a soldier, follows his orders and never questions his assigned duties. Sadly, he hasn't much of a life as of last year he became a widower. His wife, a Chinese, had cancer I believe." He lit a cigarette blowing a plume of smoke to the ceiling added, "He is at your disposal." He went on to inform her he would be busy up to two p.m. the next day and so have him take her for a drive around the city if she desired.

Finished, they dropped down to the lounge, reuniting with the two younger men and several others he knew. There were more introductions; more cocktails and shop talk amongst the now well-lubricated group. Hotaru looked around the room. The majority were men in suits, ties loosened and voices getting louder. A couple at a standing table were stone-faced and silent in this din and she wondered what unfolding tragedy prompted it. Looking at the blankness of the woman, she felt she could relate.

Finally, breaking away from the loud group, he told her Iwao was outside awaiting them, and, exchanging numerous farewells, helped her with her coat. They exited the restaurant, meeting the iciness of the Tokyo night.

In the street, Iwao opened the rear door, standing in the cold as if it had no effect on him.

In the back seat, they both shivered as they adjusted to the warmth of the seats. Hotaru let a small gasp escape her lips as she felt his hand siding up her leg to her upper thigh. Iwao was instructed to return to the Park Prince and he said "hai" as they pulled away.

He broke the silence and asked Iwao, "How do you like Miss Hotaru? She and her sister are successful businesswomen who own their own clothing shop." Hotaru felt that he needed Iwao to know she wasn't just *another*. "And beautiful too, neh? Well-named...a *firefly*, is she not?"

Iwao dipped his chin and made a sound in his throat. His eyes caught hers in the rear view mirror and she felt his embarrassment at being asked for validation. She wondered if he felt hers.

Exiting the car at the hotel, he was unsteady on his feet using Iwao's shoulder as a stabilizer. Hotaru helped by putting an arm around him and turning to Iwao, asked him for assistance; the pout on his face indicative of how little he wished to render it. Together they piloted him through the lobby and once at the elevator, both took a deep breath from the exertion. At her door, the older man turned to her.

"I'm sure you can manage this from here. I've no doubt you're more experienced in this than I." And touching the brim of his cap, turned and briskly left.

Containing her anger at such a rude remark, she managed a terse smile, entered the room and helped him to the bed. Hotaru took a bottled water from the mini-bar and handed it to him. Nodding his thanks he drank from it, half the bottle disappearing. She stood above him. What a difference a week had made. He stood, and removing his coat, came and took her in his arms, whispering in her ear, "Last week was very fine."

His hands on her back were pressing her to him.

Later, as he snored, his words came back to her and in that moment, she couldn't have disagreed more, as the smooth lover of the week before vanished. Later, on the floor, she discovered his medication of blue pills that seemed to have fallen from his jacket pocket. Obviously they helped him last week but in the face of his alcohol consumption, not so much tonight.

THE NOTE on the coffee table was an apology for the previous night *but* the promise of a better night. And then there was the itinerary for the day to include when Iwao would deliver her. Frowning, she carelessly tossed it back on the table and looked at the breakfast menu. She had a decision to make and didn't want it on an empty stomach. It was midmorning when she called Iwao on his mobile and requested him to pick her up. He would arrive in approximately thirty minutes. She was ready.

Iwao's breath was visible as he came through the automatic lobby doors and out of habit brought his gloved hands up to blow on them. Seeing her, he noticed there was something different from yesterday. Hotaru, in navy wool slacks, a turtle-neck of the same hue, boots and her heavy winter coat, walked to him, her face blank of emotion and barely made up. She brought her roller bag to a halt and leaned the handle towards him to take it.

"Put it in the car," she told him, her voice flat. When he took hold of the handle, she kept walking. She disappeared outside before Iwao could react. By the time he got to the car, she was already settled, her window cracked for her cigarette smoke to escape. Storing her bag, he entered the car, removed his cap revealing a perfect grey flattop. He turned and meeting her eyes, she simply said, "Drive."

"Am I taking you to Shinagawa?" Iwao asked. It was the first time this had happened. Her silence continued as he automatically started towards the station. She stared stonily out of the window.

"Kamakura," she said softly, speaking to the window.

"Huh?"

"Kamakura. You're at *my* disposal and Kamakura is the destination," she said with finality.

"And you don't need to tell him. This is my day and I'm taking it." And so, he rerouted and hoped the traffic wasn't bad.

They drove in silence with Hotaru just gazing and thinking the cold had the city in an embrace and she felt it a kindred spirit; surrounded and filled with millions of souls but lonely and full of dreams.

"You're the first girl to do this," he told her.

"Do what? Escape?" she smirked.

"Yes, the first to come out ready to leave."

"Is that a fact? Perhaps they should name this Hotaru Day. Maybe I'll start a trend." Now she was bordering on sarcasm. "They can name a ship after me: the *Hotaru Maru*. Don't you get tired of ferrying all of us *bimbos* to and fro? What sort of job is that?"

He seemed to bristle at her last comment. "It is my job, and so I do it."

"Well, now you have me. Hotaru the firefly, and no kidding, my light is burnt out and I let it."

There followed an intermission of silence again. Finally, Iwao cleared his throat.

"When I was a boy, we would wait until dusk to see them in-flight. They're so slow that at times they appear to be suspended in the hot, humid air in quest of a mate. Of course we'd put them in a jar thinking we could create a lantern. Every child in the world believes that."

Hotaru remembered being teased about her name. She kept that to herself. Iwao changed lanes after seeing overhead signs to their destination. He continued, his voice softer, "My aunt would make my cousins and I empty our jars telling us we were disrupting their harmony, the synchronicity they gave us. We didn't understand that but she would warn us about needlessly altering their lives for our amusement. She'd say, 'Leave this sparkle of fireflies alone. Just watch them. Be still like a hummingbird and learn.' But, we were very young boys — who ever heard of a nine-year-old sitting still? When she and my mother went inside, we continued our collections. I see what she meant now."

Hotaru smiled at his story as she watched the scenery. She turned to his semi-profile in the front seat, "Do you still feel like you're catching those fireflies now? Collecting sparkles of them for him and the others so that we can be their temporary lights in a jar for the coming darkness of middle age? Have things really changed for us?"

He played a collection of Beethoven's piano pieces.

Closer to Kamakura it started to snow; swirling flurries that turned into slower, heftier flakes that stuck to the windscreen and then flew off. There was a backup of traffic into the city and they tried in vain to avoid the ongoing annual festival that Iwao remembered was for good luck in commerce, and of course, renewal. Hotaru insisted on visiting the Daibutsu at Kotoku-in shrine. There was urgency on her part to see it. After many starts and stops while weaving through the throngs of festival attendees, they parked close to the entrance of the place, the peaceful bronze giant sat in the lotus position.

Walking in the falling snow, they entered the almost empty area where Amitahba sat in infinite serenity. After Hotaru purchased their tickets, a small bunch of joss sticks and her paper omikuju fortune, Iwao followed her, pulling his grey overcoat tighter. He stared at the fierce Nio statue. Hotaru went ahead alone up the steps to the giant urns of burning incense and joss.

Placing her palms together she recited a silent prayer, a plea for strength. She saw Iwao, off to the side. Hotaru lit three sticks: the creation, heaven and earth.

Hotaru had moved to tie up her omikuju fortune that she read next to hundreds hanging silent in the snowy air. It bode well for her in the coming year and feeling better, she turned her head so Iwao couldn't see and caught a snowflake on her outstretched tongue. Smiling at this silly and spontaneous act, she was satisfied.

They looked up into the slow motion cascade of crystals. Their eyes met.

"I know something happened inside you during your preceding journey. But that's over with." He raised his grey eyebrows.

"Yes, you're right, there's nothing in Tokyo for me, and you as well, my stone man. I would appreciate a drop at the station. I have a ticket to amend, as I wish to return home." Her voice had lost the edge it had in the car.

They drove to the station; the tumult of the crowds outside did not invade the peace in the car. At the station, he retrieved her roller bag and handing it to her, bowed deeply from the waist. She leaned down and kissed him on the cheek lightly and said "Sayonara." She took two steps and then turned to watch him once more.

Checking his work mobile, he saw eight missed text messages and held it up for her to see as he easily tossed it into the city trash receptacle. Her smile was barely discernible, but he could feel it. She thought of the *last* prayer he spoke, audible to her, his gruff voice much softer. He asked forgiveness from all the fireflies of his youth, and then the fireflies he'd contained in this gray Mercedes jar, stifling their fire, and altering their lives as he did his own.

Mee Mamak

V. S. Lai

"Klang!"

A metal plate clattered onto the greasy floor. Misshapen lumps in a murky yellow liquid oozed out from under the overturned metal plate, its contents unrecognisable from the original construct of the best dhal and roti canai served on Jalan Ton. It was not easy for the mamak restaurant to lay claim to this honour. The fact that it was the only restaurant on Jalan Ton, and the only one serving mamak food were not the reasons. No. Its crowd-pleasing mee mamak was another gem on its oily laminated menus.

That night, all of the forty four-seater purpose-built tables that were bolted to the floor of the restaurant were filled with the buttocks of diners. Buttocks of all shapes and sizes, some covering the round chairs perfectly, some registering not even a metre whilst others spilled over the sides barely contained by the straining cloth that encapsulated their flesh. Buttocks also perched on rickety plastic chairs at tables disgorged onto the five-foot way outside the restaurant and on to the surrounding roadside.

The owners of these buttocks were the most disparate bunch of people anyone could expect to descend upon Jalan Ton, from the richly adorned to the simply clad, the topmost and lowest specimen of present day society. However, their external appearances did not guarantee that their internal qualities were of equal measure.

Under the unflinching brightness of the fluorescent lighting or in twilight darkness for those seated outside, all the owners of these buttocks had one unifying purpose. To fill their stomachs with enriching sustenance, and their souls with the comfort and fleeting assurance that for just a microsecond they were part of a greater collective worshipping at the feet of the Mamak God. They were not simply mere drops of grease clinging on to the clammy floor of the universe, only to be washed out in the final cleansing when the lights had been switched off and the shutters closed. But enough of these background fillers. Let's bring our attention back to the main event of the fallen plate.

The metallic *klang* of the plate landing on the floor sliced through the chatter of the buttocks. Sorry. Diners. Not buttocks. Let's repeat that again. The metallic clang sliced through the chatter of the diners that sounded like countless out-of-tune radio channels playing all at once. Silence blanketed over the entire restaurant. All heads turned towards the table located in the far corner, including the waiters in their neat little caps.

Even the cook who was spinning the roti canai dough turned his head. A piece of dough landed onto the hot iron skillet in the shape of a letter M or a possible S. The cook glanced at his misbegotten masterpiece and thought of his beloved wife Mina and his secret Instagram crush with the handler name Susanna0003, all within the time span of a second and a half. He would have liked to have dedicated a second more to Susanna0003 but he was as realistic about the prospects of wooing that influencer as he was about his prospects to wriggle out more pocket money from his wife.

"Look! You see what you did?" a man said. "Why you always like that?" He gestured to his female companion, who was standing next to the mess on the floor. Her face was red as an overripe papaya and her eyes brimmed with tears.

As if feeling the weight of more than one hundred and sixty pairs of eyeballs on him, the man averted his face away from the curious stares of the on-lookers. But it was too late. The on-lookers had already cast their hooks onto him, their eyeballs firmly on the crosshair that was on him. This real-time drama playing out in front of them was far more entertaining than the high definition 2D drummed up events playing out on the 40-inch flat screen TVs mounted on the wall. After all, nothing beats the full force of the impact of 3D on the sensory organs, not even when said organs had already been satiated from the blessings of the Mamak God.

Even our heroine, Hui Yan who was seated at the front, far from where the excitement took place, looked up. She had been locked in battle with her archenemy, the taukwa, over the plate of mee mamak. The outcome was forgone even before the battle had been fought. The taukwa had staked their claim all over the plate of noodles.

"Stupid couple," she said. "Can't they see that I'm doing something important here?"

The offending plate of mee mamak in front of her was an affront to her sensibilities. She had instructed the waiter in clear and concise terms that no taukwa was to be added to her order. Instead, it had come resplendent with many of them – brown cubes of fried tofu with their wrinkly exterior and white innards draped artistically in and amongst the noodle strands. There had even been a centrepiece of taukwa pieces arranged in the shape of a star and the sides of the plate were ringed too with taukwa.

Someone had gone to great lengths to create this work of hellish art. Once she counted how many taukwa pieces there were, she was going to blast the waiter for his forgetfulness. It didn't matter if she had a betraying thought that the star was cute. Every piece that she counted meant a step further away from the deliverance of the bliss that she had been longing for all day.

Hui Yan took a deep breath and re-started her count. "One, two, three..."

"Like what? Like this?" the woman shouted.

"Klang!" Another metal plate joined its sadly dented partner on the floor.

The audience's eyeballs were getting sore from the intense workout, as the argument swung back and forth between the woman and the man. What would happen next? Would the man retaliate by smashing another plate? The gamblers amongst the audience placed their bets. The odds were against the man. Once the woman switched on the waterworks, the man was bound to lose.

Hui Yan however was not amused. Her right eye twitched again. She massaged her brow and sighed. It was the thought of mee mamak that had sustained her throughout the day. Without it, she would have crumbled into a million useless pieces in front of her project team members. Today had been the worst day in the three years she had worked as a management consultant. Not one of her team members had come to her rescue when she had been unfairly blamed for not having carefully verified the research data. It was not wholly her fault and her teammates could have stepped in to explain. So much for three years of working day and night together, united in heart and purpose for the success of the project as she had naively thought.

"Oh mee mamak. If it hadn't been for you, I would have been lost," Hui Yan crooned. The silky yellowish-brown noodle strands sang to her with its intricate intertwined patterns, patterns in which she could lose herself and shed her worldly problems off her frail shoulders. The aroma from the freshly cooked noodles wafted, inviting her to step into its cocoon. But she couldn't accept the invitation because taukwa had tarnished the mee mamak and only untainted mee mamak could help ease the bitter tang of betrayal that still burnt her throat. The couple's untimely quarrel didn't help matters.

Unfortunately for Hui Yan, the fight between the couple had escalated to Level Two after the second plate of roti canai landed on the floor. The couple had dug into their battle stations on opposite ends of their table, shooting murderous stares at each other.

"Can't you even get a simple thing right?" said the woman who pointed to the sole surviving dish on the table. "You should know by now I have to have TAUKWA in my mee mamak!" She broke off into a fit of tears.

The waterworks had been turned on. Money switched hands as the winners won their bets.

"But I did order it with taukwa la. In fact, I told them to put extra," said the man.

He strutted around the table and puffed out his chest like a peacock fluffing its feathers when being attacked. As the woman's sobs ascended the operatic scale, the metaphorical feathers of the man slowly drooped. His defence had fallen on deaf ears. The woman was whipping herself up into a frenzy. Agitated, she waved her arms around and stamped her foot.

"I know it, I just know it. You don't love me anymore," she shouted. "Now that your bitch at home finally gave you sons, that's all you care about!"

A piercing silence from the audience registered after that shout, as though a deluge of dhal had overpowered them. Infidelity had mixed into the rojak of hysteria, confusion and despair. Bets were placed on whether the man would own up or not. The odds were evenly split.

"See, I told you. Lucky you come out with me tonight," a girl whispered to her friend. "It's better than those lousy fairy tale love dramas with the obnoxious CEO and the Mary Sue archetypal girlfriend that you love to watch."

Her friend did not acknowledge the remark. Her eyeballs were firmly glued on the arguing couple. If events followed the common tropes of Dramaland in which The-Male-Lead-Had-Betrayed-The-Innocent-Female-Lead, The Second Male Lead would swoop in to rescue the day. She scanned for this possibility. Alas, her hopes did not materialise. There was no movement from the people seated around her, whose attentions were fixated on the arguing couple, other than a cat that stretched luxuriantly in his corner and curled into a ball.

The Male Lead's face turned ashen. He rushed to the woman and tried to put his arms around her. She resisted but allowed herself to be held while raining a series of blows on his chest.

"Don't cry la ok? My sweet, sweet angel, no need to cry la," the man said. "I only love you. How can Bonnie compare to you? She is nothing next to you."

The woman burrowed herself into the man's embrace. Her fierce sobs soon quieted down under the man's firm assurances. The couple remained entangled with each other, in silent communion. The audience waited and waited. Was this how it was going to end? Some of the women in the audience reached for their tissues. They felt sad for poor Bonnie who waited at home for this incorrigible rogue and who bore sons for this unworthy man.

With the drama over, a dispirited air hung over the audience. It had been a disappointing end to what could have blossomed into an exciting spectacle. Everyone returned to their own monotonous conversations, except for Hui Yan of course. Her conversations with herself, even when she was depressed, had never been monotonous. But things were not over for her yet. In fact, they were just beginning to turn around for the first time that day.

Hui Yan had arrived at a momentous conclusion. One that had been triggered when the tearful woman shouted "taukwa" during her argument. A gleam shone from Hui Yan's eye, so bright it combined the wattage of two of the fluorescent lamps lighting the restaurant.

Hui Yan said to herself as she patted her chest, "See, Hui Yan. You must always be positive. Things always work out in the end."

Encouraging oneself in the third person was important to Hui Yan. There was nothing more enlightening than hearing her own voice speaking to herself. She bounced up from her chair, almost toppling it over in the process and held her plate of mee mamak at the edges. No way were her hands to come into contact with the taukwa pieces that ringed the sides.

She marched down the narrow path between the crowded tables, towards the back of the restaurant where the lovey-dovey couple were seated. Past the weeping ladies who had just been crying for poor Bonnie and were now laughing at cute cat videos on YouTube, past the Dramaland girls who were arguing whether it would be a BE or HE for their lead couple and past the poor cook who was still toying with the idea on whether he stood a chance with Susanna0003. No one paid any attention to her.

Hui Yan arrived, unannounced. The couple were staring into each other's starry universe with their arms knotted around each other's neck. Hui Yan sighed. She didn't know how long she could wait before she got noticed. It was time to engage in definitive action. She placed her own plate down on their table and took their plate instead.

"Yah!" she shouted as she examined the couple's order of mee mamak.

This plate had not a single taukwa in it. Their orders had been wrongly served by the waiters, as she had suspected. At this point, Hui Yan finally caught the couple's attention. It was impossible not to dismiss the intense and unsettling vibes emitted by Hui Yan as she conducted a detailed quality assurance check on the couple's order of mee mamak, vibes that sent scorching rays into the couple's universe extinguishing the flames of love.

"Ooi, what you doing?" asked the man, staring at Hui Yan. His look was questioning yet wary, as if Hui Yan was wielding a knife in her hands.

Hui Yan looked up irritably from the most perfect plate of mee mamak she had ever seen. The patterns formed by the silky strands of noodles, untainted by taukwa, were drawing her mind in. She now knew how a man or woman dying of thirst in the desert felt like when he or she unexpectedly came across an oasis. Hui Yan had to wrench herself away from the plate in her hands to focus reluctantly on the impatient couple.

"I think the waiter mixed up our order la. I ordered no taukwa in mine but it came with that much." She pointed to her plate on the couple's table. The woman took one look at the artwork of taukwa displayed on the plate and squealed in delight, throwing herself at the man.

"I'm so sorry honey bunny. I know you always remember everything I say and like. I will never doubt you ever again," she squealed. "You even got them to arrange the taukwa into my favourite star shape!"

The man's face turned red and his eyes teared as he hugged the woman tightly. Hui Yan rolled her eyes and shivered in disgust. She couldn't understand how anyone could flaunt their affections in front of the whole world. It was just too bad for her that there was more to come.

"Honey bunny, sweetie angel, you know you are the most important thing to me. You are the only star in my sky, the brightest diamond of my heart. Oh my darling," the man gushed.

Hui Yan could not withstand any more of this gruesome display of affection, not when the perfect dish of mee mamak in her hands was beckoning to her with the calls of a siren. She quietly edged away from the couple but froze when she heard what the man had to say next.

"So what if Bonnie finally give me sons? How can you think yourself on the same level as her? She is only something I found on the street, took pity on and brought her home. You are my queen forever," the man said.

Hui Yan tightened her grip on the plate of mee mamak, so much so that the plastic plate was in danger of cracking. She turned around and marched back to the couple. She did not know who Bonnie was, what type of person she was and, in all likelihood, their paths would never cross. But she could not let this woman be scorned behind her back. Someone had to stand up for her. She would if no one else would. Bonnie would not suffer the same fate she did today. She could not believe how shameless the man was. Obviously, he did not have a moral bone in him.

What Hui Yan set forth in the next few seconds was worthy of a Nobel Prize study on the effects of gravity on mee mamak and its aerodynamic properties. If the study had been made, it would have paved the way to a breakthrough on the next generation of human aviation.

The mee mamak launched from the plate like an athlete at the burst of the gun, as Hui Yan lobbed its contents towards the couple. The pair made for an easy target, entwined as they were like a thread of knotted string. The mee mamak sailed through the air, its strands flailing and fluttering like a living organism of hairy elements. As the mee mamak approached its highest peak however, it separated into different clumps. Some clumps dropped midway, falling short of their intended destination. But enough of the clumps were fortunate to survive the perilous journey, splatting squarely onto the couple's face and hair. The couple sprung apart and spluttered while pulling greasy bits of mee mamak from their hair.

"Oi! What is wrong with you?" the man barked at Hui Yan. The woman was in hysterics trying to pull out strands of mee mamak from her hair.

Without the need to be primed with a trailer alert, the surrounding diners excitedly jumped back into their front row seats. The commercial break was over. Excitement grew amongst them. The show had resumed with a new addition to the cast. What was going to happen next? There were whispered conversations as several groups within the audience broke into fevered discussions. Some of the women who had wept for Bonnie earlier, applauded at Hui Yan's action. To them, justice had been served.

Hui Yan glared at the indecent couple in front of her. She stood with legs apart, head held high like an avenging angel. Exhilaration surged through her. In this moment, she had never felt so right before.

Despite this, she couldn't help but observe that the mee mamak actually complimented the woman's hair colour as the overall effect of the noodle strands were like hair extensions. It seemed wicked people were gifted with the natural ability to appear pitiful. The thought irked Hui Yan even further. She bore down over the man and drew to her full height. All one hundred and sixty-eight centimetres of it over the man's one hundred and sixty-nine.

"Don't you feel shame? How can you say all those things to her while your poor wife sits at home taking care of your sons for you?" said Hui Yan.

"Crazy woman," the man retorted. "I don't know what you are talking about. Stupid ah!" He turned his back to Hui Yan and soothed his distressed partner. "Don't cry baby, just ignore her. No point talking to crazy people." He tried to clear the mess in the woman's hair, but the strands of mee mamak clung on stubbornly. The mee mamak were not about to give up so easily after having discovered a whole new purpose — in their otherwise insignificant lives — as hair extensions.

Hui Yan didn't let up. She continued to lecture the man on his infidelity and lack of morals until he finally erupted. Hui Yan's unexpected actions, thus far, was totally against her retiring nature. Even her friends always had, time and again, told her she had to speak out to avoid being taken advantage of. If it hadn't been that bitter tang of betrayal that still burnt her throat, she wouldn't have acted out in this manner. It was just unfortunate that she had chosen the wrong moment to embrace this life-changing advice. And it hadn't even been for her own sake.

"Stop! Stop! No more, no more. I really cannot stand you going on like this. What's your problem? What did we do to you, man? We don't even know you!" said the man.

"I pity your wife and since she is not here, I can only help her to scold you because I cannot tahan your lack of human decency. I'm sure everyone around here agrees with me." Hui Yan waved around at the audience.

Everyone was quiet. The audience was called upon to interact with the drama playing out in front of them. What were they to do? Suddenly things were not as amusing as they had first thought to be.

Their eyes skidded away from Hui Yan and the couple and pretended to be absorbed in their food.

"What wife? I'm not married," said the man.

"Huh? What? You have the nerve to pretend. Your Bonnie. You even called her a bitch."

The man roared with laughter, clapping his hands in glee. Hui Yan flinched. The laughter hit Hui Yan like a slap on her face.

"That's because she is. Bonnie is a bitch... oh you so funny. Standing there like so righteous like that. I tell you. Bonnie is my dog!" said the man.

Laughter erupted across the entire restaurant. The audience dropped their pretence of being absorbed with their food. They poured themselves into the laughter, glad that they had not been called upon to weigh judgement when Hui Yan had appointed herself as Bonnie's champion. Hui Yan turned rigid. Blood rushed out of her face as the waves of laughter rolled her over and sought to bury her alive. She held on barely but nearly lost it as she realised a graver error had been made. Hui Yan looked down at the plate in which it had once held the most perfect mee mamak she had ever seen.

"Oh, the injustice of things," Hui Yan muttered. Their sacrifice had been so in vain. Now she would never know how it tasted.

The shutters would soon fall upon the events of this night and buried under successive waves of new buttocks filling up the seats. As for Hui Yan, her life would never be the same again. The unknown taste of that perfect plate of mee mamak would haunt her in the decades to come. But for the rest of the diners, they would meander their way home nourished in body and soul with the reassuring certainty that the Mamak God would be awaiting once more when the shutters come up again.

Courier to Seoul

M.K. Eidson

I'm the courier for a US Department of Defense software installation and testing team headed to a military camp in Seoul, South Korea in 1994. It's my job to carry the software to our destination and then carry back classified sample data derived from the testing. I'm the only one on the team certified as a courier. I have an official document requesting that certain items I'm carrying be exempted from examination by airport personnel.

On arriving at our destination, we're greeted by a friendly American face, a man we'll call Adam, our liaison for our visit with the South Korean military. He's happy to see us and has a van waiting to take us to our hotel. He inquires as to our flight. I'd slept through most of it. The highlight for me was a stop in Tokyo, Japan, long enough to change planes. No sightseeing, but I could now say I'd been to Japan. Before this flight, I'd never been outside the United States.

Adam comes for us early the next morning. We pile in the van and head for the camp. The other three members of the team hope to successfully run their software on real data collected at the camp before we return to the US.

As only the courier, I have absolutely nothing to do between our arrival and departure. A South Korean officer we'll call Lee is assigned to babysit me, primarily because he speaks fluent English. I had tried learning Korean before the trip, and had succeeded in learning the pronunciation of symbols but the meanings of most words still elude me. Thus, all our meaningful conversations are carried out in English.

My token efforts to converse in Korean are pathetic. Officer Lee takes me to a nearby museum. Outside, a Korean couple are being married in the shadow of a World War II bomber. It's lovely weather for a wedding. A sign stuck in the grass carries a phrase in Korean, with no English translation. I read it aloud. Officer Lee looks impressed, nodding his head. "You read that well."

I shake my head. "But I don't know what it means."

He's been speaking English for a few years and I only started trying to learn Korean six weeks ago. I'd bought books and tapes. Korean words were easy to pronounce, so why hadn't I learned more in those six weeks?

The sign, Officer Lee informs me, says, "Keep off the grass." We'd walked right across the grass next to the sign. The bridal party is on the grass. It seems no one cares about what the sign has to say, whatever the language.

Even when I know the meaning of a Korean word, it isn't always clear to Officer Lee that I'm trying to speak his language. A vending machine offers beverages for sale. I point at a label on the machine, 우유, and say, "Ooh you."

He looks at me strangely, a bit hurt. "You don't remember my name? I'm Officer Lee."

"No, no," I say. "I know who you are." I point at the label again, putting my finger closer. "Ooh you."

"Ah. *Milk*. Yes." Perhaps his chuckle is a bit forced.

At times my pronunciation proves humorous to Officer Lee. I

utter one of the few phrases I've memorized. The Korean spelling is 안녕하세요. It's pronounced "annyeonghaseyo," which is how I think I've pronounced it. Laughing, Officer Lee tells me I'm speaking with a southern accent. He doesn't mean southern as in South Korea vs North Korea. He means southern as in the southern portion of South Korea. I'd never imagined there might be different dialects. Who thinks of these things when struggling to learn a language?

A NUMBER of American soldiers are deployed to the installation. Some of them have been here for a few years and picked up the language. One of them, whom we'll call Mark, accompanies our team to a convenience store. Mark finds something of interest he wishes to purchase but doesn't know the price. He brings it to the counter and begins rattling off questions in Korean. The attendant rattles off answers. There's a back and forth between them. Real conversation. I'm so jealous of Mark.

Other aspects of life in South Korea are completely outside my experience as an American. One day, Adam drives us to the demilitarized zone, the DMZ. He shows his identification to gain passage into a restricted area. Then we drive a while longer. Eventually we stop and pile out next to a wire fence — there's a long building on the other side of the fence. We don't go there. Beyond the building is another fence, and beyond that a number of soldiers carrying rifles. They eye us like they want to shoot us. "Don't go beyond this fence," says Adam. Like we would even consider it.

ON ANOTHER DAY, Adam asks if we'd like to go hiking. Back in the US, I've enjoyed hiking on Billy Goat Trail in Maryland. Every time I've gone, a few other people are also there, though not many older people. The trail winds through the woods, up a hill, with some narrow rocky paths overlooking a canal. There's little in the way of walkways to guarantee your footing or of steps to make it easier for you to climb the hill. At Bukhansan National Park, the peak Bagunbong features a walkway with steps for climbing the steepest parts. The walkway is packed with hikers, young and old, some using canes. It's a good way to get exercise, but as I start up the slope, I can't help but feel distracted from the natural beauty of the place by the walkway and the masses. For me, much of the joy in hiking Billy Goat Trail is communing with nature. Climbing the walkway up Bagunbong is like being in line at an amusement park, but there's no ride at the end of the line. It's only when I'm off the walkway and can put all the people out of mind that I'm able to enjoy the view and lose my breath to it.

There are days I'm on my own. I walk about Seoul, just taking in the sights. Gardens. Temples. Statues five times my height. These are grand sights, with lots of red and gold and age, like nothing I've seen in the US. One day, after taking in some such grand sights, I encounter dark green sludge oozing from holes in a wall, sluicing over a sidewalk that otherwise looks relatively new. I walk in the street to avoid stepping in the gunk. It doesn't have an odor, but looks toxic.

Everyone walking the sidewalks is dressed for success. I don't see one male who isn't in a suit. A noticeable number of people wear medical masks covering their noses and mouths. I find out later they wear them for a couple reasons. Some of them might have allergies, and they wear them for their own protection. But most of them wear masks because they aren't feeling their best, and they're doing what they can to protect their fellow citizens from whatever illnesses they might have.

Then, in the US if I were to see an American wearing such a

mask, I'd wonder if they were a doctor or nurse who'd forgotten to take it off before going on break. I can't count how many times I've gone to the office and a sick coworker also comes in, spreading their germs, with no concern for others, while trying their best to convince everyone, especially themselves, they aren't sick. Then they get worse, and other people get sick then half the office ends up taking sick leave because one obstinate sick person didn't have the courtesy to stay home.

My hair is long, hanging below my shoulders. All the males in their business suits walking the sidewalks of Seoul have short haircuts. The South Korean ladies I meet treat me like a rock star because of my long hair. I have my picture taken with an attractive Korean woman happy for me to put my arm around her like we're best friends. Her smile is bright in the picture. After leaving, I wish I'd asked her to dinner. I think she would have accepted.

Another Korean lady I have a picture taken with says she'd love to have dinner with me. An older woman in the shop acts excited for the younger woman. I'm excited too. I'd love to talk over dinner with a young English-speaking Korean lady and get her perspective on the differences between our cultures. Unfortunately, the young lady already has plans to meet a girlfriend that evening, and she can't break them. Her negative response saddens me to an unexpected degree, so much so, I feel it on my face. The older lady says, "Aw," and the younger woman's eyes dim in apology. I feel bad that I've made her feel bad. I'm no longer a rock star.

When the rest of my team that night says they're going out for drinks, I go along, even though I seldom consume alcohol. Once we're seated, I don't drink much but as the night wears on, I feel the need to visit the restroom. I'm surprised by the lack of urinals. I do my business in one of the stalls and then wash my hands at the sink. I stand in front of the mirror, staring at the person who is me. I'm a fish out of water. I've been two weeks in a foreign land, and I'm anxious to be back in familiar territory.

A couple of people enter the restroom. They glance at me, but say nothing, and go into stalls to do their business. They're both women. What are women doing in the men's room? They act like what they're doing is completely normal. This South Korean culture is so crazy.

I return to my table. One of my coworkers, whom we'll call Jeff, leans over to me and whispers, "I think you went in the women's room."

Oh. I look at the restroom doors. Standard gender symbols mark them. How did I get it wrong?

Those two young ladies weren't fazed by my presence in the women's room. They'd taken it all in stride. They hadn't blushed or fainted or freaked out like many women in the US might. Maybe it was my long hair. Maybe male rock stars in South Korea are expected to do whatever they want, no explanation necessary. I'm a rock star again.

THE END of our stay approaches. To show their appreciation for our work for them, the South Korean military honchos feed us bulgogi and kimchee. I've never tasted anything so good as bulgogi. I resolve to find a South Korean restaurant back in the US where I can eat more of it.

They give us each a long-handled pipe with a small bowl from which hang golden tassels. It's like a peace pipe. I don't know what's supposed to go in the bowl, but it's too small for tobacco. I don't smoke and have no intention of using the pipe, but it's cool they're giving it to me.

They turn over the tapes with classified data I'm to courier back to the US. And then they're done with us. *Goodbye, farewell, get off our property. Find your own way back to the airport.* Adam's boss explains that's how the South Korean military is. As long as we're of value to them, they treat us like royalty. Once our work is done, they can't allocate any further resources to us. We're no better than any other American tourist at this point. Not even Adam can help us, despite him being American. It might have helped if they'd mentioned this earlier. Now we're all out of sorts, not able to think straight. Can we even use their phone to call a taxi?

I clear my head and remind Adam's boss I'm here as a courier. If our team is left to our own devises in returning to the airport, the South Korean classified information I'm carrying is vulnerable. I'm officially requesting assistance in protecting *their* information in my custody while *en route* to the airport. The point is, I'm still providing value to them, and would appreciate them recognizing it. I've been here the whole time waiting for this moment, when I could fill the role for which I came. The rest of my team might be finished with their work, but I'm only halfway done with mine.

The argument wins them over, and Adam takes us to the airport in the van, the same van used to drive us to the DMZ and to the mountain to go hiking, neither of which were required as part of the job, but were allowed before the software installation and testing were finished.

On the plane, Jeff says to me, "I'm glad you're couriering those tapes."

Sure, we'd have managed to get back to the airport anyway. But we were all stunned by the incongruity of how the South Korean military were treating us golden one moment and were completely oblivious to our existence the next. They hadn't shown any great concern about spending too much money on us. Theirs was a way of thinking completely foreign to us Americans, a way of thinking that made perfect sense to them, but left us baffled in the extreme.

I WONDER how South Korea has changed. Does sludge ooze out of walls and flow across new sidewalks? Does the military lavish bulgogi and peace pipes on their visitors and give their visitors a ride to the airport after their work is done, even if they aren't carrying classified information back to their home country? Are Americans with long hair still treated like rock stars?

I still wish I'd asked that first young Korean lady to dinner.

Treacherous Strand

Lynett Khoh

Familiar voices echoed outside Lei's room. They were hushed, subdued by a heavier weight than usual, but unmistakable. Lei had heard Mummy's voice too many times to know when she was upset; and it was always in Dad's nature to be strident, even when he was whispering.

"What about Lei—"

Dad's voice grew louder.

"—She has to be there."

Lei gnawed on her nails. She could almost see Dad's bulging eyes and that hostile shade of reddish-brown festering on his face whenever he was upset. *Or drunk. Or both.* Her mind picked up speed, tuning in and out of sounds throughout the house: static crackling from the ancient radio downstairs, creaking joints of an old ceiling fan, laundry rumbling in the washing machine.

Please don't come in.

"Don't bring Lei into this," the fight sparked in Mummy's voice. "She won't do it. You of all people should know. Isn't that the entire reason why you promised we'd stop talking about your mother? To protect whatever respect Lei has left for her?"

Lei froze.

Her parents hadn't argued for a long time. And when they did, especially when they did so in secret, it always involved that woman.

Grandmother.

Lei wondered about her over the years. Sometimes she would come across others who resembled Grandmother, whose presence crept like a wrinkled hand down her back. When Lei was twelve, she made up her mind that grandmothers were vicious beings who manipulated their son's marriages for sport.

At least, that's what happened the last time Lei saw her grandmother.

That night, the cruel moon watched with silver eyes as Dad's tantrum struck like a hand on Mummy's tear-strewn cheek. Lei was never a spineless child, but at that moment she clung white-knuckled onto the back of Mummy's shirt. A monstrous song roared from the radio, competing against Dad's drunken wails. Lei remembered reaching for a knife and no one saw. She remembered Mummy's urging pull as they retreated deeper into the kitchen, how they leapt on their toes because the floor was a dense forest of whiskey bottle shards; she remembered pressing her back against spice-dusted cabinets to stay hidden. Blood rushing and wrist numbed, Lei asked herself: if it came down to protecting Mummy with the knife, could she do it?

The backdoor was only an arm's reach away.

"Lei, please... don't say or do anything. He'll only get angrier."

Lei should've run. But there was rotting desperation in Mummy's words as she promised that Dad was not himself, that he wasn't thinking straight, and he wouldn't remember any of this tomorrow.

Mummy was protecting him.

Why?

Lei's toes drilled into the ground. Her fingers wound tightly around the knife, willing for some kind of courage to see things through. When Dad reached the kitchen, he had morphed completely; his mouth enlarged, spewing rancid saliva droplets and sour whiskey fumes. Bitter words thundered from him like a monsoon storm. She recalled his staggering feet, barely holding up as his clumsy hands extended murderously close.

Behind him stood Grandmother, her face scrunched into a look of concern.

Liar.

Grandmother was encouraging Dad's tantrum. Accusations of Mummy being unwelcoming hissed from the wicked old woman: that Mummy had intentionally starved Grandmother by not cooking dinner on time; that Mummy intentionally forgot to do the laundry, so Grandmother had nothing to wear; that Mummy made Grandmother feel like a burden for asking to stay over; that it was all Mummy's plan to pressure Grandmother to leave.

Lei was at the mercy of the broken adults before her.; Dad was a man-child, throwing tantrums because no one shared his love and respect for his mother. Mummy, stilled into a daze, denied everything but the silly belief that her husband would come back to his senses. Grandmother insisted on an apology, a response from Mummy, any sign that showed Mummy's inferiority. And when there was none, Grandmother's triumphant voice moved to anger. She blew whirlwinds of lies, fuelling Dad's drunken fire.

"I should divorce you." Dad was too far lost in his blurry, burning rage. He spat at Mummy, "You owe my mother. Without her raising me, do you think you'd have a good husband like me? This family is nothing without her—"

Lei could have sworn Grandmother's lips curved upwards.

Her fingers tightened around the knife, holding herself back from lunging at the older woman.

"—since it's so difficult for you to respect my mother, let's divorce. You can keep the child too. Yes, you, Lei. Don't act so innocent. I know you didn't talk to Grandmother, didn't even hug her when she came through the door. I can't believe it. You two are nothing to me."

Mummy's eyes found the floor. She must've been shocked, yet she said nothing.

Then Grandmother must have grown tired of playing games. The scene before her was going nowhere and it was late, after all. The wrinkly woman feigned a loud sigh. "You're both adults. You. How can you disappoint your husband so much that he wants to divorce you? And son, you shouldn't say that in front of your daughter. I just wanted to visit my son's happy family, not see you two fight and get divorced. You should be ashamed of yourselves."

Grandmother acted mighty like she had saved the family from ruin. She announced her decision to leave at once, not wanting to witness the fallout of Lei's family. *More like she wanted an easy way out*, Lei thought at the time. Though Dad hadn't sobered up, his already reddened face burned a tinge brighter, as if embarrassed by the sudden ceasefire. Humiliation crushed him so much that he drove off into the night with Grandmother and some clothes.

Thankfully, the woman never visited again.

But Dad. It took him days before he returned with shame scored deep in his bones. And surely enough, Mummy forgave him as quickly as she moved on from his betrayal that night.

Lei never did.

The years gave Lei lots of time to think about that last visit from Grandmother, and about Dad who had since picked up the nasty habit of breaking plant pots whilst staggering home as a howling drunk at two in the morning. More than once, Lei wondered if she had spoken up that night, if she threatened them into listening with the knife in her hands, maybe she could've talked some sense into Dad or maybe even put Grandmother in place for turning Dad against Mummy. She thought of it a couple of times, but it would never work out. No. It just wouldn't seem like a sincere attempt to fix things if Lei looked as if she was going to stab someone. Besides, she would've given Grandmother another reason to blame Mummy.

Lei would then shove these thoughts away in the back of her mind. Each night since, Lei prayed that Grandmother had her fill from that incident and was content enough to never return for more.

Now, from inside Lei's room, her parents' voices grew distant. Whatever they said next became too muffled to make out— not that she was trying. Lei was grateful for Mummy's interjection. And yet, she couldn't stop thinking about her parents' unpleasant exchange. What was happening? She wanted to tell Dad she was scared, like how daughters turned to their dads for protection against harm. But it was obvious that he was the harm; he was going to make her go somewhere, or do something. With Grandmother.

What if Mummy failed to stop him?

White, steaming panic surged in Lei's head. Mummy had sounded firm earlier, and Dad rarely fought against Mummy's decisions but there was no telling whenever Grandmother was involved. Dad's heart only had space for one woman at a time. And Mummy never stood a chance against that woman.

It was early afternoon when Mummy slipped into Lei's room, smuggling along the outside warmth.

Lei had hidden from her parents all morning, passing it off as though she slept in. The air inside her bedroom thickened like roux, even her sheets twisted and lumped like mush. The room was an icky concoction of musk and condensation. Yet, Lei found herself comfortably wrapped in the denseness of it all. She would have stayed in bed a little longer if not for Mummy who bared her teeth so much her words came out as snarls. "His mother had the nerve to call. They spoke as if nothing happened, as if we're still family, as if we always were. Isn't it clear we want nothing to do with her? He should have made it clear—"

"He *is* one of them, Mummy." Lei's words were nimble, delivering a carefully strung message, one that crossed somewhere between a reminder and plea. "He doesn't want us anymore. He said it himself, you remember?"

Silence followed.

Lei almost believed she had convinced her mother.

Instead, Mummy shifted across the room and fiddled with Lei's curtains.

"He said he was sorry," Mummy whispered in a voice so low, it almost sounded like defeat. Almost. Though trembling, Mummy continued to defend him. "He apologised to me. I know what he did was wrong but if you're looking for more reasons to separate this family, then you're not going to find them. He's still my husband. Still your father. And we need him: a family cannot hold without its base."

Lei readied her tongue.

She had a sharp one and was quick to use it on anyone, even family. Grandmother once said it was a nasty trait she inherited from Mummy. So maybe, just maybe, Mummy might finally see that they were supposed to be on the same team.

But Mummy's tongue moved faster. "What is the main virtue we follow in this house?"

"Virtue?" Lei ran a finger along her bottom lip. "I don't see how this—"

"孝. Xiao. It's the virtue of respect for your parents," Mummy said. "I raised you better than this. I raised you to value our family, to be a part of it, to protect it. It is your duty to respect your father, even if he is wrong."

A bitterness curdled in Lei's chest, but she wasn't about to let Mummy win. "So your husband has a duty to respect his mother, even if she hurt us?"

Though Mummy was quiet, her anger seethed into the air around them. And before Lei could amend her words, Mummy ripped the curtains wide open. The sun's white-hot rays struck past the windows and broiled Lei's skin.

"It's not the same," Mummy's tone took on more of a scald.

Of course Mummy was upset. She hated being compared to that woman. Lei's grandmother raised children to compete with each other for resources like vicious rats, and the woman took pride in this. Aunties and uncles from Lei's father's side of the family seared with jealousy over each other's success. They ruthlessly scrutinized from the side lines as their own kin suffered from hardships. Yet, as self-serving as they were, Grandmother had raised them all to worship her — even Lei's father did so. She was the matriarch.

Mummy would rather die than become that woman.

"She's unwell." Mummy uttered, sitting at a cautious inch away from Lei, on the bed's edge. "It's bad. Your aunt kept calling... I think it might happen."

Lei wasn't sure how to respond.

With concern? With pity? Those weren't what she felt. She was shocked, sure, but nowhere near being worried. Then again, Lei didn't feel the need to hide her emotions. After all, Mummy had always shared the same sentiments for the wicked old woman.

"About time," Lei said.

Mummy smiled. It wasn't like the sneering one on Lei's face though, it was heavier — the way someone smiled just before they'd say something they wish they didn't have to. "She wants to see us."

"No." Lei's skin went grey. "He promised! He said we didn't have to see her anymore. He said that he won't force us to—"

"She's dying, Lei. Your Dad won't let this slide."

Lei couldn't meet Mummy's serious gaze. No. She didn't want to. She didn't care if that woman was going to die, that her last wish was to see her entire family. It's not fair. *He promised.*

"I know you still keep scissors near your bed—"

Lei's toes curled taut, pinching at the sheets.

"—and I know you lock your door when he says he'll be home late because you don't want to see him drunk. But you have to let go of what happened. This family... our family should move on together. I want us to be happy, don't you?"

Lei lowered her eyelids; she couldn't find it in her to respond. *Mummy had been hurt enough.* It was a losing battle for Lei; Mummy must have known that. But the whole thing wasn't their fault and Mummy was ridiculous to act so. Even if Lei agreed to mend things, and wanted to, Grandmother should be the one begging. Dad too. They started this. They should be the ones asking to move on.

Lei's thoughts weighed down on her, sinking her deeper into the bed. Mummy knew it was too much to ask, she could see it in Lei's tensed brows but was determined to have her way. Sensing that the conversation lulled, Mummy stood up to go.

"So you're... you *want* to visit her?" Lei finally asked.

Mummy looked at Lei. "You have to, too, if this family is going to heal."

Have to, Lei thought. *Was that man all that mattered to Mummy?* It saddened Lei that Mummy was leaving her behind, that Mummy insisted on holding on to Dad as if their flimsy marriage was her only lifeline.

"Our family will get better," Mummy said with a vile surety.

"But Grandmother hates us, she might—"

"Our family *will* get better."

Then Mummy walked out of the room. Lei should have said something after that night. But she hadn't. Now, Grandmother had made the first move. She wanted to see Lei's family again.

Peeling off the sheets, Lei recalled the fear, an ugly feeling that twisted around her bones, how she wanted everything to pass. And now the chance had finally presented itself.

"I forgive them," she breathed into the empty hallway, practising. "I forgive them."

As Lei descended the steps, she overheard Dad venting to Mummy downstairs. "If your daughter can't even show some respect to my sick mother then who gives a damn about how she feels!"

Lei drew back from sight.

She felt like an idiot, hiding when she hadn't done anything wrong. Her throat burned just from listening to Dad's lips, smacking on something oily as he muttered his disapproval. If not for Lei's nose that twisted in disgust, she would have convinced even herself that she was ready to move on. Her toes coiled against the tiled floor. *I forgive him*, she reminded herself. For Mummy's sake, she had to face Dad, even if it meant playing dumb. So she hopped down the stairs, focusing all her weight on that last step.

Thump.

That shut Dad up. She watched him straighten, his chewing grew quieter with every padding of Lei's feet— which only made her angrier.

Lei joined her parents at the dining table. Fury flushed across her cheeks as her attention remained directly on Dad, who was now too guilty to meet her eyes. Instead, he looked over and said to an equally thin-lipped Mummy, "Your soup lacks something."

"Oh, does it?"

"Yes. It doesn't taste authentic. You did something wrong."

"Maybe," Mummy laughs politely.

"Yeah."

Neither of them talked about the things that really mattered: Grandmother's request, the closure that was long overdue, or even how Lei felt about everything. They just sat there, mundanely conversing about Mummy's white radish soup.

Lei tried to ignore the sound of metal cutlery scratching at ceramic bowls. It didn't help those other sounds in the room, like the buzzing rice cooker and the squelching of food from Dad's mouth shot straight up her ears. Lei felt a tightness pulsing at her temples.

Briefly, Dad looked at her and said, "You should start your day earlier, Lei."

"I haven't been sleeping well—"

Then Dad's attention turned to Mummy. He casually spoke, dismissing the previous conversation as if it didn't happen, "Maybe you didn't season it. There's no salt."

Mummy always seasoned her cooking.

His chewing, down to the way he inhaled air with a sharp whistling sound, prickled gooseflesh beneath Lei's skin. She remembered a time when her younger self had beamed along to Dad's radiant laughter. He had the kind of laugh that hummed into others, the dizzying kind that tipped a person over their toes, yet they still wanted more. But the man currently sat before her was not that Dad. This version of Dad gobbled messily like pigs ate slop. He hadn't even noticed how uncomfortable Mummy was, how she responded to his berating statements with only a tight smile.

"Yeah, you didn't put in salt," Dad repeated.

You should have never come back, Lei wanted to say. If Dad hadn't believed Grandmother's lies, this wouldn't have happened.

Gusting anger blew away all warmth from her body, leaving her lightheaded enough to say the words she meant to conceal, but was now spoken with an unyielding weight. "I'm not going."

Mummy put down her spoon. "Lei—"

"No!" Lei stood abruptly. Her nose scrunched at the pitchy 'o' that sounded from her lips. Lei was scared. But the words had already come out her mouth. She glared at Dad and spoke through gritted teeth, "You know what I tell myself every night when you don't come home? I say maybe everything will get better; Grandmother will have no reason to be in our lives anymore."

Lei could hear her voice rising as Dad's face darkened.

"Then I hear your drunken body dragging itself into the house. And I realise, we're never going to get better—"

"Enough!" Dad's eyes bulged.

"—because you weren't mature enough to deal with your lying mother, so you drank and smoked your problems away, just like you continue to do now!"

"Lei, please..." Mummy spoke this time, eyes moistening.

Lei bit on the inside of her cheek. "You knew, didn't you? That night. You knew Grandmother was lying."

"You have no idea how difficult it was for me," Dad replied immediately, but they were the wrong words: *excuses.*

Hot, throbbing anger blurred Lei's vision.

"Was it easier to hurt me? To hurt Mummy? You could've done the right thing." The words came out quavering, but her unforgiving eyes locked on Dad. "Just, please... let me stay home."

And there, Lei surprised herself.

She didn't intend for her anger to reduce so quickly—she didn't expect to beg. Dad must have been shocked as well. She watched as the man shrunk into his chair, hollow-eyed, defeated. Though his face remained hideously reddish-brown, this was a different kind of anger. The man was embarrassed, and Lei could see guilt slipping out from between his clenched teeth. Beside him was a brooding Mummy, hurt by Lei's disobedience, no doubt. But Lei didn't care. No, she would deal with it later.

She hastened for the stairs, feet pulsing up each step.

The sun's frenzied rays flickered from each passing window to Lei's room. She thought that someday, when Grandmother became nothing but a name on a grave, Lei would grant Mummy's wish, and her family would heal. Because Dad's heart had space for one woman at a time, and Mummy only stood a chance if Grandmother were dead. So until then, Lei would remain a treacherous strand in her family. Until then, she would do so to protect Mummy, to protect her family.

The Pocket Watch Expert of Kalimantan

Patrick Burns

Indonesia is part of my territory while working in the oilfield services business and Kalimantan is one of the many islands that form part of its lengthy archipelago, running like a belt across the centre of South East Asia. Strictly speaking, it's not a whole island in itself but the major part of what used to be known as Borneo in the days of the British Empire. It shares the landmass with the two Malaysian states of Sabah and Sarawak and the super-wealthy dot on the map that is Brunei.

Away from the drilling rigs and oil-camps, this is a land of equatorial rainforest and primitive tribesmen who reputedly still shrink heads and eat human flesh. While the edges have in parts been brought roughly into the twentieth century by trade with the outside world and the search for natural resources, the interior is the quintessential steamy primeval jungle: full of flora and fauna usually seen only on television nature programs and in the National Geographic magazine.

I land in Balikpapan, the primary town on the west coast, spending a night with the American District Manager and his wife. After a breakfast that neatly merges the expatriate and local life (whole-wheat French toast, maple syrup, fresh mango and papaya 'from the garden'), I set off on a one-day field trip to a couple of oilfield camps for round-table sessions with local and expatriate service representatives and engineers.

The day is one of contrasts with its combination of routine business procedure and exotic travel. We talk about pay structures and upcoming training programs in the camps.

I SPEND several hours traveling between locations.

The first leg is by four-wheel-drive truck along rough twisting roads that wind through the penumbra of a dank rainforest. The sky is rarely visible. There are sudden movements in the massive trees and rampant undergrowth while the screeches of monkeys fill the air.

The second leg is in a small three-seater helicopter flying just above the tree canopy. The pilot, almost inevitably, is a US Air Force veteran who flew Hueys on missions in Vietnam and clearly misses the excitement. Between pointing out the campfire smoke from settlements of tribesmen, he talks about the fun they had performing aerobatics in the old war machines he flew out of a base near Saigon. I'm relieved that he doesn't give me a practical demonstration.

The second camp visit ends at about 4:30pm and I'm scheduled to take a final helicopter ride back to Balikpapan to complete the day in an eight-seater machine providing a glorified bus service shuttling oilfield personnel around the state. At the edge of the jungle clearing where the helicopter is due to land, there is even a small open-sided structure that looks for all the world like a bus-shelter outside some rural English village.

The sky is darkening and rain begins to fall steadily.

I make for the shelter amid the tumultuous cacophony of birds, monkeys and other animals rising from the encroaching jungle greenery.

There is already one other passenger sitting on the bench under the attap cover: an overweight westerner who looks to be about forty, wearing a battered cowboy hat and carrying a small backpack. We nod and begin the process of conversation as it starts anywhere in the world between strangers. He has oddly combined diction: a sibilant lisp riding over the elastic vowels and rising whine of Texas. He introduces himself as Harold Drayman, but adds that "motht folkth juth call me Blondie." I can see why as he removes his Stetson to wipe the brim.

I realize I must know who he is. Well, I don't actually know him but I know his file. Working in human resources means that I spend a good deal of time looking at the paper records of employees. Certain people stick in the mind and Harold 'Blondie' Drayman is one of them. That he works for the same company as I do, and happens to be sitting in a clearing in a rainforest in Borneo, is not as surprising as it may seem.

He is a Senior Service Representative (Level 3) working out of the Balikpapan base and ours is a big company in the oil patch with a significant presence in Indonesia. SSR3s are the wise old men of the organization. They've typically worked in oilfield service most of their lives, never progressed managerially, but know everything there is to know about pumping cement down newly-drilled well holes to secure a mile or so of hollow, vertical steel pipe in the formation: a dangerous, dirty but essential job in the process of getting oil out of the ground.

Blondie's reputation and general eccentricity precede him – both on paper and anecdotally. Although a well-paid expatriate on a rotation assignment which would normally have him working four weeks out of Balikpapan followed by two weeks back in the States, Blondie rarely leaves Indonesia, preferring to take his breaks in Surabaya on Java where he has a local wife and children.

By all accounts, he has become a practicing Muslim, devoutly following religious observances while maintaining one foot conveniently in the western world. He keeps a Vespa scooter at the Balikpapan base and is often seen riding around town – his long, butter-colored hair dragging back from his head. He's viewed as a gentle giant type, but with a temper when prodded, and his colleagues regard him with a mix of amusement and respect.

While I make it clear to Blondie who I am and that we work for the same company, I don't tell him I'm forearmed with much of this knowledge. He is in a quietly expansive mood having just completed his four weeks "on" and is looking forward to "a little R & R." Nevertheless I'm more than a tad intimidated by this strange man who has chosen to live such a different life and I wonder what we can possibly have in common to talk about while we wait.

The helicopter is due and I check the time. My wristwatch – a cheap fake Rolex – has given up the ghost. Until I can find a replacement, I carry an old gold-plated pocket watch that belonged to my grandfather. I pull this out from the depths of my overalls.

Blondie gives a low whistle and says, "That thure ith narth. Lurkth lark a Waltham fum here!" I'm not quite sure whether he is lisping the word 'Walsam' or if the watch is a 'Waltham'. I've never inspected it properly but a closer look at the small logo just below the 'XII' numeral on the dial tells me it's the latter.

I'm impressed he can tell the make of the watch from just a cursory glance over my shoulder. He explains that the shape and style are typical of Waltham from the late nineteenth century. I pass the timepiece to him and he opens the back and pulls a small magnifying loupe out of his pocket to inspect it more carefully.

He tells me it's a fairly basic piece with just the minimum number of jewels and that the case is Canadian. I am amazed not only by his knowledge but also by being in such a strange setting learning about my grandfather's watch. The trees drip, monkeys whoop forlornly and our genteel conversation about timepieces seems out of place.

We pass an enjoyable ten minutes with him telling me an awful lot more about the watch than I suspect I would ever have been able to find out myself. He says it can't be earlier than 1882 but it's not the fabled 'Railwaymens' Waltham which has special features required by those working on the railroad in the US in the heyday of steam. We both wonder how my grandfather, a Yorkshireman who worked in the steel industry all his life, could have acquired an American watch like this.

At one point, he asks me if I'd like to get some idea of how much it's worth. He proceeds to undo the straps on his backpack and, to my astonishment, pulls out a thick, heavily thumbed catalogue. The name of this tome escapes me but it seems to contain a vast amount of data about old watches. He runs his finger up and down columns, checking the reference number stamped on the watch's interior structure and tells me he's fairly certain it's from 1888 and is valued in today's market at about $250.

My initial reserve about his oddness falls away as I warm to his enthusiasm for the subject and total disregard for the circumstances in which we are having this bizarre exchange. Our conversation is gradually beaten into submission by the increasingly loud drumming of the approaching helicopter. Blondie may look the stereotypical redneck Texan oilman but that's as far as it goes. He tells me, "Itth been a great playthure meeting you an' you look after that purdy watch."

We climb aboard and the noise prevents any further conversation. There are two people already in the cabin section behind the crew and we make two more stops to pick up additional passengers. Everybody looks tired and in no mood to chat. The only interaction above the clatter of the rotors comes from the pilot as he speaks to invisible ground staff while ascend.

We arrive at Balikpapan and it's just about to go dark – a process that takes barely minutes this close to the equator. Blondie nods and smiles as he runs over to a waiting truck and I hang around for a few moments to watch the helicopter's departure. It rises up twenty feet, dips its nose in farewell, rotates 180 degrees and speeds off into the crepuscular sky, lights blinking.

He really says "purdy."

The Dog Walker

Ivy Ngeow

He took a long, hard look and then he said, "OK". David Soh had never had a dog before but then he'd never lost his job before. There was a first for everything. His 22-year-old niece Stephanie, who'd never worked a day in her life, now fancied "a change". She was going to America to "check out" a course. It was all right for some people.

She'd offered to pay him RM200 a day. Expenses on top. David was not in a position to say no. All he had to do was to keep the dog company, take him for walks, feed him. Seemed like the easiest job. He thought back when he was in PR a year ago, managing a tech firm's marketing and web strategy. He hadn't found anything else since. Soon he would be handling a dog, now *that* was a different animal.

Having to bite down on his pride, whenever he dropped by at his brother's, did not make it easier. His brother and sister-in-law ran different businesses morning to night. He never saw them. You wouldn't know they lived here. He looked around him, at the dark granite patio with a hammered finish where the dog had been padding around since living here. The dog's house alone was a palace, a mini sandstone temple with built-in Italian spray taps for washing the stainless steel water and food bowls.

There was no denying that his brother had done well for himself: a 5,000 square foot designer house with swimming pool and electronic gates in Mont Kiara, with far-reaching views of Klang Valley. A new black Range Rover, his brother's spare family vehicle. And a couple of "less rugged" vehicles such as a tiny sports Mercedes, which was Stephanie's, and a Prius (the wife's shopping trolley).

"His name is Keane," said Stephanie. She wanted a personal maid just for herself and she got two; a big dog and she got one and now she'd decided she'd *die* for a film studies course in San Francisco and that too was in the bag.

"Pardon?" said David, distracted when he looked straight into the dog's soul, if there was such a thing, and the dog stared back.

"Keane."

Keane was like a long-lost friend, found again. The dog's eyes had the sad downturned look of an ancient lion, yet he was not old. He was only four. In human terms he would be a young, fit, hot-blooded man. David chuckled at the thought. The opposite of him. He was a slight, bespectacled middle-aged anyman, an ex-manager type with no interests except lunch or golf and even that was now a fantasy, like going to the moon. His only thrill had been dragging himself to a sports bar in Bangsar Village to watch Liverpool's Champion League matches at 3am. Perfect for the unemployed. Golf, private health insurance, gym membership and lunch at the club had been the perks of his job. His world.

He stroked the dog's head tentatively.

"He OK one, Uncle. You can sayang him. If he don't like you, you will know straight away one."

"OK," David laughed. Keane's tail, wagging continuously, slapped Stephanie's thigh. His jaw hung open in a drooly smile. The dog shut his large sad eyes like it was rare to be shown affection from anyone, apart from Stephanie who was now "too busy". David's hand moved to tickling the dog's neck which David enjoyed almost as much.

Keane was an enormous black and copper-colored Rottweiler, Shar Pei and something else mix, which gave him his huge melted candle look. His neck alone was the size of a small motorcycle wheel. Stephanie was already his third owner as he was abandoned, abused by various other dubious owners and then finally brought to the animal shelter. No one knew where he came from originally. Stephanie felt sorry for him, adopted him from the shelter six months ago, sent him for training, and now had decided she needed to party for about two months in California.

David took on his new "job" with the gusto and enthusiasm of discovering a new bike hobby. After Stephanie left, he went from his modest apartment in Sunway every day to his brother's Mont Kiara resort-style mansion. He picked up Keane and drove around in the Range Rover. They went everywhere together, mostly exploring nature reserves; caves, big parks, long walks. David started enjoying avoiding people while improving his fitness. Why on earth did he ever need a gym? Dumbbells were dumb. Dogs were smart. He already started to feel odd stabs of grief. When Stephanie got back, he'd have to say goodbye to Keane.

Sometimes he waved to neighbors, acquaintances and other dog owners or walkers. Maybe he'd walk dogs as a career. Working his first 3-hour shifts before 9am, getting fit, taking care of animals. Never having to schmooze or talk to colleagues or arrange meetings again. Lunch on the go. Keane didn't like to sit around panting in kopi tiams. David imagined himself doing job applications and LinkedIn all afternoon with the TV on low and the aircon on high. Then back for another 3-hour shift of more dogs, from 5 to 8pm.

He shopped for food at the vet (none of that rubbish from Carrefour), weighed the right amount for Keane's breed, age and weight, showered him every two weeks, dried him with a fluffy extra-large beach towel that he bought from Jusco in a pack of three. His brother and niece would surely give him a reference. Alia, one of

Stephanie's personal maids, was relieved. Indonesian and Muslim, she did not want to care for canines for cultural reasons.

One of the places he liked to explore with the dog was the hills at around 5 am when Bukit Kiara Park was cool and calm, with the hum of insects and birdsong. David would turn left after the Pizza Hut and start the steep ascent before finding a parking spot for the Range Rover. Keane was keen. He'd always jump out of the car, casting a glance of approval towards David before he dashed into the bushes to sniff around and find treasures such as the scent of a jungle rat or a flying squirrel in the dense, ancient rainforest.

After almost two hours of hilly jungle exploration, occasionally David would buy takeaway breakfast on the way home, prata or chee cheong fun at the TTDI market before peak hour traffic started to build. Also it was probably his only chance in this lifetime to show off the Range Rover. He was almost 60 and had been hanging on for his retirement package from the tech PR industry before shit happened, so why shouldn't he show off the Range Rover? He always got ta-pau because he knew most people wouldn't welcome an enormous and not very handsome-looking dog into their cafe or kiosk. Though of course, to David, who was not in the least biased, Keane was cugly. Cute ugly.

One morning, when it was still dark, it started to drizzle after they arrived in the park. Mist covered the paths a few meters in front of them. David proceeded with caution but Keane relied on his sense of smell and confidently strode off looking for marks and scents of anything he could chase or actually catch. A long-tailed civet cat, a fox.

David looked up at the trees. They were at least 50m high. He had his waterproof hooded walking jacket on. He pulled the zip all the way to the top and tightened the knotted toggles around his neck, so that the hood stayed on, not slipping back. He checked his phone was on full charge, as he'd need a torch at some point. In some parts of the forest, it was eternally dark from the dense tree canopy. He glimpsed a faint figure in the misty distance. Surprised, he stared. It was unusual for this time, when day looked like night. Keane let out a low growl, and his hair stood, that motorbike-wheel neck stiff as steel.

David felt a chill. Keane had changed. Icy sweat poured from David's brow, steaming up his spectacles. A tourist guide in Sarawak had once told him an Iban proverb: "when you know the jungle and a friend very well, you know well this is not the jungle and the friend you know."

Keane suddenly charged off towards the ghostly figure without even a glance back. The copper-colored, short-haired body bolted into the darkness of the jungle. "Keane! Keane?" David shouted. "Come back! Oh God. Keane!" The dog did not return.

A few shrieks. Then it stopped. David waited. Was it a monkey? He shouted the dog's name again, as he ran through the dense forest, between the fallen trunks, over roots, dead leaves, probably even snakes. There was no path; this was the real jungle, no one had come with a parang and cut out a nice tarmac walkway. It was covered in thorny undergrowth and branches. It was hard to tell what was plant or what was space in the darkness.

David tripped and fell. He hit his head on a log branch protruding at an odd angle. He felt the hot trickle of blood turning cold against his forehead skin when he touched it. "Keane," he moaned. "Where are you?" He got up and tried to run to where he thought Keane went. His phone. Where was his phone? He had to find that too. It must have dropped out. "Keane!" he screamed.

The dog returned, calm, wagging his tail. "Oh my God," he said. The dog's jaws were wet, dark, glistening. "What did you do? What the hell have you..." In his jaws was David's phone.

David held his breath. He stared at the dog, unable to read his expression. He took the phone from the dog. When David shone the torch of his phone, Keane's grinning teeth were covered in blood.

He gasped sharply and his hand flew to his forehead.

The dog led him by looking at him and walking, walking and looking back at him. Shaking, he followed the dog.

As there were no paths, the dog jumped over the uneven ground, roots and bushes while David had to climb his way over, covered in cuts and bruises.

The dog stopped.

Something like a lying human form twitched on the ground. He switched on the torch on his phone. "Oh shit," cried David, his voice trembling. "Oh shit, shit, shit," he roared. He clamped his hand over his mouth, the other still shining the phone torch. He leaned towards the bulky figure. A man. A fly already landed on him and buzzed like a little doorbell. "Oh God, Keane, what have you done? No, no, no. Oh God." David's knees had gone soft as tofu, and he lost his balance.

He reeled backwards, light-headed. He vomited white froth which ran over his waterproof jacket. It tasted of acid and diesel. His stomach was empty. He had been looking forward to having breakfast later before returning the dog to his brother's house. After David was sick, he sat down on a log and calmed himself. Rain fell on and around them. He stared blankly, telling himself in a trance-like voice, "Don't black out, Uncle. Don't pass out. Wake up."

Minutes passed or maybe half an hour. He had no idea how long. He steadied himself while looking at Keane. "What did you do, Keane?" he wept. "I can't believe it. Why, Keane, why?"

He checked the man's pulse. Nothing. They sat with the man for a while. His face was a mess, like pasta sauce or a pizza. No one would be able to tell who this was. Keane had completely taken off the man's face: his nose and lips were missing, his teeth exposed in a horrible monkey grimace. His neck was severed. Was that a windpipe? David leaned towards the rest of the body and peered.

In the man's hand was an umbrella. It was half open. The man had huge walking boots, a tracksuit and a baseball cap with some team logo. A walker. He obviously had started to open the umbrella and it was extended to the second extension point. It started to rain. Gradually bigger proper drops fell, which penetrated the dense foliage.

He held and glared at the man's hand: slim, wet, cold.

It was a white man.

HE LOOKED at his phone which calmed him for a second. “Keane,” he said. “Let's cover him up. We'll come back later.” He got branches, twigs, huge palm leaves the size of his 60" TV. Keane wagged his tail and assisted him in gathering material and covering the body.

He drove like a tyrant on acid. Adrenaline coursed through his veins and every breath he exhaled was an attempt to retch. Oh no. He knew the disastrous consequences. They would take Keane away, put him down. David would be in court in some stupid suit he last wore at a team meeting. No more dog walking or any work at all for David. Stephanie would not talk to him. No one would. He was hideous as the dog. Both monsters. Pariahs. They went back to the Mont Kiara mansion. Breakfast was definitely cancelled now. He had lost his appetite. No maids appeared. He pressed the remote control and the electronic gates of hell slid open. They were both wet and stank of mud. The rain had washed off the blood on David's cut when he fell over, the vomit, everything.

Thunder roared as David traipsed across the manicured lawn, kicked a dropped frangipani flower and raided the gardener’s store room behind the palace that was Keane’s kennel. The dog followed and watched him. David found the biggest shovel he had ever seen. Naturally his brother had to have the biggest and best of anything, including gardening tools when he didn’t even do any gardening. He then put a kerosene lamp, a waterproof oilcloth sheet and the shovel in the back of the four-wheel drive. “We're going back, Keane.”

David dug for two hours in the downpour, which, by softening the ground, had made it looser. And there were no walkers or trekkers in weather like this. Great. When he thought it was deep enough, around 3 feet, he simply rolled the body into the grave. The next stage was easier than the first. *Grave-digging was now a new update for his LinkedIn profile*, he grimly thought, *under Volun-*

teering. After the body was buried and the grave well-concealed with the original assortment of tree branches, foliage and giant leaves that Keane had brought, David thought he'd move an entire small tree, roots and all, for good measure. He planted it in place and made it all natural, no bare earth showing. When he looked back at the dog, he swore. He couldn't believe it. The dog was holding in his jaws the bloody corpse's baseball cap. What. The. Hell. He would have to dispose of it ASAP. He snatched it from the dog who surrendered the cap dutifully.

HE DID NOT GO BACK to Bukit Kiara Park. He dreamt of the man every night. In some dreams, the faceless man talked to David and Keane, like friends. David woke up each time, gasping and trembling. Every day, palms sweating, he checked the news online in the Mail and Straits Times. He also had kept the baseball cap that Keane had clung onto. Manchester United. He had not noticed the logo at the scene of crime though it was familiar enough from those days of watching a stupid match and being handed a beer and a bowl of nuts at 3 am in a sports bar on Jalan Telawi 1. It seemed like another lifetime. He snipped the blood-splattered baseball cap into a thousand picccs with scissors and put them into 3 different municipal bins in TTDI.

A week after the incident, The Star ran a missing person appeal. A 65-year-old tourist from New Zealand was on a two-week holiday with his children and grandchildren, and staying at the Bukit Kiara Equestrian and Country Resort. It appeared that he did not come back to the hotel seven nights ago.

According to BBC, a family friend said Tim Vale, despite his mental health issues and the medication he was on, enjoyed being out alone in nature. The friend also said the family had called him for breakfast that morning but he was not in his room. Sri Hartamas OCPD Supt Mohamad Nor Ali Hishamuddin confirmed the family, "comprising a couple, an elderly man and a 10 year old child" had checked into the resort a week ago. "However, the family lodged a report after they found that he was missing at 8.30am the following morning," he said. A police team assisted by personnel from the Fire and Rescue Services Department had conducted a search in the area. "We are continuing with the search and we have also informed all district police chiefs to assist," he added. "Anyone with any information needs to contact the Sri Hartamas police desk."

Days went by, perhaps another week. He lost track. No news from his brother, sister-in-law or niece. They were busy living their important and hectic lives. David's eyes were bloodshot. He was unable to concentrate on anything. Meals, TV, football. He had lost weight and looked old. He was too ill to go on any more long walks. He only needed to stare at the dog and tears came. Keane was possibly the only thing he'd ever loved. How awful it was to find out this way. He'd never loved his wife and there were no children. They separated five years ago when he was 54. She'd had enough, as he had, so he didn't blame her for that.

Guilt consumed him. He observed Keane swallow meals as before, with a normal appetite, a sense of resignation, duty and dignity. Never blame the dog. Always blame the owner. But Stephanie was not in the country. How could anyone be blamed but him?

Seven weeks with Keane. Now it was all over. He wasn't able to put that poor family out of his mind. A holiday of a lifetime in KL? Not so much. He knew he had to say goodbye to Keane and confess his crime at the Sri Hartamas desk on Jalan 26A. He was looking the directions up on Googlemaps when he noticed that a WhatsApp message came in. Stephanie was arriving the next day. She said she was just leaving Los Angeles International. Would he be available to pick her up at KLIA at 8:20pm the following night? He replied OK. She sent her flight number.

Right, he thought. Stephanie would never forgive him whether or not he owned up so he might as well. Just as he shut his WhatsApp, his Facebook newsfeed came up with a photo of the missing man, Tim Vale. He had not seen the photo in any of the other tabloid news he had been scouring.

David's heart banged like a drum.

It was not the man.

He brought the screen in his hand nearer to him as though he was back in the forest that day. This was a bald man with glasses and far older than the man Keane killed, who, when the baseball cap fell off, had a lot of dark hair and was relatively young. In his 30s or 40s.

A more chilling realization came to him: who the hell did Keane kill? He found no more missing persons reports. "Keane. Shower time. Chang ek leow," he said in Hokkien. Stephanie said the crap previous owners didn't talk to him. At the training school she had sent him to, Keane managed to learn some basic words, like lai (come), cheh (sit), khoon (sleep), chiak (eat) and of course, chang ek (shower). Suddenly, it felt precious. He wanted to protect his secret language with Keane. It might be their last day together.

"I WANT to talk to you about the dog," he said driving Stephanie home from the airport.

"Yes, Uncle? But I am very tired now." She yawned. "Not going to ask me how was San Fran?"

"No, I need to ask you something else."

"What lah?"

David stammered. "W-what... why... what happened to Keane in his previous life?"

"Uncle, why did you not ask before?"

"I didn't know what to ask. I have never had a dog."

Stephanie hesitated. "Wait... what's happened?"

David was choked up. He had to pull over at the next toll booth. He was prepared to tell Stephanie. Everything. But first he said quietly, "Is the dog from a shelter?"

She didn't answer.

"IS HE?" he shouted.

"NO," she yelled back. "I didn't want you to know. He is... you won't tell my daddy, right? Promise me you will not tell him anything?"

"I won't. Why should I? I have not talked to him in years."

Stephanie smiled sadly. "Keane's previous owner is... called... Mike Thurton. English. A bastard in Bangsar. He was my..."

"Oh... you— were—?"

"Just a fling," she said sullenly.

David did not reply. He did not care. He just cared about Keane. After a slight pause, he asked, "Why is he awful?"

"Mike lived alone, loved long walks. Nature. Had the boots, the kit. But he is violent. Abusive. I don't know why he started beating Keane. Mike inherited the dog from his ex-wife. That is why I am the number 3 owner. The wife went back to the UK. He used to punish Keane, with an umbrella. And to this day Keane freaks out and growls when he sees an umbrella, any umbrella, especially if it's the extendable, foldable kind. I tried to report Mike but he threatened me too."

She shuddered and shook her head, burying her face in her hands. David thought this was unusually sensitive for Stephanie, perhaps she was tired from the flight. She took her hands off her face and looked alarmed.

"He OK?" she bleated. "Everything— OK?"

"Of course he's OK. Having the time of his life."

"Oh, Uncle! I'm so happy to hear that." She clapped like a child, with grateful wet eyes as if being told she would be going to Disneyland.

"What was Mike like?" Asked David. "Was he into football?"

"Yaya. He's English, lolz," she said without a trace of irony or a laugh.

"What team did he support?"

"Uncle. I hate football. Please take me home now. I am tired," she whined. He started the engine and they set off.

"I just have one more question," he said as they pulled out onto the highway.

"What lah?"

"Can I keep Keane after tomorrow?"

"Oh sure, I can't have him back. I have signed up at the University of California San Diego. Yep! I am going to be making films! Is that cool or is that cool? Watch out, Sundance! But now tell me why you were upset?"

"I wasn't. Your dog missed you, that's all."

"No, he so does not, lolz."

She shut her eyes on the rest of the journey home. They arrived at Mont Kiara. David pressed the remote and the electronic gates slid open. As he parked and got out, the dog came racing from his sandstone mini-palace.

David went to wake his niece. Keane barked and wagged his tail on seeing Stephanie. She opened her eyes. "I just remembered, Uncle," she said, "it might have been Manchester United."

First published in Singapore as "The Dogsitter" in The Best Asian Short Stories 2021.

Buaya Tembaga, Bujang Senang

Mason Croft

There were reports of crocodiles in the city. The sightings came quickly, one after another and all within a week, as if the riparian marauders had arrived in a pack and dispersed among the waterways. One crocodile was discovered drifting through a residential storm drain, another spotted swimming up the Klang river in full view of the fishermen on their skiffs. They were horrifying creatures; each two or three metres in length, their skin thick dermal plates of ridged, clay-coloured scutum, with long trailing tails and glossy, reptilian eyes. Despite appearances, they posed no threat to the ogling crowds that gathered along the riverbanks whenever one surfaced. They merely sized up their onlookers, grinned and disappeared beneath the brackish waters, leaving only a ripple on the calm, flat surface.

The urban frenzy that followed, however, shook the city. Citizens were terrified. News spread like orchard fire through community phone trees. Fire stations and police departments lit up with calls. The Department of Wildlife launched an investigation. Several ministers made statements; warning signs were posted near riverbeds and beaches, and mothers escorted their children to school with mobile phones in their pockets, fingers twitching above speed dial. The paralysing fear of being eaten alive — once a real possibility, if the urban legends and folktales of the carnivorous buaya tembaga were to be believed — had left the collective consciousness. City folk had forgotten this was once the land of crocodiles.

Such city hysteria barely registered on the island of Tioman. It was peak season and I was working as a dive instructor. The seas between the island and the peninsula were level this time of year, not prone to sudden swells and squalls, and even with the seasonal influx of mainlanders, daily life proceeded untroubled, as it does, in the sleepy backpacker district of Kampung Air Batam — "Kampung ABC" to the locals.

I had just returned from touring a group to Teluk Kador off the north coast and was cleaning gear in the back. It was midday and the sun shone overhead, bathing the dive shop in heat. Outside and on the narrow concrete path that ran the length of the village, a passing scooter-sidecar gave several short beeps, no doubt clearing a few holidaying pedestrians out of its way.

I wore shorts and nothing else, rinsed the sea from my salt-crusted legs with the hose, and prayed for a breeze to cool me down as I worked in the still afternoon. For every wetsuit I soaped, scrubbed, and hung to dry, I took a long pull from a Tiger can I kept in an icebox on the gear shelf. By the fifth suit I was lightheaded so I sat down and watched the banana trees droop over the back fence. Behind them I saw shivers in the bush — a group of mynahs, maybe, a hornbill on the branches, or monkeys — and thought to move the dive bags inside but decided it was too hot. In front of the shop, another scooter beeped, this time louder and closer.

Someone was here.

I threw on a shirt and walked through the darkened shop, ducked under the hammock where I slept each night, and approached the front door. Through the screen I could see it was Rafie on his scooter.

He leaned over the handlebars, his long, thick hair tied behind his head, and peered through the window. He caught sight of me and beeped the horn again. "My friend," he called out, "this heat is wretched. Even the monkeys refuse to climb trees. This is a sign, you know. Come, let's go to Kak Bayar's and cool down."

"Too early for your poetry," I said and stayed in the shade of the shop. "How was yours this morning?"

"Same same ay. Sunburned and hungover. Some cute ones, some not. One guy puked at 20 feet. Barely got his respirator out in time. Psi over 800. He was fine. Maggi noodles floating around his head like this." Rafie dangled a few dreaded lengths of hair in front of his eyes to show me. I smiled but didn't say anything further.

An island second passed in which neither of us spoke. We stared at and past each other, letting his last comment lounge between us like a lizard on a warm rock. I was getting used to these moments: silent stretches of time, often mid-conversation, that expanded in all directions without a trace of awkwardness. The need to fill silence was unnecessary here. It bordered on untoward. It was a new impulse, a Tioman way of talking. Rafie picked at his shirt, then asked "You coming? Or you got cold beer inside?"

I shook my can, showing it was empty. "Another sign," he gestured to his seat. "Hop on, I must kacau Hakim at Kak's anyway. He has my package from Mersing. Been waiting for it since tourist season started."

I thought of the unwashed wetsuits out back, macerating in their neoprene brine, and the stacks of dive gear I'd not yet dealt with. Used to be the thought of a job unfinished was a fishhook to the throat. Pre-island life had distilled in me the barbed notion that time was measured in seconds and every task undone loomed as large and monolithic as a skyscraper. I learned to recognise these thoughts as remnants of city life. Now, an ocean apart, I easily breathed them away.

I said to Rafie "Give me two minutes."

We motored along the village path towards Kak's, bumping past wilted wax palms and single-story beach huts built on stilts. Rafie sounded the horn to clear our way of tourists or packs of long-tailed macaques. Kampung ABC was built into the few parcels of land between where the ocean stopped and the steep, jungle-covered mountains that formed the centre of the island began. Narrow properties filled with huts, guest houses, "chalets," and family-owned shops snaked along the western shore, each covered with roofs of corrugated metal and spray-painted red, white, black, like banded corals on a sea krait.

We passed a group of men carrying lengths of lumber towards a small hut near the treeline. I saw from a distance the hut's roof was caved in from a fallen palm tree. The force had buckled the rear stilts and pitched the hut backwards on its foundation. It reared up at the workers who gathered before it, goading them to come closer. Beneath the porch the soil was also upturned: lush, pulpy mounds of dark dirt, stones, cigarette butts, rotting coconut husks. Exposed, the ground underneath was in full view of the sun and steamed in the afternoon humidity, looking arable, volcanic. I wanted to thrust my hands deep inside and move the earth around with my elbows — another impulse I'd noticed since arriving on the island — but knew my neighbours would think I'd gone off the end.

I recognised some men among the group. The doctor from the clinic, the owner of the sundry shop near my bungalow. "Is this why the shops were closed this morning?" I asked. Rafie nodded. He stopped the scooter and walked over to the man directing the work. The two spoke briefly, the man shrugged, and once the customary island second had passed between them, Rafie came back to the scooter and said our help wasn't needed. The call had gone out in the morning while we were on the water and within an hour, enough volunteers had brought the tools and lumber needed for the repairs. The community always rallied to defend their own whenever trouble came. I waved at the workers as we mounted the scooter. They raised their hands to me in response.

As we pulled out, I noticed something to the right of the hut — a cluster of palms that towered near the fallen trunk, each one poised to topple on the other homes nearby. "They're not going to bring down those other trees?" I asked. They teetered in the wind, swaying drunks on pedestals, the sound of bending wood echoing out to sea.

Rafie gave me a look. "Why, man? Nature gonna break in when it want to anyhow."

He revved the engine. We continued on.

KAK BAYAR'S BAR, Sunset Bar, was tucked into the far end of Kampung ABC on a quiet and unremarkable stretch of sand. Next to it were cliffs of jagged rock, an igneous division between Kampung ABC and the Muslim side of the island, where liquor was sold but no one drank.

We set the scooter near the back entrance and walked towards the beach. Kak Bayar sat behind the bar on her stool next to the cash register. She was brushing her teeth, dipping her toothbrush in a nearby beer mug of sudsy water. Rafie went to talk to her while I took a seat at the other end of the bar and faced the ocean. He showed her a news article on his phone about the crocodile sightings in the city. Kak gave a frothy, full-mouthed laugh and spat into the mug. "Like you," she said to me, the latest city-dweller to move to the island. "Scared of the jungle."

"Did you ever see any?" Rafie asked me.

I felt a faint tug in my throat, then it went away. I shook my head. "The only crocodiles I saw wore suits."

I'D MOVED to Tioman five weeks earlier and already most of the memories of city life had turned to monochrome in my head. This was common for newcomers, I'd been told, but truthfully, even as I lived them I remembered very little of those years. They felt abbreviated, condensed, as compact as a postcard. I grew up in the suburbs where we looked both ways and saw grey concrete in either direction. After graduation, I moved a short distance to the city. I worked a vague marketing job I didn't fully understand. I accumulated stuff, then more, and more. I lived in a condominium with a pool, a tennis court, a steam room. I dated a woman with a pretty, frictionless name that could be spelled any number of ways. Ashley. Ashli. Ashleigh.

Time elapsed with blistering speed and excruciating slowness. In a blink, five years passed and felt like twenty. I realised a want, a hollow and immeasurable want, one that gave as much satisfaction to me as sea water would to the dehydrated, had swollen under my skin.

Soon after, I left the city with the same abruptness I'd left the suburbs and appeared in Kampung ABC like flotsam after a typhoon. When I tried to suss out a reason why, all I could come up with was this: there was so little I could remember or account for in the last two or twenty years that it made just as much sense to leave because it meant I'd be somewhere else when I woke up in the morning.

HAKIM, Kak's barman, came out from the kitchen with a tray of burgers and set two in front of us. Rafie showed him the crocodile article and they laughed. When Rafie asked Hakim about the package, Hakim pulled a small bundle of rolled newspaper from beneath the bar. He glanced at Kak, who was busy glaring at the sun, and slid it over to Rafie. Rafie pulled the package into his lap and unrolled it. Inside, glinting like a silver tooth, was a stainless-steel butterfly knife.

I stared at it, unsure how to react. The sight of a violent piece of metal in a place like Sunset Bar dislodged me. It didn't jive with the place. Cocktails were served with tiny, candy-coloured umbrellas. Bob Marley played over the speakers. Rafie flicked it open and turned it over, inspected the sharpness of the blade with his thumb, then slid it in his waistband and pulled his singlet over his shorts. He counted out two hundred ringgit and handed it to Hakim, then picked up his burger and tucked in like nothing had happened.

"What the hell, Rafie?" I felt uneasy. I wondered why he needed a blade like that. It wasn't for diving. We had argonauts and fogcutters to cut through fishing line, wires, sea kelp, whatever; utility knives built for a purpose. A butterfly blade was made to cut other things. If Rafie carried one then there must be reason to, and I wondered what threats he knew of that I'd missed. Was this island really that dangerous? Was I still so city that I only saw bright waters and tall palm trees and couldn't detect what was lurking beneath the surface? Should I start strapping an argonaut to my waist too?

Hakim, sensing my discomfort, held my wrist and spoke in a hushed voice. "We had trouble the other night. A group of tourists got rowdy and I stopped serving them. One guy pushed me. Rafie almost stepped in but Kak calmed them down pretty good. Got skeevy a bit. You weren't around."

His last words stung but he was right. I knew Hakim didn't expect me to be there; he was just stating a fact, but still I felt distanced by what he said. I thought of the men and their lengths of lumber, how they gathered to repair that destroyed home, and how they grew smaller in the scooter's side mirror as we raced away from them. My face flushed but I maintained my anger, which I turned on Rafie, pointing to his waistband. "So you need that?"

Hakim tilted his head, the Tioman version of a shrug, and said, "Kak can't solve everything, man."

"Wish we had a crocodile instead," Rafie laughed. I studied Kak on her stool. She was picking her teeth with a fork.

"Kak stopped them?"

IT WAS our first night drinking at Sunset Bar when Rafie told me Kak Bayar was a badass bitch. Everyone on the island knew it. "Don't cross her or you'll be sent to the deep," Rafie had warned me. Rumour had it she once sank the supply boat of a liquor agent who cut his vodka bottles with water. It seemed plausible then, but looking over at this short, middle-aged Malay woman now and thinking of the gentle, untroubled interactions I'd had with her since arriving on Tioman, I couldn't see it.

I liked Kak, from what I knew of her. She was uncomplicated. Didn't speak much. I never saw her off her stool. With a full view of the bar, the kitchen, and the beach, her stool was where she commanded Sunset Bar, directing her staff with nods, or, when that didn't get their attention, short barks in a voice like shovelled gravel. She shifted in her seat only when a customer approached the bar to settle their bill. Her staff would yell "Kak! Bayar!" and she'd look up from her register, her grin wide and toothy, clasp their hands in hers and say, "Come again."

Mostly she sat in silence, tranquil as a water lily, blunt as floating driftwood, and watched over her stretch of sand. If she was indeed a woman who could put grown men in their place with a few words then I didn't have as strong a measure on these people as I thought.

Maybe I'd overreacted with Rafie and the butterfly knife, too. I assumed the worst and shouldn't have. It was clear I didn't know Tioman well enough to work out which threats to take seriously, or when a bark was more persuasive than a bite. Not yet. Still, I was angry with myself for not being at Sunset Bar that night. This tiny island was my home as well.

Rafie and I ate our burgers and watched the bar staff set up for the evening. My belly grew full. The more I thought about the butterfly knife, the more I wrote it off. Rafie was acting paranoid. The idea of needing teeth on this island felt like another remnant of the city, an old piece of meat stuck in my gums. Hakim placed two more cold cans in front of us. My bar stool sank further into the sand. A breeze drifted through the banana trees behind us, smelling sweetly of salt, and any fear of what I hadn't yet encountered on this island disappeared.

There were no crocodiles here.

SUN SET like the fade out of a song. A pleasant twilight settled on Kampung Air Batang as the bar filled up with customers. On the stool next to us, a tourist ordered a bucket of beer for himself. At a nod from Kak, Hakim lit tea candles and placed them along the bar, then the low tables scattered about the beach where customers sat in pairs and sipped from their bottles.

Rafie and I were several rounds in, talking about crocodiles for the better part of an hour. Rafie was leaning hard on city folk, saying we scared too easy and hadn't seen a real 'saltie,' when he asked me, "Have you ever heard of Bujang Senang?"

I shook my head.

"Biggest saltie in history. He killed many people. Famous in Sarawak. Watch—" he leaned past me and yelled, "Hey! Kak! You know Bujang Senang ay?"

Kak was mid-conversation with a young, dark-haired girl seated opposite her at the bar. I didn't recognise the girl but guessed she was from the island. Kak shifted in her stool, paused long enough to say "Scary," then turned back to the girl. Everyone around the bar agreed. When he saw he had an audience, Rafie ramped up the dramatics.

"Bujang Senang was a nightmare. Over six metres long. Teeth the size of my forearm. A long, white stripe down his back. He hunted the Batang Lupar river for years. Mum always tell us 'Hurry home or Bujang'll get ya.' They say he catch over forty people and ate them alive. Even now I hurry when I go over rivers. They tried to catch him many times, ay. Professional Iban crocodile hunters. Guys my father knew. They loaded up longboats and searched the rivers with their parangs. They hunted Bujang for a decade and never found him. Hell, they even brought in a white man to track it—" Rafie waved a hand at the tourist next to us, "—some Uni professor from the US, and still Bujang would not be caught. Funny ay. Load up boats with men and machetes and roar out into the mangroves and find nothing but silt."

"Crafty bastard," I said. I crumpled my fifth can and motioned to Hakim for another.

"Yes. Here is why. Bujang Senang is no crocodile." Rafie leaned closer. His eyes flashed yellow and black in the candlelight. "He was a man, a warrior, killed by his enemies, his body thrown in the river. Some say he got cursed by the river spirits to return as a saltie. Others say a bomoh bring him back from the dead. Whatever you believe, he came back to get revenge on his attackers. When he finish them, their sons and daughters. He kill for generations, but I was not afraid of him. I knew I would not be eaten."

Hakim stopped fishing beer mugs out of the freezer. "Wah such confidence, you. Why not?"

"Because my friend, there are times when a man is more likely to be eaten."

"When they're near a river?" I quipped, which Rafie ignored.

"Bujang Senang attacks when a man is punik. Puuunik." Rafie drew out the 'u' sound, pushing his lips towards his nose. "Sarawak word. It is..." He searched for an answer at the bottom of his beer. "When you go to a friend's for dinner and there is no food. Or when you buy a tool and then you want to buy another." He tried to find a better example. The tourist slipped on his elbow and caught his head before it slammed onto the counter. I noticed the large number of bottles lined in front of him. Rafie snapped his fingers.

"Punik. When a man wants and does not get."

It was last call. Sunset Bar began its slow wind down for the evening. I heard the rustling of palm leaves high above us but couldn't see them, the distant beep of a scooter-sidecar, the jungle bending into the darkness of the hills. The tea candles flickered as Kak took notes in her ledger, still talking with the young girl on the other side of the bar. She gave a nod and her staff began closing the kitchen.

Rafie and I sat in silence. Our beers grew warm in our hands. After returning from his fourth trip to the toilet, the tourist beside us tried to climb back on his stool. He misjudged the distance and sent it crashing into the side of the bar. I jumped in my seat. Hakim and the kitchen crew stopped their cleaning. Kak eyed the man from her corner. He straightened up and tried to brush it off, righted the stool then, teetering over again, sat down in another stool as if it were his own. He picked up a bottle another customer had left and took a sip. It was empty. "Hey, my beer's gone. Who drank my beer?"

We looked at him. He was lanky, his shoulders and nose burnt raw pink, with thinning hair and a long forehead. His hands looked soft. He looked like city folk. I clenched a fist and felt my nails dig into my skin. Once smooth and plump like his, my hands had gone hard from the sun and salt water. He leered at the dark-haired girl a few seats away. "Was it you? Did you drink my beer?"

This was said with a bit of a wink — the girl was pretty, after all — but the droop of his eyelids and the oil in his voice made him sound aggressive. The girl spoke to Kak in their dialect.

Kak motioned to the beer bottle next to him. "No, that your beer. That one. You in the wrong chair."

Seeing his mistake but unwilling to acknowledge himself, the man took his beer and grumbled "Yes, well. Lucky for her then."

Everyone thought that was the end of it but a few minutes later, he was back to ogling the girl, flirting loudly across the bar. She was drinking plain soda water with lime and picking at a plate of fries. I wanted to ask Rafie if she was from the other side of the island but was afraid the man would hear and direct his attention towards us.

For her part, the girl was ignoring his advances, half listening out of one ear. When it sounded like he'd finished, she'd offer him a faint smile. Kak, still on her stool, kept a steady gaze. If she was waiting for the man to move closer, she gave nothing away. She made no ripples in the distance between herself and him.

He continued. "Hey, you. Thought that was pretty clever, huh? Trying to take my drink." He snickered like it was a good joke, but when the laugh was not returned, he grew agitated. "What's the matter, don't feel like talking?"

Kak laughed to fill the silence that followed. "You're drunk." She tried to play it off. "How about another beer?"

The man stared at Kak like she'd grown a snout. He scoffed at her, this squat, middle-aged Malay woman, then to the girl he slurred, "How about it? You want to drink with me?"

"Man, she not interested," Rafie said.

Over his shoulder the man said, "Mind your own business," and took another pull from his bottle. "Who's this lady, your mother?"

"Don't talk to her," Kak Bayar said. Her tone shifted. Imperceptibly to the man but noticeably to the rest of us. Rafie stiffened in his chair. The kitchen staff peered out from the service window. Hakim had one hand on the counter, the other below the bar, his shoulders taught. Customers on the beach turned to look at Kak, who everyone knew was a badass bitch, and watched. Kak shifted in her stool. She laid an elbow on the counter and leaned sideways as if she were gliding through water. She never took her eyes off the man.

"I'll talk to whoever I want!" he raised his voice and slammed his fist on the counter.

"You want one more?" Kak gestured to the cooler behind her. "We have Tiger and Carlsberg." In her mouth the words were ground bone. Rafie's hand was under his singlet and clenching what I knew was tucked in his waistband. I didn't know if I should move or stay between him and the tourist. I looked for exits. Was the clinic still open at this hour? If not, where would we take him if he got hurt? How hurt do you have to be before you have to go to a real hospital? By speedboat, the mainland was two hours away and no pilot would take that risk at night. Tioman was a distant star to civilisation.

Ignoring Kak, the man kept at the young girl, wading deeper into brackish waters. "What about you, huh? You're an adult, you can make your own decisions."

"She not your type."

"I think she's just that, ain't you, pretty girl. So, how about it eh?"

Kak Bayar grinned her crocodile teeth. "She fourteen."

"What?"

Kak repeated. "She fourteen."

I watched the man's words get stuck in his throat. Whatever he planned to say next was yanked back down into his gut with a chain. In an instant he cowed, mumbled into his beer and didn't speak again to the girl. She tilted her head and went back to her plate of fries. The tension in the air released.

I heard again the lap of the water on the shore, the putter of a fishing boat in the distance. Customers went back to their conversations, the cooks back to the kitchen, and peace settled upon Kampung Air Batang. The man left without finishing his drink and stumbled off towards hostel row. We watched him teeter down the concrete path on leaden feet. All around him the thick foliage shimmered, the banana palms shook, and the sunburnt gleam of his bald head grew dimmer, dimmer, until the jungle swallowed him whole.

When I went to settle my bill, Kak Bayar smiled and held out my change. I stepped closer and she snapped the bills into my palm with both hands, patted my wrist and said, "Come again."

I was still rattled from the encounter at the bar. I told Rafie I needed to clear my head and that I'd walk back to the dive shop. Before he took off, I stopped him and asked, "Did they ever catch Bujang Senang?"

He picked at his shirt. "Yes. Finally. Took thirteen men with nail guns. A shame. They put his skull in a museum in Kuching. Maybe I take you one day."

We said goodnight. I walked back under bare starlight, the reflection of moonlight off ocean waves lighting my path home. When I arrived I stumbled at the first step, knocked my shin into the staircase, and crashed onto the porch. Leg throbbing, I sat down and inspected where it hurt. I pulled my leg hair back, probing the area with my fingertips. No cut, no blood, only a dull hum of pain.

Above me the stars winked, black sky stretching like a blanket over Tioman, and I had no desire to go to sleep yet. Instead, I laid on my stomach, pressed my belly into the lumber, felt the wooden slats pinch my skin, and peered under my deck. I tried to see through the darkness, past the support stilts and dead husks, into the rich soil in the corners, and searched for a flicker of movement, for a dangerous and dark and scaled reptile with sharp ridges along its back, the frozen, forever grin of a forgotten piece of memory.

I called out, announcing my presence to whatever threat was hiding beneath. I lay there and waited for a response, some sign that the island acknowledged me. All that came was the buzz of the cicadas, the lap of the waves, beneath my belly nothing but the beams and stilts, the smell of rot, the far corners disappearing from view.

OBE in my Office

Y.K. LIM

`10 July 2017. Full Moon Party.`
`Koh Phangan, Thailand`

Zonked on beer, melding with 30,000 fun-seekers shuffling on the beach and moving rhythmically to the music banging from giant loudspeakers on the mile-long Hadd Rin Beach, I clambered up Mellow Mountain to chill with a shroom shake and watch the fiery orange orb dip slowly below the horizon.

It was my 25th birthday.

I remember waking up, at about 4:00 AM. Or did I? I was hovering about 1.5m above my weary body on my dorm bed. It lasted only a few seconds. Then, I felt as if someone had dropped a heavy box on my chest and I was thudded out of my bed. Fear gripped me. I ran to the bathroom, looked in the mirror, thinking the face wasn't mine. My still unwashed neon-coloured face then split into a double-hooded cobra, hissing at me, and I freaked out.

I woke up on the bathroom floor, my head throbbing from the previous night's inebriation. I lay there trying to recall the night before on the beach and on Mellow Mountain.

"How did I get back to my room?" It was 5:00 AM and my

dormmates were still not back. They were likely knocked out by the liquor and shroom shake just like me, lying on the beach somewhere, waiting to see the sun rise again for another day and another night of wild, frenzied Full Moon partying.

LOOKING BACK, that must've been my initiation into OBE— Out of Body Experience. I researched online to learn more and got in touch with people in the OBE community. I experimented with gong baths, yoga nidra and Robert Monroe's patented audio sounds. It was tough at first. When my subtle self or soul left my physical body, I was frightened. Sometimes I freaked out, fearing that the fine silver cord linking my ethereal form to my physical body would snap and never return, like being lost in outer space — forever.

I trained myself rigorously, for two hours a day, for about a year. At first, I could only leave my body for less than ten seconds. After five months, I was able to stay afloat longer and moved further away from my physical body. Once I saw four arms growing out of my subtle body, making it six altogether. Another time I nearly fainted in mid-air when I saw my willy taking flight and my subtle body flying after it in hot pursuit. When I thought I had gotten it back, I realised that it had been there all the time: it was my mind playing tricks on my eyes. At that moment, I knew that I didn't have to stay afloat in one spot; I could move about or wander as I please — well, almost. I couldn't move too far away because there was the danger of crossing into another realm. I'd tried to push myself beyond my 21m limit but each time when I saw or sensed the danger, I recoiled and turned back.

MY OBE, which used to scare the hell out of me, is now something I've come to terms with. I see it as a way of relaxing myself, what non-

OBE people would refer to as "letting your mind wander." This is why I'm writing this story to share with you my maiden OBE experience outside the confines of my house. Now, sit back, put on your headphones, and join me on a short "mind-wandering" trip in my office.

Wednesday, 13 May 2020. Cyberjaya, Malaysia

5:00 pm. It's that time of day when you know you've done enough and you're looking forward to going home for a good rest or meeting up with friends over a beer or two before heading home. I've just finished my writing quota for the day and I have thirty minutes to kill. I work in an online publishing house where I write short stories and comic book stories.

Headphones in place, I recline my seat to a relaxing angle, and play the Beatles' *Lucy in the Sky with Diamonds* on my smartphone. The moment it hits the first line in the chorus, my subtle body is triggered into leaving my physical body. It's weird to be a floating CCTV going around the office observing my colleagues, unobserved. I know this is like spying on my colleagues; yet, this first astral travelling outside my house is both exciting and intriguing, and I'm curious. However, there's one thing I will never do and that's venturing into the Ladies'.

For the uninitiated, please allow me to share something. During an OBE, the subtle body rises from the physical body; the floating body, face down, is aligned to the body in repose. I sit in the first row closest to the window; so, where I'm sitting, I can see the whole office, including the manager's at the other end. My subtle body, hovering over my physical body, is turning around like a flying car on a mission. Yes, I almost forgot to mention this: my year-long training has got me to the stage where I can navigate my soul car in whatever direction I wish.

Sitting in one corner is another writer busy tapping on his smartphone. I hover close to his left shoulder — close enough for me to see that he is doing some auction trading of old coins and currencies. Suddenly, he turns to his left as if sensing the presence of someone. Seeing there's no one, he continues with his business. Sitting behind him, Adrian, a graphic designer, is drumming the table, humming and enjoying himself, while watching a music v-log. In the next row, a programmer is playing a popular online game. Two illustrators are discussing some sketches with a writer for an upcoming comic series. Then I hear a buzz from someone's phone. Ah! It's the gorgeous graphic designer from the Philippines. She walks right through me and — if only you could see me — my ethereal form's shimmering with ecstatic delight. Upon recovering my balance, I turn around just in time to see her lovely booty swinging teasingly behind the meeting room door to take her call.

Or so I thought.

You see, when I'm out of my body, my sense of hearing is sharp, and my vision, although I'm short-sighted, is high-definition. I can hear the drop of a pin, and my eyes can pick out the tiny mole on your face almost 20 m away. As soon as she's in the meeting room, I pick up the sounds of muffled words escaping through the tiny, narrow gaps of the glass door.

"Oh darling, I love you so much!"

"One day you're going to get us both into trouble!"

"Oh come on, Lyn! Only one kiss, please...?"

Then the smoochy-moochy sounds of two lovebirds. I'm tempted to just go in and watch but decide to hold myself back. Well, I don't want to be called a voyeur by my OBE friends. And also, someone might notice the excitement on my physical body. Even in that state of excitement, my ears manage to pick up a teensy buzz which sounds like static electricity. Having identified the source of the sound, I zoom over to Jess, one of our sub-editors, who sits in a quiet nook by the window. What's she listening to? It's definitely not music.

Now, I know Jess quite well as we've been working together for the past three years. I write the stories and she does the editing before it goes to the chief editor. At least once a week, she joins us during lunch break; otherwise, she brings her own food from home, which is mostly vegetarian. Knowing that she's a Theravadan Buddhist, I immediately make the connection: she's doing her Vipassana meditation with the aid of the audio.

Watching her meditating, breathing erratically in and out, I recall the conversations I had had with her about her Buddhist belief and meditation, and I've come to the conclusion that she's somehow gone astray in her meditation. This is apparent in some of the things she says which can sound a little kooky. Over lunch one day, she confided in me that she was being followed by Special Branch officers who were out to get her over some treasonous emails she had sent to the FBI. Or, like this unfinished email that's on her desktop monitor:

> Dear Mr Stevenson,
>
> I would like to congratulate you on the successful premiere of your new movie, Kungfu Panda. However, I regret to say that you have plagiarised the ideas from a short story I wrote about an obese panda and how he becomes the unlikely hero who fends off a Shaolin martial arts exponent attacking his village. Is it a coincidence that your protagonist is Kungfu Panda and I've named mine Shaolin Panda? There is more...

John Stevenson's movie was shown in cinemas worldwide in 2008, and she's writing to him *now*. Poor Jess. I wish I could get into her brain and try to smooth the neural kink that's making her a little daffy.

From where I'm hovering, I can see my body in repose, slouching in the chair, a light blue mask over my cheerless face. Suddenly, I feel the urge to go to the washroom. In an instant, I'm there, entering the toilet cubicle from the top. Just then, I realize that I can't answer nature's call in my ethereal form, but it's too late. From my vantage point, I can see Zack, one of our animators, sitting on the toilet bowl, drooling over some tantalizing images of exotic women in various poses of nudity on his smartphone.

"Oh shit! The smell!" I blurt out.

As soon as I've uttered those words, I know I've succumbed to my conditioned reflex again. In a flash, I'm out of the WC. I turn the corner of the wall that separates the WC from the office only to come face to face with my boss.

I'm, like, 10 cm from his face, eyeball to eyeball, we're breathing into each other's face, my spirit body floating and retreating to make way for him to enter the WC. He has the strange, lost, zombie-look in his eyes that tells me he is not his normal self. If you've seen someone with those rolling, glazed eyes walking like an automaton, you'll know what I mean. Just when he's about to push open the WC door, I swerve to his left to make way for him — which I don't have to, of course.

"Something's not right," I say to myself.

You see, when you're in the state I'm in now, you see things that your physical eyes don't see, and hear things that your physical ears don't hear.In my OBE adventures at home, I've seen ethereal beings, which in the physical world we often dismiss as someone imagining or seeing things. I can't even believe I'm telling you this because I'm quite a sceptical person and often scoff at friends who have a penchant for sharing ghost stories.

My ears pick up the sound of someone chanting in a mix of Arabic and Malay and I hear the boss's name mentioned. I find myself suspended just above the right shoulder of the person responsible for the chanting — or more accurately, incantation. The tall, six-footer IT guy, Duke, is notorious for shirking his duties or responsibilities. It's a well-known fact that by virtue of noblesse oblige, he is appointed the IT manager of the company; he's paid to *goyang kaki*, shake legs in the office without having to do any work. As the company has been implementing some 'Covid-19 pandemic' cost-cutting measures, he must have been worried that his contract may not be renewed. Perhaps his Arabic is not so good.

There's more Malay in his boss-hexing incantation which makes me privy to what he's chanting.

"O Deep Purple Jinn. Bless my soul. Bless my health. Bless me with good life. Bless me with good health and prosperity. O Deep Purple Jinn, grant me this wish. Protect my job. Cast a spell on *Datuk Rusdi* so that I can keep this job for as long as I want. O Deep Purple Jinn. Thank you, thank you for your blessing and protection. Thank you."

Then he sweeps his hands over his face, opens his eyes, and I catch sight of the aubergine-hued jinn with big round eyes and pointy ears hurriedly leaving from behind the 32-inch desktop monitor. We lock eyes and I perceive that it is a little embarrassed that it has been caught in the act of abetting someone in this hexing job. Upon opening his eyes, Duke reaches for his mouse and enlarges the screen of a site that he had minimized earlier.

It's a YouTube video about the controversial Muslim TV evangelist Dr Zakir Naik's 2017 visit to Universitas Pendidikan Indonesia in Bandung. A young woman in the audience stepped up to the mike during the Q & A:

"Dr Zakir Naik, you have said before that if Muslims have to choose between two leaders, a Muslim and a non-Muslim, even if the latter is a better leader, they should choose the Muslim leader. My question is this: Is that *dakwah*, religious propagation, or destruction?"

In response, Dr Naik asked instead, "In what way is the non-Muslim a good or better leader?"

"Well, he does charity work, helps the poor and has built mosques for Muslims," she said.

Dr Zakir said to the woman, "Of what use is the building of mosques if he doesn't pray?" He added that Muslims must choose a Muslim leader even if the non-Muslim is a Mahatma Gandhi or a Nobel Peace Prize recipient. "A Muslim leader who has *iman,* belief in the Quran, is far superior to a non-Muslim leader."

In other words, don't choose a kafir, and if Muslims do that, "they will not get the help of Allah except by way of warning," he proclaimed to thunderous applause from the audience.

Engrossed in the video, I haven't noticed the sumo Assistant HR Manager lumbering into the room, heading in our direction and slapping her big, pudgy right hand on Duke's shoulder where I've positioned myself, precipitating an airquake, and my momentary loss of balance. She then bends down close to Duke's left ear and whispers: "Congratulations. HR Manager would like to see you tomorrow at ten."

By now, my body has slid further down my seat and I open my eyes to see Madame Dada, the matronly 60-year-old expat instructional designer, standing beside me, thrusting her index finger into my ribs.

"You were mumbling something. Exciting dream, eh?" she teases.

Next time, I'll have to be more careful.

Riding the Killer Fish

Sylvia Petter

It was a Sunday and I was in the kitchen musing about falling in love with a leprechaun when—

"Banzai!"

Globs of green squelched through the air as Ben landed feet first in the shivering jelly of summer fruits. "My *chartreuse*!" I shrieked only to shake into giggles as I recognized the kimono-clad leprechaun planted arms akimbo in my dessert.

"Oh, Ben. I've missed you so," I blurted. "How's the rainbow business doing? Why are you dressed up like a Samurai?"

Ben climbed out of the bowl of Bohemian glass. He shook as much as he could of the sticky substance from his feet and legs while keeping the hem of his blue and white weave gown hitched high enough to let him get to the edge of the sink without tripping. There he sat, his little legs stretched out to rinse under the running water of the tap I had turned on. "Lots of rainbows these days. But you can't work all the time," he said with a grin. "Sorry about the jelly. Couldn't resist," he twinkled. "All those colors. I was exploring old Japan when I thought I just had to come by and tell you all about it."

I mopped the mucky matter from the kitchen top and took off

my soiled red gingham apron. "You could have landed more discreetly," I scolded, suppressing a smile. "Look at all this goo."

Ben ducked his head: "I know. I was trying to keep ahead of the thunder. You know how they do it?"

"Do what?" As I uttered the words, I knew I was caught once again.

"Make the thunder, of course," he said. "They use dried fish hide stretched over the drum, about the size of a timpani drum, but they have three of them. Then they rumble the padded sticks across the hide and let it roll. When they go against the scales, that's when the lightning crackles along with it. When they do it across the scales, there's just that low rumble. And there'll probably be a rainbow following it."

I stared at him. I had no idea who "they" were, but somehow, for the first time, I did not want to ask.

"And the only way to drown them out," he said, "is to pierce the hide with a terrible scream."

"But there hasn't been any thunder, Ben," I said, brushing a strand of hair from my face.

"I know. I just wanted to try it out. Just in case ..."

He was doing it again. The crazy pictures and adventures, the looping in and out of honeysuckle whims. I hadn't even gone back to the book of verse, the one in which I'd found him snoozing in amongst the musk roses. I hadn't dared go back to open it since the day he'd left to shin back up the rainbow in search of pots of gold. Some things were better left alone. But it was as if he'd heard me missing him.

"It was your chartreuse, I couldn't resist," he said. "Full of rainbow colors, plump apricots, raspberries ripe with juice, crisp green apple slices, smiling strawberries crowned with fresh and tangy leaves of mint. I just wanted to bounce about in it."

"Well, we'd better rinse your kimono and hang it up to dry. You too, by the looks of it." I pointed at the curtain rod and swept the sunny cotton fabric to one side. "Go and sit up there, out of the way while I clean this up," I said and hung the dripping kimono, twice the size of the breadth of my hand, over the kitchen doorknob.

Ben took a deep breath and leapt up to the curtain rod, making it in one go and clinging with hands and feet. Proud, he balanced, hanging by the knees, his eyes half closed and his shiny sheaf of barley hair dipping down like silk.

"I'm a sloth," he said, swinging to a stop. He closed his eyes and pretended to be asleep.

I stared at him. He hadn't changed.

"We ate raw fish, you know," he said and flick-flacked onto the kitchen counter.

"Who's we? And when was that?" I asked and knew I'd been baited again.

"In old Japan. Down by the village with Anjin-san. Chopsticks aren't easy. They're not rounded in Japan and things slip off if you're not careful. Sushi's fine though; you can spear it. Ever tried?"

I had never eaten raw fish before coming to live in Japan. Not that I wouldn't have dared, but where would I get raw fish in the middle of the countryside? Anyway, I'd never even been to a Japanese restaurant back then, although there were a couple in Geneva.

"You know, they even have bars there now where little boats carrying all sorts of fish delicacies and morsels float past before your table to tease your fancy. I could take you to one," he said leaving questions in the air.

I felt the familiar tug and wondered whether I would ever be able to dismiss this strange little man. "Ben, we've been through this before." Hadn't I sent him on his way to be about his business, to look for his pots of gold. Hadn't he left me last time with a tear in my eye as I watched him climb up a rainbow?

"Why can't I...?" I said.

"You can," Ben said, climbing the set of condiment shelves.

Holding the silver pendant dangling from my single hoop earring, he stepped gingerly onto my right shoulder.

"Grow up, I mean."

Ben nuzzled my earlobe and I pretended not to hear the dull and distant rumbling that signalled he would have to be off. "One day you might even ride a killer fish," he whispered, and then he was gone. I raised my eyebrows and shook my head.

Time went by, my career took off and Ben entered my mind only rarely. I was working in Tokyo for a UN setup and had even developed a liking for raw fish. So when I was asked to go and do precis-writing for two weeks at a conference in Kyoto, I jumped at the chance.

My colleagues from the Geneva HQ had been allotted hotel rooms near the conference site. I was living in the country and coming in at the last minute, so in a way, I was a free agent. In the short time I would have in Kyoto, I wanted to do things properly, the old way. So, I booked myself into a ryokan. I would take off my shoes, walk barefoot on a tatami-covered floor and sleep on a futon. I would wear a yukata, sip green tea and eat sushi. I would go native. Suddenly I thought of Ben. He would surely approve.

Don't eat the blowfish, the Geneva mob said. *Don't touch the Japanese, don't hug them. Thumbs up is not what you think.* I laughed. What did they know? I still wasn't fluent in Japanese but I no longer tripped over clichés. Thinking of the advice I had given them in return that alligators might work as a mnemonic for how to say thank you, I ventured out on my first night in Kyoto.

Restaurants on the main road near my small side street were lit with bright lights that reflected off the pink plastic prawns and tuna sushi pieces in their windows. I suddenly felt very lonely. Plastic sushi was not what I wanted. *Ride a killer fish*, Ben had said.

I walked around the block. Close to my ryokan, I saw what

seemed like a small restaurant. A banner with calligraphy floated down the wall next to a warmly lit window. I peeked inside. Behind a small bar, a man was skilleting food on a long hotplate. Two other men were perched at the bar. Behind them were three very low tables. Two were occupied by a man and a woman. One place was left at the bar.

I pushed open the door and said hello. The man behind the hotplate nodded. I gestured with my fingers that I wanted food. He nodded again and pointed to the last seat at the bar. Then he pointed at the skillet: a mixture of thin slices of meat and rice, scallions and tomato. I nodded. In no time, he had placed a steaming plate before me and poured a clear liquid into an earthenware cup. I accepted the chopsticks he offered, and he smiled.

I ate studiously, concentrating on working the shiny pointed sticks. They were just as Ben had described. The liquid was sake, and it made my cheeks hot. I could feel the man watching me. I ate the whole dish and opened my purse. He took ¥1,000. Alligato, I said. He nodded. I returned the next evening. The man's name was Mitsui-san I was told by a patron who spoke some English. Mrs Mitsui appeared. She passed me a dish, watched me eat, nodded slowly.

THE NEXT EVENING, they were waiting for me. Mitsui-san placed a tiny bowl before me. Fugu, he said. Fugu means blowfish, but the words that flashed across my mind were hara-kiri, sayonara, killer fish. I didn't have the Japanese vocabulary so with my finger I mimed slitting my throat. But I'd paid my bills, written my letters, paid up my insurance, said my goodbyes. Besides, wasn't I immortal? Hadn't Ben told me?

Blowfish is supposed to be served only in specially licenced restaurants because improperly prepared it kills instantaneously, painfully. What was more important? A certificate from experts or trust in my host? Or the certainty that my time could not have come yet. I suddenly knew I wanted to ride rainbows.

My gaze clung to the look in Mitsui-san's eyes. I feared for a second. Then Mitsui-san put a finger to his lips. *Shhh,* he said and smiled at me in a way that made me reach out, spear a sliver of fish, bring it to my mouth. It tingled on my tongue with the thrill of taboo. I knew something would happen, and then it did.

A wave rolled beyond the constraints of language. Mitsui-san's eyes told me that I had passed the trust test. He didn't need to be licenced to know how to serve fugu. I swallowed and smiled. I made the sign of circling finger and thumb to make it look like a lowercase b for "bon" as I'd say in Geneva. But here, the sign would have to do even if my hand was trembling. Mitsui-san's wife patted my hand and poured a beer for herself, for her husband and for me. Kampai, they said, and we all laughed.

I ATE with the Mitsuis every day. On the day I left Kyoto, we hugged. We exchanged gifts. I gave them a story I had written about a leprechaun eating sushi with a Samurai in old Japan. I'd had it translated into Japanese. They gave me a lacquered clay tanuki, a plump raccoon dog to bring me luck. Luck had been with me, and I had fallen in love — with Japan.

An earlier version of "Riding the Killer Fish" was first published in the charity anthology New Sun Rising, stories for Japan, Raging Aardvark Publishing, Australia, 2012. The "Old Japan" excerpt was first published in Yomimono, Japan, 1994, and included in the story "An Imaginary Friend" published in Thema, USA in 1997, and in Sylvia's collection, The Past Present, IUMIX, UK, 2000.

Shark's Best Friend

Rumaizah Abu Bakar

Endless layers of pointed white teeth raced towards him. A big grey tail flipped over his head. Salty water filled his throat. He lost his footing and coughed hysterically.

Danny

Danny sat in his office in the dark. He ran his palm over his damp pony tail. His neck and shirt were drenched in sweat. His secretary had switched off the air-conditioning when she left hours ago but he did not have the energy to get up.

He stared at the two framed photos on the wall.

Visitors loved to see the first image of him lying down at the Sipadan beach with a baby shark. Its caption was heartwarming: 'My best friend'.

The second piece was a photo of the villager's boat that he used for his fieldwork. His islander research assistant had proudly raised it in the sand as a monument in his honor. A tribute was printed on the body of the boat: 'Datuk Dr Daniel Ong – Shark's Hero'.

He would undertake the Presidential post for Shark Lovers Asia Pacific and in due time earn big bucks and international fame. He had already eyed a few potential residential areas by the beach in New South Wales, Australia. His children would continue their secondary education at an international school. His wife would enjoy a socialite life with the other expatriates' spouses.

SYLVIA

Sylvia first met Danny when she came to the Oceans Without Sharks exhibition ten years ago. She seemed engrossed with the big panel illustrating the 63 shark species, their local habitats and their challenges to survive in a cruel world.

Shark Lovers had collaborated with the Selangor State government and a pool of sponsors to create awareness through scare tactics. Disconcerting shark-themed masterpieces by various artists and photographers leapt from the four walls of the hall. Visitors gasped at the vivid visuals of sharks in distress, bleeding, lifeless, and lying in various stages of suffering.

Sylvia faced a blown up image of a finless shark. The creature seemed to look out with sad eyes. Her hands went to her mouth when a man approached her.

"The shark was in so much pain," he said. "It was hard to live without fins. Imagine having our limbs ripped off. That is why nobody should ever, ever eat shark's fin."

She turned to look at him.

"Did you know that sharks have become an endangered species?" he continued. "You must have watched *Jaws*. Actually, there have only been three local incidents of shark attacks within the last 40 years. Sharks don't usually eat humans. It's is the other way round." He gave her his most charming smile. "Sharks are top predators that stabilizes the marine ecosystems. They tend to eat the old, sick or slower fish and keep the fish population healthy. If they become obsolete, the humans' seafood supply chain crashes too. So, you see, sharks are not dangerous. In fact, they are important to the survival of the human race."

Sylvia tugged her printed dress and smiled shyly. "Yes, I know. It is a sad reality. I learned about the ocean food chain during my lectures." She told him that she was just fresh out of university with a degree in Marine Science.

"Awesome! Welcome to the wild." He took out his iPhone and showed her the photo of him lying down at the Sipadan beach next to the baby shark. "I've swum with sharks for 15 years," he said. "These beautiful creatures are my friends."

"You're such a hero," she said, in awe.

"I'm organizing a regional sharks' conservation workshop in Kota Kinabalu next month. If you like, I could arrange for you to go."

She seemed surprised. "Really? But the airfare to Sabah is so costly. I can't afford it. I haven't gotten a job yet."

"No problem." He grinned. "We'll have you on board as a junior conservation officer. That is if you are interested, of course. Your travel and accommodation cost for the week will be all taken care of."

"But— but I have no working experience."

"My dear, none of us did when we first started. We learn on the job."

A month later, she sat next to him on the three-hour flight to Kota Kinabalu. They dined at his favorite Chinese restaurant at the city's waterfront boardwalk. The stunning vermillion sky and jazz music made the perfect setting for them to unwind and get to know each other.

He enticed her with the special dishes. "Say no to shark's fin! These vegetarian alternatives taste just like the real thing. Ooh... it's good. The broth is rich and spicy."

"The glass noodle fin is much cheaper too," she agreed. "It's all about prestige anyway. Shark's fin has no taste. It's ridiculous to fork out a hefty amount for something so bland."

Danny cringed, recollecting his younger days as a junior conservation officer. He had made endless visits to the food premises along the river. He persuaded the owners not to serve shark's fin. He persisted for years until most of them agreed to sign a pledge to protect the species.

However, he did not have the same success with his own family. He stunned the guests with his epic toast at his elder brother's wedding.

"Congratulations to the bride and groom. Thank you for keeping Malaysia on the list of top ten shark goods' producers. We don't just murder them at our own sea. We import dead sharks from abroad to fulfil our endless greed. Well done!"

He bowed and walked out of the event hall.

His father had not forgiven him for embarrassing their family and disrespecting their tradition. Shark's fin soup was a delicacy at Chinese banquets. To forbid the dish was a disgrace to their ancestors.

Sylvia listened intently to his series of confessions. It was almost midnight when they returned to the hotel.

They only got to hang out in the evenings as their days were filled with work. He was entrusted to moderate most of the four-day sessions. The younger participants seemed to find him inspiring and uplifting. After all, he did initiate the Malaysian chapter of the world's renowned shark-saving organization. He was also the first person in the country to complete a doctorate in shark conservation.

Sylvia had been cautious of him at first. "My dear, life is not all about work," he'd said.

She soon relaxed and talked about herself, pouring out secrets that few knew. He listened, or at least he pretended to. On their last evening in the city, she spent the entire night in his hotel room.

Once back in Petaling Jaya, they went to karaoke sessions with their other colleagues in the evenings. She sat next to him and joined him in singing the oldies. She moved onto his lap after they had too much to drink.

DANNY

He was careful not to be seen alone with her, unless they were outstation. He told his wife that he was going out with his staff to build a good rapport with them. She was too occupied with growing her image consultant business to notice the change in him.

Eyebrows started raising at work. People noticed and talked behind his back. His loyal secretary fed him the latest gossip, showing him what was shared on multiple WhatsApp groups. He chuckled.

Still, they dared not mess with him. They had each experienced the wrath beneath the humble and friendly façade.

Instead, they let it out on Sylvia, dumping work on her and blaming her for their mistakes and own poor judgement. Her immediate superior gave her a low annual performance appraisal rating.

She left on her own free will. She was a discerning writer and a dedicated researcher, her media articles requiring minimal editing. He was happy to see his byline at the end of a series of fascinating sharks' advocacy articles that she had slaved over for a year.

SOFI

Sofi and her team members conceptualized and organized the Shark Lovers fashion show five years ago. They reached out to the best designers in the country and convinced them to contribute their chic clothes and accessories for a noble cause. High heels and belts with fins, dresses with teeth-shaped sequins, and shark-motif scarves were among the creations auctioned at the prestigious fundraising event.

Their triumph caught the attention of shark conservationists worldwide. Sofi was invited by The Shark Lovers' Regional Head to apply for the marketing manager post that was recently vacated.

She appeared serious at the interview in a crisp pants suit and plain hijab. She took the panel through her pack of well-illustrated

PowerPoint slides. They were impressed. She stood head and shoulders above her competitors.

She would lead Shark Lovers' image revamp exercise. After two years, awareness of the organization would increase significantly, and donations would come pouring in.

DANNY

He would, in turn, become redundant way too soon. He put on a friendly and encouraging demeanor when she consulted him. "Everyone calls me Danny. No need Datuk or Doctor," he assured her.

They chatted at the small round table at his office. The large windows opened up to a cluster of mango trees along a stretch of tarmac road. The worn out building in the seedy part of Petaling Jaya was all they could afford with their non-governmental organization budget. He did enjoy having occasional visitors from the wild though. The security guard had found various species of monitor lizards, snakes, mammals and amphibians at their open air car park.

Danny found out that she was flying to meet their Sabahan colleagues and planned a trip to coincide with it. He asked his secretary to book a room at the same backpackers' place at which she was staying. He would tell Sofi that he tried to stretch the donors' money by reducing expenses where possible. He was the kind of leader who walked the talk. It was still more comfortable than his cramp rented flat in the suburbs when he started working in the state.

He saw her having breakfast at the courtyard café alone. He asked to join her on the wooden bench. They sipped cups of hot black Kopi Tenom while he cheerfully shared tales from his rough marine expeditions in Sipadan.

SOFI

Sofi was impressed that he learned the local island dialect and won over the hearts of the tribal leaders. Soon, she forgot her professional conduct and lowered her guards. She began to see him as a heroic icon. He should be highlighted in their brand revamp exercise.

She valued his guidance. He was among the first conservationists dedicated to saving the endangered sea creatures. She felt honored to work with him.

DANNY

He poked her plan bit by bit and slowly swayed her away from her original ideas. After all, several more television appearances focusing on him would not hurt. During their annual fundraising review session, he subtly pointed out to the board of trustees and donors how much she had wavered from the plan. He said that it was understandable due to her lack of field knowledge. Her forte was marketing, and not conservation.

Satisfied that he had ruined the trustees' confidence in her, he informed her that they would not be renewing her annual employment contract. She would leave Shark Lovers in ten working days. He stepped into her portfolio temporarily just in time for International Shark Day to take the credit.

He did not reply to her email protesting his action, copying in the trustees. She had sought legal advice and demanded that they meet up to discuss. He could see the upcoming accusation of a major sabotage.

He knew the trustees had called her and all the senior staff for an investigation. He did not trust any of them. They then took turns to interrogate him. It was surreal. He felt as if he was participating in a reality television show. He was smashed like a shuttlecock by the team of eight men and women from all corners of the packed meeting room.

He stumbled out six hours later, shaken and disoriented. He had covered his trails well. They could not dismiss him.

He did not expect his young lover to return and haunt him a decade later. He blamed the #MeToo social movement for it. Women all over the world had come forward to share their sexual harassment and abuse experiences openly. It had inspired Sylvia and half a dozen former female employees to do the same.

She stood quietly at the entrance of his office. She was clad in a pink *baju kurung* and appeared more matured than when he last saw her. He heard that she was married with two children. He had no idea who her husband was and could not believe that the timid woman would be strong enough to lead and win a war against him.

Alleged sexual misconducts did not look good for the head of a noble organization dedicated to saving sharks. Donors were appalled. The federal and states' government officials were horrified. His conservationist peers from the entire region turned against him and rallied to have him removed.

For the umpteenth time, poison pen letters appeared to tarnish his reputation. A petition to sack him was raised yet again. Enough members of his staff summoned their guts to sign it.

The beep of a WhatsApp message startled him. It was his estranged younger sister. He had not seen her for eleven years.

> You should come tomorrow. No shark's fin. Daddy canceled the main dish. His friends threatened to boycott my wedding. Come! Everybody expects to see you there. HERO!

She ended her message with confetti.

He stared at the two framed photos on the wall for a while.

Maybe he should go. It might make him feel like a hero once again.

He grabbed the embossed beige envelope on his desk and left the office.

HIS NOSE AND THROAT HURT. He struggled to push himself back up to the surface of the water. The cold wind punched his face. He took a deep breath and calmed down. The gray creature swam around him. He remembered his best friend. It had been a while since they last hung out. He gave it his biggest smile, and waved.

Last Exit to Bugis Street

Ewan Lawrie

My father was part of a tiny RAF support unit off the Bukit Panjang Road. The 100 or so British, Australian and New Zealand Air Force personnel lived and worked alongside the Singapore Air Force at Tengah in the mid-70s.

I was on holiday from a boarding school in England. We should do some decoding here: if I were the kind of person you have assumed I am from that statement, it would have read quite differently: "It was the long vac and I was spending it with mater and pater."

Or something very similar. My father was an NCO, a Warrant Officer. This puts me as far as the moon away from someone who ever spent a "long vac" anywhere.

I was 16 and for the first and only time my older brothers Derek and Trevor were in Singapore too. Derek had just finished a tour of Northern Ireland. He'd got an 'indulgence' flight on the trooper aircraft which flew direct into Tengah Air Base, which still took a few RAF transport flights. People were stationed at Gan in the Indian Ocean and occasionally manufactured a "sports trip" to Singapore so they didn't go completely mad. Or *Doolally* as people said then, although the number of people who'd ever served in India would have been very few, by that time.

Derek had a month off before he had to head back to join his Royal Corps of Transport unit in West Germany. We'd never got on awfully well, I have to admit. The five years between us was unbridgeable until I turned 25. Most likely that was my fault.

Derek had to sit where he could see the exits from a room. Even in the Married Quarter on Tengah. He took up golf that summer and still plays now, nearly half-a-century later. At Tengah Golf Club, he would sit outside on the terrace, with the wall of the building behind him, after a round. He arrived changed and borrowed clubs from an Aussie next-door-neighbour. Anything to avoid going inside. The sight-lines weren't good.

Trevor – or Trev – was a deck officer in the Merchant Navy: deep sea, ore carriers. He'd been dropped off in Singapore on the way back from Australia. Nine months at sea, except for a day here and there, loading and unloading. Most times, as the most junior officer, he'd pull the worst watches or even duty officer if the port was half-decent. Whatever, he was due leave and he was spending the month with the "olds" too. He was planning to fly back; British Airways, if they couldn't get him the cheap flight on a trooper.

I'd flown out on Singapore Airlines. A millionaire for a day. If you haven't guessed, the RAF paid the fees for the school and three trips a year for the school holidays. I spent half-terms with various sisters of my dad's, but that's another story. Or three.

Which leaves my sister, Maureen. Maureen was at school on camp with all the Aussies and New Zealanders. Her accent was interesting. The school was terrible.

My parents played golf and socialised in the ANZUK Sgts' Mess. I have photographs of my dad in tropical mess kit. He looks smart as ninepence and as uncomfortable as a cat in a cage full of dogs, the eyes staring: looking — as they did in every photograph — like the eyes of someone begging to be rescued. Exactly the way they did in real life, once the Alzheimer's came for him.

One afternoon, the three of us, my brothers and I, we got on a rackety diesel bus and followed the fog of two-stroke exhaust fumes down the Bukit Panjang road until we got to the Bukit Timah Plaza and then jumped in a taxi.

"Take us to Chinatown," Trev said.

We'd promised we'd be back at ten p.m. "A sailor, a soldier and a schoolboy went to Chinatown..." It sounds like the start of a joke. Maybe it was, maybe it is.

By the time we got there, it was after five. So we decided to go somewhere to eat. We chose Fatty's, on Albert Street. We *were* tourists, after all. The only food I ever had that came close to being as good, was in 1978 when Alice Leung took a gang of us to a Chinese restaurant in Newcastle, where she had to translate the whole menu. We were the only Caucasians there.

That was not the case in Fatty's. We were the *only* people there. I say in, but back then, there was no in. There were trestle tables on the street. It wasn't busy, of course. Too early for the drunken sailors and the visitors from Hong Kong. They just kept coming with food and Tiger beer. Trev said he was paying, but by the time we stopped eating two hours later, my brothers had agreed to split the bill.

It came to 27 Singapore Dollars. About a fiver then, since you ask. Trev paid.

I don't know who suggested we go to Bugis Street. I'd heard of it; of course I had, I was 16. At least, one of the VIth Form boarders at my school had been in Singapore up until a few years before. He didn't tell me the whole story, of course. Or even much at all really, just told me to listen to some Lou Reed song. I'm sure you can guess which one.

Surprisingly, I wasn't that drunk. All the food had helped with that. Nothing like noodles, rice and dim sum for soaking up beer, even the fire-water that was Tiger Beer, back in the day. It was about a half-seven, quarter to eight. Sunset had been and gone. The lights were bright on the street. Neon tubes crackled, fizzed and some fizzled as we walked down Albert Street to the corner of Bugis Street. Further down from Wing Seong's — as we never once called Fatty's but should have — the mopeds and tri-wheeled delivery vans' exhaust fumes overcame the smell of garlic and fish based "wok-kery". Nowadays, the slightest whiff of a two-stroke engine's fumes takes me back to Singapore.

Bugis Street was still quiet. Most of the servicemen still scattered around the island at Seletar, Tengah and other units called it "Boogie" Street. I smile every time I hear Baccara, as I did the first time, when it was a Euro monster hit, barely a year later. I understand all of that area is pedestrianised now. There were a lot of tables to negotiate in your vehicle back then. Some of the bigger saloon cars and taxis drove very slowly down the street. Sometimes they picked someone up, after a conversation through a passenger-side window.

About half-way down, we took an empty table. Derek took a seat where he could see both ends of the street and the entrance to the bars on both sides. He kept his head 'on the swivel'. The table stood outside some neon declaring the bar's name to be '*The _ello _earl*'. Trev pointed at a building across the street just at the corner of Bugis and Malabar. It was a toilet block.

"That's where they used to do it; on the roof of that building," Derek sniggered.

I said, "What?"

"The dance."

"Who did?"

"*Royal* Navy types," Trev said. "At least until the local police arrested those Aussies a couple of years ago. Don't reckon I'll ever see *The Dance of the Fiery Arseholes* again."

My brother looked as though he thought that might be a pity.

We ordered beer. It came, but it wasn't Tiger, though. I couldn't read the characters on the label and there was no pinyin to be seen on it anywhere. It tasted fine.

"Gosh," I said — people said that kind of thing then, or at least I did — "some of these women are very tall."

Some of Derek's beer came down his nose. But they were. And also very beautiful. Without exception.

A man placed two further chairs around our table, making it a table for six, although there were just the three of us. He wasn't exactly glowering, but he looked like he'd last smiled when Lee Kuan Yew was at Raffles College. I thought one of my brothers would tell the guy that we weren't expecting anyone else, but they didn't.

Three women sat down. My brothers looked sideways at me and nodded at each other.

"Just a photo," Trev said.

He might have been speaking to our brother, but the woman next to me answered in a voice as deep as Lauren Bacall's after a whole pack of cigarettes, "Especially him, huh?" She flicked the fingers of the hand not holding the cigarette at me.

I looked from one brother to the other, "What did she mean by that?"

She leaned over, put her hand on my chest and then sat in my lap, when I fell back in the chair. My brothers and the other two women let out peals of laughter, although a couple of the bells sounded cracked.

The waiter with no smile brought a tray of brightly coloured drinks over and the women took one each. The girl on my knee held the drink in her cigarette hand and raised the other arm overhead and clicked her fingers loud enough to hear from across the street. Which somebody clearly had.

His smile was the first thing I noticed. It was as if the man and the waiter were yin and yang. He was dressed like Hollywood's idea of a press reporter from over twenty years earlier. The only thing missing was the piece of card marked 'press' in his hatband. Yes, he wore a hat. A trilby or something. And a tweed suit. It must have been 75º F in old money. There wasn't a bead of sweat on him. He had a camera slung around his neck, one of the latest Polaroid models. The man was well-dressed, but he didn't look *that* well-off. The other two women went off in search of better company, as the sound of American voices rose further down the street.

By this time, Mai-Ling had her arms around my neck and was whispering in my ear. What she said after her name, I couldn't quite catch. My face was flushed and I was praying that Mai-Ling would just sit still for a moment. The flash went off and it was like a switch had been flicked. The woman towered over me and held her hand out.

"Twenty dollar, Singapore. Five American."

"For what?" I said.

"For me," she said. "Photographer get different money, thank you."

Twenty Singapore dollars was half of all the money I had, but I handed it over. Mai Ling stuffed it down the front of her tight, high-necked dress. She turned to my brothers. Maybe she'd noticed some resemblance, although I never have.

"Nice boy, your brother. Did not feel me up. Maybe got shock, huh?"

I watched her walk down the street to the next bar. Then I closed my mouth.

The photographer was holding out the photo, waving it intermittently.

"Another twenty, for your souvenir, kid."

Derek paid the man and handed Trev the photo.

"I think I'll keep this, for now," he said, before stuffing it into the breast pocket of his batik shirt.

I mumbled something. Trev said he'd post it to school for me, from wherever he was next in port. "Maybe I could impress my friends with it," he added. He never did send it, though.

I didn't say much until we flagged a taxi for home a half-an-hour later, back on Albert Street, where we could expect a more reasonable fare.

"She was beautiful, eh?" I said.

My brothers shook their heads. Derek mentioned that Lou Reed song. He had an album with it on, back at the barracks in Germany, he said. Trev told me I needed to watch *Some Like It Hot*.

I did watch it, about a year later, with a VIth Form Film Studies group.

You know what? Nobody IS perfect.

A Father's Son

Sandeep Kumar Mishra

The mourners were not plentiful on the day of the funeral. Charvik Sharma had not been a popular man in this life, having dedicated very little time to cultivating and maintaining relationships. Sahil, his eldest, watched the people move about in respectful silence, occasionally stopping with one of his siblings or mother to offer quiet condolences while the chanters continued through their mantras. Some made their way over to him, but he had nothing to say to them in return.

Everything was too fresh — Sahil wasn't sure how he felt about his father's death yet. He hadn't even seen his father for at least ten years, having left to live with his aunt while still a boy.

He looked over at his mother, his brother Ishaan, and his sister Shaleena. His mother looked sad at least, but Ishaan and Shaleena looked as numb as he. He wondered what the past ten years had been like for them and if their father had changed at all since failing Sahil.

He would never forget the first time his father struck him. It was a miserable, humid day, the air so wet that you could almost taste it. Charvik was home, classes having been let out, and was especially short of temper.

Sahil, still a small child at the time, refused to go outside to play. "It's too hot," he remembered protesting. "I'll melt!"

His mother had gently but firmly encouraged him to go outside anyway. "You won't melt, I promise. But you really should go outside. The sun is good for you."

"I don't want to!" his little voice rose.

"Sahil, my darling, please go outside." His mother looked around, fear coloring her face. It was the first time Sahil could recall seeing his mother afraid, though it would not be the last.

Charvik appeared around the corner, his face an oncoming storm, and Sahil understood his mother's fear.

"What is the meaning of this noise?" It was less a question than a demand.

Sahil ventured a reply. "I don't want to go outside."

The baleful gaze Charvik leveled at his son burned into the young boy's soul. "I heard your mother tell you to go outside. Why do you stand there mewing?"

"I—"

SLAP.

"Do as you're told. If I see you in the house again before supper, you will get it twice as bad!"

Tears ran unchecked down Sahil's face, and he bolted through the door before his father could rebuke him for those, too. Oblivious to his surroundings he fled off into town, and did not dare return home until well after dark.

"Sahil?"

Sahil glanced over to find his sister standing beside him, her previously numb expression now one of concern. "Yes, Shaleena?"

"I just... I wondered if you were all right. You've barely spoken a word since coming home."

Home. This was not his home anymore, and hadn't been since he had been sent away. "I'm fine. Just a little impatient to be done with this."

Shaleena nodded. "You and father never did get along."

Sahil gave her a glance. "You say that as though I am unique in that respect."

She shrugged slightly. "He... tried, I think, to make some small amends. He never apologized, not in as many words, but he was... softer." She hesitated, as though weighing her words. "I think he missed you."

Sahil scoffed. "I find that unlikely."

Shaleena was quiet for a long moment after that. "Well, I missed you at least. And I'm glad you came back, even if it's just for this." She briefly touched his arm, then moved back towards their mother. He allowed his mind to wander again, passively listening to the chants and watching the dancing flames of a candle.

"I know your father was very cruel," Sahil shook his head and looked over to where his Aunt Shashi was addressing him. "Perhaps he will be kinder in his next life."

Sahil couldn't reply to that. He wasn't certain his father deserved another life.

"I am sorry you did not get to say goodbye," his aunt ventured again. She was a kind woman, almost a second mother to Sahil, but she was too forgiving.

"I am not." The first words Sahil had spoken since the funeral began. "We said everything we needed to say to each other a long time ago."

A YOUNG SAHIL stood nervously in his father's cramped office. Their small house afforded little space for their growing family, yet Charvik refused to give up this room. Sahil had no idea what it was for, he just knew that his father's claims to it meant that he and his new brother Ishaan would be sharing a room.

"Your brother will be your responsibility," he remembered his father saying, eyes intense and hard. "I expect you to take the responsibility."

Sahil didn't speak. He knew by then that discussions with his father were not truly discussions; they were just brief moments when his father bothered to remember he had a child long enough to impart specific instructions. Any words on Sahil's part would earn him a backhand, and that was if his father was in a decent mood.

"That means helping your mother feed and change him, teach him, and—"

"Keep him out of your way?"

The words were a mistake — Sahil knew that before he said them, but sometimes he couldn't help himself. He stood defiantly as the fury entered his father's eyes. He would feel the repercussions of that remark for a long time, and remember them even longer.

Sahil wasted no time after the traditional ten-day mourning period to get back to his life. The fact that he even had to take ten whole days off irritated him, and he was unreasonably short with his family because of it. He wanted to leave this house and its memories, to get back to his own wife and child and job, and to burn the past away just as the body had been burned.

On the tenth day, his brother found him alone and sat beside him. Sahil looked over skeptically; he and his brother had never been close and disagreed often, hardly speaking to each other these past days.

"I assume you plan to leave with the sun," Ishaan began, not looking over.

"Before the sun, if I can manage it. I have a long ride home and the earlier I start, the earlier I am back where I belong."

Ishaan shook his head. "You never cared for home."

"You make it sound like I chose to leave in the first place," Sahil countered, frowning.

"Perhaps not. But you did choose not to come back."

"Father—"

"Damn it, Sahil, this isn't about Father!" Ishaan stood suddenly with this outburst, spinning so he looked down at Sahil. "You left more than Father behind! You left Shaleena and Mother too, or did you think being sent away to school freed you from your responsibilities as eldest?"

"I checked in when I could. Everything was under control, and Father didn't want me back besides."

Ishaan threw his arms in the air. "Typical Sahil. Always running from Father. If you only gave him the respect he deserved, perhaps—"

"You want to talk to me about respect?" Sahil was standing now. "You call abusive behavior worthy of respect?"

"He was our father. He deserved your respect regardless." Ishaan began to head back inside, but paused in the doorway. "But I see you won't listen to me. You'll just run, like you always have."

By sunrise on the eleventh day, he was packed and ready to go, not even staying for breakfast. He had nothing more to say to his mother or siblings, and they had lived the past ten years without him. There was no reason to stay here any longer. So he quickly and quietly slipped out of the home of his childhood to catch the first train of the day and refused to look back.

As he walked, his thoughts wandered. He looked forward to home, that the train was running on time, that his wife, Viha, had set aside some dinner for him, and a thousand other thoughts like these — anything to get his mind off and moving forward.

He was so focused on putting the past behind him that he didn't notice the football until it was almost too late. With a small yelp he bobbed his head to the side, narrowly avoiding a head-on collision with the flying ball. He shook his head, startled and confused, and looked around for the ball's owner. He spotted them: a young boy who was smiling apologetically, and his father who was laughing just down the road. The father jogged towards Sahil.

"My apologies," he began, still laughing a little. "My son and I like to come out for a little game before I have to go to work, and we are unaccustomed to sharing the road so early."

Sahil took a moment to gather his wits before answering. "Ah... it is all right. I was not hit, so no harm." His eyes drifted back to the boy. "You two do this... often?"

The father nodded. "Most mornings. I work long hours, so I cherish the moments I can. Surely you understand?"

Sahil looked back at the father.

"Sahil, why does father never come out to play with us?"

Sahil didn't turn to look at his little sister. Shaleena was barely five, but already she was noticing that their house was not like the houses of some of her friends. Her father was practically a stranger to her, only seen at meals and on holidays. *No great loss there*, Sahil thought with no small measure of distaste.

"Because he is too busy," Ishaan said when it was obvious that Sahil had nothing to say.

"Busy with what?"

Ishaan paused. "Work, I guess."

Shaleena clearly didn't understand, but filed the information away nonetheless and pressed on to her next question. "And why is he so sad?"

This got Sahil to speak. "You think he's sad?" Shaleena nodded and Sahil scoffed. "Why do you think this?"

"Because he never smiles. Sad people don't smile."

It made sense, in a little kid logic sort of way, but Sahil had trouble picturing his father's constantly dour expression as anything but angry.

"He isn't sad," Sahil said finally, frowning at the football by his feet. "I don't know what he is, but he isn't sad."

This confused the little girl more but Sahil chose that moment to kick the ball and she took off after it, screaming with joy. Ishaan looked at Sahil and frowned. "Don't speak of our father like that."

Sahil rolled his eyes and watched Shaleena run. "Why not? It isn't like he's around to hear us, and even if he was, he never listens to anything we say."

"But—"

"I don't want to hear it, Ishaan. Come on, let's catch up to Shaleena."

GIVEN THE EARLY HOUR, the train station was thankfully quiet and Sahil managed to purchase his ticket and board with minimal wait. He also had his choice of seats for the long ride ahead of him. Settling his luggage above him, he sat heavily and sighed, thankful to be on the way home at last. The rest of his day promised to be an easy one, as it was nothing more tedious than waiting until he reached his stop that evening, then getting a cab to take him home. Comforted by these thoughts, he drifted into a light nap as the train began to move.

When he stirred a few hours later, he noticed the car was significantly more crowded than it had been, with nearly all the seats outside of the one directly beside him taken. He also noticed a lone man who, noticing that Sahil was awake, was headed his way.

"A thousand apologies, sir, but is that seat taken?" He indicated the seat beside Sahil.

"No. Please, sit." The man nodded his thanks and situated his own luggage, pulling out a well-worn book before stashing the bags, and settled into the seat. Sahil's eyes were instantly drawn to the cover.

The man noticed Sahil's attention and held the book up for better inspection. "I take it you are familiar with *Songs of Kabul*?"

Sahil startled. "Oh... ah... not as such. Or rather I have not taken the time to read that particular collection myself. Someone... I knew, did. Spoke of it very highly."

The man nodded and began flipping through the pages. "It is a good book. If you have any love of poetry, I highly recommend it."

"I shall keep that in mind."

"Are you a student of poetry?"

"I teach a high school literature class and occasionally write my own pieces. Nothing worth publishing, but...."

The man nodded. "It's nice to put thought to paper?"

"Exactly. And poetry has always been special to my family."

"What are you reading?"

Sahil looked up from his own perch across the room from the conversation, watching where Shaleena had approached their father's armchair and interrupted his reading with her question. He instinctively tensed, waiting for the cold dismissal or fiery rage at being disturbed; the first would cause Shaleena to run away hurt and Sahil to follow so he could calm her down, and the second would be directed at Sahil for not keeping her distracted in the first place. Either way, it was about to become Sahil's problem.

Yet Charvik did neither. Instead, he'd looked up slowly and studied his daughter for a moment, as though trying to remember who she was and how he should react. Then he'd closed his book in order to show her the cover. "This is a book of poems. Can you read the title?"

Shaleena had squinted at the letters. "*Songs of Kabir*?" She spoke slowly, careful to get every word correct. Sahil couldn't help but be a little impressed. He hadn't realized her reading skills had progressed so far.

Charvik had smiled at her, and Sahil had frowned in confusion. "That's right," their father had said, sounding pleased. "Would you like to read some poems with me?"

Sahil looked back down to his own book, but he couldn't focus on the words anymore.

That was the kindest he'd ever seen his father behave towards anyone outside of their mother. He'd watched and listened as Charvik read to Shaleena, poem after poem after poem. He hadn't grown tired, or annoyed, but rather he'd seemed almost... happy.

"Are any of these by you, Dad?" she'd asked.

Charvik had paused at that question. "No. I have written poems, but I have not been so blessed as to have them published."

"Maybe someday?"

"Yes," he'd said, a wistful look in his eyes. "Maybe someday."

HAILING A TAXI TO take him from the train station to his home didn't take long. It was already much later than Sahil had hoped to arrive home, as a scheduling mixup with a different train had caused a delay of nearly two hours, and he was now more anxious than ever for the comfort of his wife and bed. As he was driven across the city, the driver made occasional attempts at small talk, most of which Sahil answered with polite but short replies, doing his best to avoid a protracted conversation. One comment, however, caused him to pay attention.

"Are you excited for the start of Deepawali tomorrow?"

Sahil blinked. "That's tomorrow?"

The driver nodded. "I love Deepawali, personally. Well, specifically the Feast, but the entire festival is fun."

Sahil glanced at the driver's bulky figure and guessed that the man did not save feasting for the festival alone.

"Hurry, Sahil! Father wants us to be among the first visitors to the temple!"

Sahil groaned, stretched and tried to rub the sleep from his eyes. "The... temple?"

"Yes, the temple!" Shaleena was entirely too excited and loud for this early hour. "It's the first day of Deepawali!"

Sahil shook himself more fully away and swung his legs over the side of his bed. *Deepawali.* He smiled a little as Shaleena scampered off, her mission accomplished. Father was always in high spirits during religious festivals and holy days; his usual dour expression lightened and stormy mood calmed. He might even be persuaded to give his children treats, so long as all the proper observances are met.

"It is a holy day first and a festival second," he would solemnly intone. "Be respectful of that."

And they were. Quiet and respectful, they said the correct chants to the best of their abilities and answered every question Charvik had for them about the origin of Deepawali. Then, finally, the religious observances were finished and it was time to decorate.

Their house was never so clean as it was during Deepawali. And between Shaleena and Charvik, it was harder to find a house more thoroughly decorated, either. A hillside's worth of flowers were braided together and hung on every door frame and window. Sahil looked at the flowers and frowned. What was it about flowers and a stupid festival that suddenly made his father so cheerful? Why couldn't he always be like this?

He wanted to tear all the flowers down.

Sahil slipped quietly into his home, unsure if his wife was awake and knowing their infant son was not. He paused just inside, seeing the flower decorations all prepared for Deepawali. A frown tugged briefly at his lips, but he shook it away; the holiday had never done him any harm. Setting his luggage down in the entryway and taking off his shoes to make as little noise as possible, he made a quick walk of the house.

Everything was spotless. His wife had done an excellent job keeping up with the cleaning, even with the added responsibility of their newborn. He smiled slightly as he paused by the dining room table, laying a hand on their son's highchair.

He moved into his office and saw everything was just as he had left it. It was, by agreement, the only room she didn't routinely clean, as Sahil had his own method to the seeming madness. He knew where everything was and that was the important part. He looked over his papers, his bookshelf, the grading pens and the half-finished poems, and he frowned.

It looked remarkably like how he remembered his father's office being laid out. How had he never noticed that before?

"Am I becoming my father?" The question was asked quietly, barely even whispered, as though Sahil was afraid of the answer. Were not all men their fathers' sons? What hope did he have to build a better life for himself when he mirrored his father in even this tiny detail? In what other ways had he shaped himself after a man he... he what?

He missed. Here, in the darkness and the silence, he missed his father. He missed the idea of his father, that connection he saw so often, just that day coming home from the funeral. Someone he could talk to, someone he could play ball with, someone who led by example and listened to the worries of his children.

Charvik had never been any of those things for Sahil, but he'd seen glimpses of that man in the way Shaleena interacted with him, and wondered if he had changed at all after Sahil had left. If he really had missed his son as much as his son now missed him, as Shaleena had suggested.

"It's too late for regrets," Sahil told his ghosts. "He's dead. Whatever that may mean for him, it means to me that he is beyond reach." Forgiveness and healing were beyond Sahil's reach; there was no saving Charvik's memory or salvaging the relationship. But Sahil was more than his father's legacy. He would prove that, to himself and to his family.

Sahil left his office and its ghosts and headed up the stairs. He paused midway up to look at the pictures hanging from the wall — him and his wife on vacation, on their wedding day, on the day they brought their son home for the first time. They were happy in those pictures. Sahil knew true joy in every moment captured and it showed. He thought back to pictures of his father; Charvik had rarely smiled in person and never for the camera. Even in the oldest photos he'd looked serious and stoic, never expressing joy in his life.

"I am not you," he whispered, wondering if Charvik's spirit could hear him from wherever it had gone. "I will not be you."

He finished climbing the stairs, bypassing his own bedroom to check on his son. The child was asleep, oblivious to the presence of his father, and Sahil smiled down at the small bundle. Resting a hand on the side of the crib, he made his son a promise. "I'll do better. I swear, I will do better."

The floor creaked softly, and Sahil looked over his shoulder to see his wife, wrapped in her dressing robe, squinting sleepily at him. "Sahil?" Her voice was barely audible, and he quietly crept over to her after a final look at his son. "I didn't hear you come in." She squinted at him again, then reached out and touched his face, concern taking over her expression. "You're crying! What's wrong?"

Sahil cupped her hand and smiled. "Nothing. Come, let us go back to bed. I am ready for today to end and tomorrow to begin."

The Deepest Heart

San Lin Tun

Holding his debut book in his hand as if it were a blue sapphire, Naing felt quite elated with his nascent accomplishment. He reflected on the time he had spent to reach this level. It was over two decades. *Phew.* He remembered he scribbled down his ambition to be an English author on the back page of a text book when he was a high school student and it seemed a tall tale.

That time he was fortunate to attend a private tuition class arranged by his classmate when their school was closed for summer holidays. His classmate, Tin, called Naing to ask whether he would like to join a conversational English class at his place. Naing readily answered that he would love to attend because he wanted to learn English well and it was once in a blue moon for him too. Since then, he had developed that aim in life and he often looked at the expressive line again and again to remind himself of his determination.

In their family, Naing was the only person who was passionate about learning English. His parents, being devoid of good schooling, worked hard to support his education by setting up a grocery shop. Mostly, Naing had to rely on himself whenever he found difficulty learning English. Naing knew that he should be well-versed in English when he grew up. That would vouchsafe him to fit in at a high position in the government administration and he could deal with educated people to raise his social status and to mingle in the elite circle.

Naing met his first English teacher U Tun at his friend's house and he liked the way the teacher taught English to them. The teacher used the Progressive English Course for them. Even though he graduated from Rangoon University three or four years ago, Teacher Tun had been studying English with a well-known Rangoon University alumni couple who opened a private tuition classes with meager fees for learners. Naing's respect for U Tun enhanced when he found out that U Tun learnt the rudimentary of English in jail when he was detained for his involvement in the political activities of 1974.

When he came out from prison, U Tun picked up his disrupted university course and graduated, majoring in psychology. As a habit, U Tun got up early in the morning and revised his English almost every day. Knowing his teacher's unflinching effort, Naing was encouraged and he decided that he would do the same. U Tun was punctual and he used a very good method to teach English. With his guidelines, Naing became worry-free for his English, enjoying it; his decision to be an English writer was augmented and secured.

HIS STRAIN of thoughts was disconnected when the publisher U Myint patted gently on his left shoulder. U Myint assured, "Ko Naing, I thought you like the book cover illustration and everything."

Naing nodded his head, thanking U Myint for bringing out the best quality book to the public.

U Myint said, "Here are the rest of the royalties we owe you. How many complimentary copies do you want for your friends?"

Naing said, "Twenty copies. That would be enough."

U Myint smiled at Naing's self-restraint reply and complied, "All right, I will take care of this." The deal was as simple as that.

SOON NAING LEFT The White Swan Publishing House office and hurried home. On the way, he called some of his friends and shared his success with them. A tinge of excitement in his voice was noticeable. He made an appointment with them on the following Thursday morning at a usual teashop where they sat together.

On a whim, Naing stopped at a place where less people were present and he turned to the frontispiece of the book and read:

Dedicated to those who taught me English, especially Sayar Tun.

But his mind wandered back to the past in which a series of episodes popped up like a fluttering of flashbacks.

"NO, you cannot be a writer. NO WAY. If you become a writer, how will you survive?" Naing and his father did not see eye to eye. Naing was stubborn and hardly yielded. He knew that there were other writers who lived well. His father totally objected to his ambition and said sharply that he could not be a writer and instead should pursue a secured profession. Since that day, his father stopped talking to him.

The teenaged Naing had to put up with the distress. He faced an impasse and wondered how a seed could sprout without proper attention. He did not receive any encouragement from his family members. Naing decided that he would show his capabilities one day. He made up his mind that he needed to spend more time on reading English books. Since then, he had saved up his pocket money to buy English books and a high pile of books was a witness to his discipline. His parents did not consent to his pastime. They thought that he was wasting his time and money and assumed that he was just a dreamer.

Naing knew that if he wanted to excel in something, he had to be crazy about it, only focusing on his goal. That meant that he had to live with it. Wherever he went, whenever he ate or slept, he had to live with that mindset. It was like testing one's ambition with one's fate. If he threw his dice of fate wrong, his life would be down in the drain. He believed that self-confidence was the decisive factor in winning a game.

In reality, it was harder and trickier. It was easy to get frustrated or despair whenever he faced difficulties and debacles. At that time, he thought that his life was done. He did not want to do it any longer. Artistic people tended to falter when they faced difficulties. To get back on their feet would surely take time. Their lives were as miserable as they could be. Naing was not an exception.

AS A TEENAGER, Naing learnt his English by simply looking at the Oxford dictionary without proper guidance. He followed everyone's advice. When someone said to him that he should memorize all the words in the dictionary, he did. It was a blind chase, leading him nowhere. He tried every way to improve his English. But, his improvement was not apparent although he tried really hard. He needed proper guidance and methods.

Through luck, he met some people who knew English well. He remembered Mr G Minus who was a master sergeant in the British Army and he was like a living dictionary. When Naing met him at the central train station, they sat on an iron bench and Naing asked Mr Minus some words he did not know when he read the *Reader's Digest*. Mr Minus readily explained to him the meanings and Naing was amazed at his knowledge.

Over a pot of green tea and pea cake, Mr Minus briefed Naing. Mr Minus was weak in Burmese. When he explained new words to Naing, he explained in English, not in Burmese. Naing learnt a direct method from him and a number of good things from Mr Minus such as the way to memorize words with rhyming patterns which were used in older days of the educational system.

Another person who bestowed good knowledge was a dedicated English grammarian who elucidated Naing on eight parts of speeches and incurred a good foundation of grammar in him. With his clear-cut explanations, Naing's English improved and his fear in grammar went. Most of the English language teachers in his town normally used *High School English Grammar* by Wren and Martin, *Nestfield's English Grammar and Living English Structure.*

To read all these grammar treatises without a teacher was like cleaning the Augean stable. After his matriculation and his sophomore years, Naing took up a general English class taught by a well-known teacher who preferred American English. Naing learnt American idioms but he still did not know how to end a sentence because he was negligent of sentence structures.

THE UNIVERSITY STUDENT Naing found another middle-aged man, a former headmaster, who was an expert in English grammar. When the ex-headmaster explained to Naing about sentence structures, Naing understood all the functions of English sentences. The man used the subject and predicate section of High School Grammar. Naing could now see the whole scene of English sentences and connect the two parts: the eight parts of speech with composition. His knowledge gap was totally bridged.

Since then, Naing understood that types of sentences could be linked if one really wanted to excel in composition. Naing started to collect rhetoric books to improve his writing skills. His obsession in learning English was so immense that he had collected ELBS English language books. He thought that he had more than a hundred grammar books in his collection.

When he could write correct and simple sentences, the graduate Naing tried to write short stories with the guidance of the books which focused on writing. Gradually, he learnt more about creative writing which was not available in his town. He decided that he should rely on himself if he wanted to write properly. Self-study was the only way to achieve his goal. He would go to British Council library to do creative writing. Bit by bit, his writing skills improved and soon he wrote short stories. Since then, he was determined to write a proper novel when the time was due.

NAING'S present novel was the result of his incessant effort for a couple of decades. He realized that his dream had come true in some way. As soon as he finished his novel draft, he showed it to U Myint, who readily agreed to publish the book in a couple of months. When he shared his news with his parents, his father said nothing, still keeping his steady, silent composure by keeping his genuine feelings from Naing. But Naing knew that his father would be proud of his work and success.

Success was not a decisive matter in Naing's career because he believed in what he did. Whether success would come to him or not, he would write more as long as there was an audience for his literary work.

THE AUTHOR NAING BECKONED to his friend when he saw him coming into the teashop on a Thursday. His friend called out his name. "Hey, Ko Naing, have you been waiting here long?" Naing looked at his friend, Lwin who smiled down at him. He then signed one of his books and gave it to Lwin, who said, "Oh, it's your first novel. I like the title. It makes a lot of sense. It will be a hit, Naing. I am very proud of you."

Nodding his head, Naing agreed with Lwin's words. During this time, the waiter boy brought a menu for them to order food and drinks. Looking at it, Naing asked Lwin what he would like to have.

"Tea, of course, with some dumplings."

Naing also ordered for himself. While they waited for other friends to arrive, they talked about the past, how carefree they were in their high school days, how mischievous they had been. In their eyes, there were glimpses of nostalgia. They knew how they wanted to preserve those good memories.

Sayar Tun's words "You have to be crazy when you want to excel in things" showed some truth. Naing built his life based on the assumption that where there was a will, there was a way. Out of his madness and creativity, he had accomplished his objective: to write a complete novel in English.

He had treaded the difficult path and valued his rewards even though he had not been paid well from his writing. His literary onset was successful. He sensed that his efforts were not in vain as he set a good example for other people who wanted to walk this dreadful path without faltering. Simply, he was a torch light for them.

In a few days, reviews of his book would appear in local journals and magazines and social media and everyone would wonder who the writer Naing was and why he wrote in English instead of his native Burmese. They would want to know more about his life and his efforts in any way.

NAING LOOKED AHEAD with blurry eyes in reminiscence of Sayar Tun. He saw more friends coming into the teashop, greeting and congratulating him until they slumped down on chairs to begin a lively and cheerful conversation about him and his book entitled *From the Deepest Heart.*

Full Moon over Tawi-Tawi

Nenad Jovancic

"'Look out the left,' the captain said. "'The grass down there, that's where we'll land.'" I actually sang this, albeit quietly, to my girlfriend.

We were about to land at Sanga-Sanga airport, on the southern tip of the Tawi-Tawi island group, and I was sure I'd made a hilarious joke, suggesting that the Philippine Airlines Boeing 727 we were in would land on grass. After all, what was visible to me through the dirty window was just a flat expanse of mud and grass and bushes. And a shack at its southern end, a crooked sign on its roof welcoming us to Bongao.

We came down hard and I still only saw grass and red soil zooming past the window as the plane shook and shuddered across the uneven surface. Yes, definitely one of my more interesting landings in Southeast Asia.

Why would two kids from Sweden, barely in their twenties, decide to travel across the globe to visit a known hotbed of Islamic insurgents in the southernmost part of the Sulu.

Why indeed, with easy access to Spain, Cyprus, and not least the Greek island of Mykonos, where anything was acceptable in the early eighties – these holiday spots inviting us, the young and hip crowd, to spend our vacation in a cheap beach hotel, with bars and nightclubs only a few steps away. Sure, during our three years together, Susie and I had done our best to ravage the Med each summer, competing with the hot sirocco winds.

But I'd always wanted something more and yearned to experience an exotic, faraway location. When one of my friends told me about his trip to the Philippines, I knew what our next destination had to be. It wasn't difficult to convince Susie, the eternal romantic. She could already see herself coming out from a turquoise sea and stepping onto a golden beach fringed by swaying palms. I got Lonely Planet's *South-East Asia on a Shoestring* and we started planning our first winter holiday, in a fabulous yet cheap location. Goodbye snow, hello sun and sea. The two of us welcoming the birth of a new year on a tropical beach, under a moonlit sky.

ARRIVING IN MANILA, we'd found a seedy hotel in Ermita that was just within our tight budget but otherwise had nothing else to recommend it. Then, tired and disappointed, we got into a pointless, heated argument.

Manila is not the best introduction to Southeast Asia, as I've discovered since. A grotty, disorganised airport, taxi drivers that rip you off and let you know it with a smile, traffic jams that make the busiest Bangkok and Jakarta streets seem like a weekend jaunt in the countryside. Then there was the air – oh, the air – or rather the lack of it. We'd never before seen anyone wear a face mask just to cross the street. Our expectations of beautiful tropical locations were shattered. And having spent close to twenty hours with the cheapest possible airline, in contortionist positions each time we tried to sleep, hadn't done anything to put us in a good mood.

We ended the argument the same way as all previous ones since the weekend we'd initially met: having fantastic sex. The act itself was gratifying, as always, but my last thoughts before falling asleep were that we'd perfected the art of quarrelling and used it as foreplay. And that sex was the only thing keeping us together.

In the morning, we agreed that there must be more to the country than its horrible capital. Somewhere like Boracay, as Susie suggested, even in those days on every backpacker's list. Or Zamboanga, which I favoured as it was the gateway to the exotic-sounding Sulu Archipelago and as far from the usual backpacker trails as you could get. We debated the options for two days while partying in Ermita bars. I proposed a compromise: buying tickets for the ferry to Zamboanga, which docked halfway at a port close to Boracay, and holding off our decision to the last moment.

Having boarded the ferry, we discovered scores of western backpackers, each with an oversized backpack and sleeping on the deck, eager to reach Boracay. During that day at sea, Susie's initial *I told you so*-attitude, aimed at me for wanting to take us to a strange place no one had even heard of, got thoroughly quashed as we chatted with our unshaven and smelly fellow passengers. Carrying suitcases instead of backpacks identified us as mere tourists. On top of that, having booked a private cabin on the ferry, never mind that we had to share it with countless cockroaches, was anathema. We were pariahs, not even wannabe backpackers.

"Fuck them all," Susie said the next day as we watched the unwashed masses leave the ferry in Caticlan. "I wouldn't want to spend five minutes with these idiots, let alone a whole vacation."

Zamboanga Port appeared as singularly unattractive as Manila.

"The weather is better here, I can see the sun. But there are no beaches. Are you sure this is the right place? It stinks." Susie wrinkled her nose as she made herself comfortable in the back of a tricycle while I helped the driver secure our suitcases.

"Trust me, you will love this hotel. I just hope we can afford it."

Despite everyone in Manila warning us about Zamboanga and the Moro guerrilla specialising in kidnapping westerners for ransom, we felt safe throughout our stay in Lantaka Hotel. A thoroughly westernised place, the hotel catered to the stratosphere of Zamboanga's upper classes in those days, yet it was ridiculously cheap compared to Manila. We enjoyed the luxurious surroundings, our dollars lasting much longer than I had expected. This was the ultimate place for a tropical holiday for a young couple on a tight budget and Susie loved it, either lounging by the pool and commandeering the bar staff, or hiring a boat to take us to Santa Cruz Island – the only place in the world with a pink beach. She was in heaven.

Two days before the New Year celebration, I found out from the airline office in the hotel that Marcos had just opened up Sulu to foreigners. I was itching to see it and got Susie to agree after a brief argument and another sex session. Once in a lifetime opportunity, I'd said, just for a day and night, then back to Zamboanga, as we didn't even know if there would be a place for us to stay.

And here we were, at the outermost island of the Philippines that you could fly to. I was looking forward to the adventure of a lifetime. All Susie wanted was a shower. Having managed to retrieve our bag in the usual airport melee, seated in an overcrowded jeepney on our way to Bongao, I was full of expectations. Our fellow travellers had informed us that there was indeed a reputable establishment in town, the one and only Southern Hotel. Ah, to me the name evoked images of grandeur and past times: an impressive entrance, chandeliers hanging from high ceilings, opulent guest rooms. Set in a perfect beach location, with swaying palms and an open-air bar, the staff milling around discretely, ready to indulge the guests' every whim.

Maybe I was too optimistic.

The dirt track the jeepney was bumping along on turned into a dirt street that sloped gently some hundred metres towards the sea, where it disappeared into the water. Rickety wooden constructions, made to look like houses, lined the street on both sides. Our first impression was of a film set for an old Western, with only the fronts and sides of the buildings put up, the walls propped up from inside the empty spaces. I'm sure that Bongao nowadays has grown into a semblance of a town, but in those days it was barely a village.

Halfway down the street, though, we could see the Southern Hotel, two storeys high and made of concrete, the only real building in sight. There was no grand entrance, however. Not even a door, just a door frame. Never mind, the interior was cool enough and yes, there was a free room for the night – the last one. We followed the receptionist upstairs to a large landing with two rooms on one side and ours on the other, and another door frame in front of us. This one leading to a balcony overlooking the street, running the length of the building. Our room was spacious, with a double bed that wasn't too lumpy. It also had an ensuite bathroom, an unexpected bonus, and louvred plastic windows facing the balcony. Hardly luxury but more than adequate for a couple of young adventurers. A shower and a change of clothes later, we were ready to explore our surroundings.

Armed with several bottles of water, snorkelling gear, and a camcorder, we set out. We started at the south end of the village, where the street ended, hoping to discover a beautiful little beach with an untouched coral reef. What we found instead were rusting cans, torn plastic bags, unmatched flip-flops – ever-present in the tropics, bobbing forlornly in the shallows – and stinking fish remains floating on top of an unhealthy mix of diesel and sewage.

Thus we turned north, towards the airport, having seen several beaches during our jeepney ride and intent on reaching them. Walking through the village, camcorder on my shoulder, I felt like an explorer capturing the sights and sounds for posterity and wished that I could record the smells as well: a mix of delicate fragrances from flowering bushes, the unmistakable odour of fish left to dry in the sun, and the ever-present smell of cooking. Even the fine dust rising from the ground had a peculiar smell and taste.

The street was busy with tricycles and tiny, two-stroke motorcycles that trailed plumes of blue smoke, weaving between scores of pedestrians and dogs. Two jeepneys were vying for the narrow space, their drivers honking the horns as the passengers looked out the windows with unseeing eyes, stoically accepting their lot. Yet, despite everyone around us pretending normality, we were not fooled. Even seeing the shacks up close, with people going in and out of a couple of these, Bongao versions of general stores, did nothing to change our initial perception. The buildings still looked surreal and put up as props, the people nothing but extras, even as they nodded and smiled shyly at us, having been dropped in Bongao overnight to confuse us.

We found our beach in the end. Warm water washing across soft sands, the reefs reaching the shore in places, teeming with fish and shells. I've travelled the world since, looking in vain for a beach as profoundly beautiful and serene as the one we discovered that day.

The people we came across on our trek were another kind of different, though. We'd see a bunch of kids playing in the dirt, Susie would wave and smile and call out to them while I filmed it. The tots would look at us in fright, eyes like saucers, and run into the nearest hut. The adults behaved similarly. A friendly nod and 'hello' from us and they'd immediately retreat indoors, eyeing us suspiciously from the door gap. Yes, we were outsiders, that much was clear, particularly with Susie's classic eighties mane – big and wavy and positively blond. Yet this differed from our experience of the settlements around Zamboanga, where women would come up to her and stroke her hair, cooing and nodding and looking up at her as if she were a goddess. To give you an idea, someone in Lantaka Hotel started a rumour that she used to be Rod Stewart's girlfriend and everyone took it seriously, pestering her for autographs. But that was Zamboanga and this was Bongao. A different world that we'd stumbled into, with only our young naiveté as a shield.

We did have one friendly encounter. On one of the beaches, we came upon an old man, nearly naked, sitting alone and mending a fishing net. We waved at him and he waved back, inviting us to join him. He was happy to talk to us, in surprisingly good English. Without a single tooth in his mouth, his pronunciation was mumbled, but we were patient.

He told us a story from his youth, about brutality and revenge.

Towards the end of the war, the American troops advanced throughout the archipelago, forcing the Japanese army into retreat. On Tawi-Tawi, the soldiers had dispersed and fled into the mangrove swamps, away from the villagers they had treated with contempt and cruelty.

Once the American troops had reached Bongao, they knew that they wouldn't need to fire a single shot. Instead, they gave guns to the villagers and let them loose. Each day, these would enter the swamps with guns and knives and proudly come back with Japanese heads held high on the knives' tips, until they had found and decapitated the last of the soldiers. The old man claimed two heads as his trophies and said that the villagers had used magic to locate the enemy, something about being aided by the ancestors, but I was sure this was only to spice up the story for our benefit. They would've known every bit of the swamp, living next to it, and would hardly have needed occult means to find their way in there.

Youth has neither patience nor time to dwell on things past. Instead, it focuses on the now, which in our case meant that we were ravenous after our adventure. The hotel had a combined restaurant and bar, the receptionist now apparently both bartender and waiter. As he disappeared into the kitchen for several minutes after taking each order, I suspected that he was also the resident chef.

After our questionable dinner, we were chilling out with ice-cold bottles of San Miguel when Susie nudged me discretely.

"Those two that just came in, are they men or women?"

I checked them out, likewise discretely. "Yes, definitely ladyboys."

As the late afternoon turned to evening, more of them arrived until they were in clear majority and we found out what everyone was waiting for. The receptionist rolled in a table with a TV and VCR player, and we were treated to a pirated copy of *Moscow on the Hudson*. The camp crowd loved it, their cheering and booing and laughing delivered with perfect timing throughout the film, as if they'd anticipated each scene. Which they had, as we found out the film was shown nightly.

Our mood took a dive for a while, as a nondescript man sat down at our table uninvited. "What are you doing here?"

"We were having a beer and watching the film. Until you interrupted us."

Undeterred, the man elaborated on his query: "What are you doing here? How did you arrive here? Where are you from?"

Everywhere we'd been, particularly in Zamboanga, people would come to us and start chatting, asking us where we were from. We were getting used to that as westerners but they'd all been polite.

Not this guy.

"It's none of your business. As far as you're concerned, we could be from Mars. Now bugger off."

The man stared at me as he took out a laminated card and slid it towards me with one finger. "I want to see your passports."

The card identified him as a member of NACTAG – something about anti-terrorism – an organisation instituted by Marcos. Silly acronym, yet menacing enough. Susie and I exchanged glances, incredulity in her eyes.

"We've come from Zamboanga to check out the beaches," I said while Susie took out our passports from her bag and handed them over.

"We're Swedish, you know," she said, as if our nationality was enough to ward off any evil.

The man ignored her while he thumbed through the documents. "When are you leaving?"

"Tomorrow morning."

"Good. Don't leave the hotel tonight, it is not safe. These

people..." he made a vague gesture, "are simple. They do not like strangers. And my life would get complicated if you disappeared."

He handed the passports back to Susie and left without another word.

Well, at least we'd found out after the fact that our tour of Bongao and surroundings had potentially been unsafe. Yet we'd survived without any incident. But as I've said, we were young and naive. Sometimes ignorance is bliss.

Still unsettled by the conversation and jittery from the adrenaline rush, we were accosted again, but this time the guy was our age. Unlike the other men, ladyboys excluded, he was elegantly dressed in smart slacks and a short-sleeved silk shirt, with a heavy Rolex on his slender wrist. And he was smiling broadly, his white teeth in stark contrast to his dark face.

"May I sit down?" he asked. "I'm Freddie, Prince of Brunei. And what are your names?"

I'm calling him Freddie to preserve his anonymity, just in case he really was who he claimed to be. The chances of it being true were infinitesimally small, but you can never know for sure in this part of the world.

I invited Freddie to sit, amused by his introduction and ignored Susie rolling her eyes. He finished his beer and ordered another round, and told us all about himself. He was living in Manila, studying engineering, and had come down to spend the holidays with his family. And yes, by the way, he was linked to the Sultan of Brunei through the old Sulu Sultanate family of which he was a proud descendant. We listened politely while we let him pay for the beer rounds, waiting for the sales pitch for surely this was a scam. Soon, he would try to get us interested in investing in a pearl oyster farm, or maybe buying an island, just a hectare or two, with a freshwater well and a perfect beach.

Nope. Instead, he tore out an empty page from Susie's diary, borrowed her pen, and wrote an introduction to the Sultan of Brunei.

Dear cousin and warmest greetings to you, it began, *please accept my friends,* (our names inserted), *as your friends, and show them your full hospitality* etc. Well, that was a surprise, and I still have that piece of paper somewhere, just in case I wanted to surprise the good Sultan with an unannounced visit.

The conversation turned to our earlier chat with the spook. Freddie confirmed that it was indeed perilous for two Europeans, one of them a beautiful woman (said with a dazzling smile at Susie), to go anywhere outside Bongao, particularly at night. Bad things might happen to foreigners. But he would gladly show us the best beaches the next day, with armed escort, if we wanted to stay another night. We just smiled, not believing a word of what he'd said.

Suddenly, he looked at his watch and exclaimed that he must leave us immediately, to his regret. Soon the dogs would be let loose in the grounds of his family compound. And once they were out, no one was safe. But he would see us in the morning, surely. After elaborate phrases, where a simple *good night* would have sufficed, and professing that we were now indeed friends for life, with his right hand over his heart in Muslim fashion, he left.

Realising that we were the only remaining guests in the restaurant, we went upstairs. Susie started another argument, about me taking her to a place where she risked her life, just because I insisted on visiting unsavoury locations. Or worse, getting raped by nasty people while I did nothing to stop it. I was on the verge of saying that in Bongao, her craving for undivided attention by males had been fulfilled, but thought better of it.

Not in the mood for another pointless sex session, I left the room. Contemplating my decision to see Bongao, and our relationship, which was disappearing below the horizon faster than the tropical sun, I went out to the balcony for the last cigarette of the day. I leaned on the railing and looked at the street below, ending to my left in the sea, its surface black and oily, the light of the full moon only enhancing its forbidding appearance.

There were fewer people in the street than in the daytime, and all of them appeared intent on getting home. Or at least somewhere else, off the street. A couple passed below me, the man striding resolutely up the street, the woman following behind, covered in white from head to toe and shuffling along, trying to keep up. Even the stray dogs were looking for a shelter for the night, mostly ignoring each other as they briefly met, not even attempting a single butt sniff. The usual village cacophony was still present but subdued.

I snore occasionally. Mostly when I have a cold, or after a particularly heavy meal combined with alcohol. I hate it – sometimes I even wake myself up – and I can't stand listening to someone else's noise. I'm hypersensitive, always have been, and can detect a quiet snorer two rooms away from me.

This one, though, was a candidate for the *Guinness Book of Records*.

My first impulse on waking up was to walk out of the room, figure out behind which of the doors the snorer was hiding, and thump on it until the racket stopped. Then I realised two things. The village was still, without any of the usual nocturnal sounds. And the snoring was not coming through our door, thus not from across the landing.

I felt Susie grab my hand. "What is that?" she asked sleepily.

"It sounds like some bastard is sleeping on the balcony, outside our window. I'll go and kick his–"

I stopped as I heard the snoring increase in volume, slowly but steadily. It was coming from the street, moving from the sea in our direction. And it wasn't the sound of snoring. How to describe it? It was a sound I'd never heard before nor since, in two distinct parts: the inhalation, which resembled human snoring – if a human had the lung capacity and vocal capabilities of a bull; the exhalation somewhere between a growl and a roar of a lion. A primitive, savage and utterly alien sound.

"It must be an animal," I corrected myself as I sat up and turned towards the window. But looking out, all I could see were roofs bathed in moonlight, the rest of the buildings and the street hidden from view by the balcony. "I'll go and check it out."

"Are you sure it's safe?"

My sensible girlfriend. Of course it wasn't safe. If this was a hitherto unknown species of the cat family – the first thing I thought of – it sounded big. There was no entrance door downstairs; the only object between us in the room and the street below was a thin plywood door. And if it were indeed a big cat, it wouldn't even have to run up the stairs. It could easily jump up on the low balcony and go through the plastic louvres. I was petrified.

So we remained in bed, holding hands, listening as the sound approached the hotel. Did it pause outside the entrance? We waited for several heartbeats, almost afraid to breathe.

Susie squeezed my hand and whispered, "I think it's moving again."

She was right. The sound decreased slowly towards the northern end of Bongao. Until everything was quiet again. Too quiet for any village in South-East Asia; this was absolute silence. Then the silence was broken.

A heartrending, drawn-out scream pierced the night, coming from the top of the street and rolling down it. It bounced off the shacks, moving towards the sea as if it'd had a life of its own, begging for mercy. Have you ever been unfortunate enough to hear the pitiful whine of a pig about to be slaughtered, aware of its impending fate? Turning into wailing, then panicked shrieks, then the horrible gurgling as its throat is cut. Now imagine that doubled, simultaneously emanating from a distressed pig and a human. Do you blame us for going rigid with fear? Whatever was going on, it was bad. Seriously bad. All I could think of was a flimsy door between us and whatever was roaming out there, with only a diving knife for protection. Yes, it did cross my mind that we might have to fight for our lives.

We stayed like that, lying like dummies and holding hands, until dogs began barking again and we heard a motorcycle engine revving. A few insomniac cockerels ventured forth the odd crows. I imagined I heard the tinkling of wind chimes carried on the breeze, but by then I was tired enough not to care if the Vienna Philharmonic Orchestra had been outside our door, going through their repertoire of Strauss waltzes. Relieved, assuming that whatever beast this was, it had gone by now, all I wanted was to embrace Morpheus.

Not so Susie. "I fucking hate this place, and I hate you for bringing me here. This is not what you promised back in Sweden. Next time, we go somewhere civilised, like Ibiza, where I can..."

I turned my back to her and shut out her voice.

Bongao in early morning sunshine was a different world. As we came down to check out, still barely on speaking terms, we could see and hear the usual bustle in the street.

"Last night," I began as I counted out the dollars, "what was that–"

"Nothing," the receptionist interrupted me. "There was nothing. Was your food good yesterday?"

"Yes, it was. I meant during the night, the sounds–"

"No. No sounds. I heard nothing." He was perfectly still, fixing me with his stare, yet his right index finger traced patterns on the desk. A lot of curves, some straight lines, and what looked like dots.

I tried again. "So we were the only ones to hear the scream?"

"What scream? Your jeepney is here now, I will take your bag."

There was no point in continuing the dialogue so we walked out and got on the jeepney, the receptionist passing us the bag. As the vehicle pulled away, I turned towards the entrance for one last look and noticed something that had not been there on our arrival. Above it, on the lintel and in bright red, someone had painted an elaborate sign, vaguely Arabic. Too elaborate for me to remember, and I didn't have time to take out the camera, but it did have a lot of curves, some straight lines, and a few dots.

WE FLEW BACK to Zamboanga without a hitch, then Manila, and finally Sweden. Not once did we mention the night in Bongao. Susie had wiped out that memory and preferred to dwell on how I had disappointed her. I was still trying to figure out what we'd heard, sure that it would have had a rational explanation.

I STILL SEE Susie occasionally when I visit Sweden. Stockholm isn't a big city, and we've remained true to some of the favourite nightlife spots of our youth. She's never visited Southeast Asia again, as far as I know, happy with the Med and its trusted charms. Nowadays she stays in posh hotels, as she can easily afford them. Spends her days with the rich and famous, her nights with young studs that find her irresistible.

Me? I'm living here, in Southeast Asia, where I've always wanted to be. Still looking for that perfect beach while telling myself that one day I'll return to Bongao to solve the mystery.

Diari Sepi Seorang Mudi

Shafiqah Alliah Razma

English translation in the following chapter

Malam menjengah kembali tatkala Sang Mentari memberikan salam perpisahan. Aku, pena dan kertas usangku masih mencari sinar dalam kegelapan. Aku masih menjadi hamba buah fikiran malamku dan ia memintaku untuk mengukirkannya pada jutaan bintang di langit. Bisiknya kepadaku, bintang-bintang itu sinarnyakan terang, nanti pasti ada yang mendengar. Jauh terbenam di sudut hati — perasaan yang mengulit ini meronta-ronta dengan jari-jemari halusnya, terus menggamit jiwa ini untuk bermadah tatkala dunia, si dia dan juga mereka, sedang enak dan lena dibuai mimpi. Tulisan berangkai dan dakwat hitam ini menjadi taruhanku. Niat di hati ingin menjadikan lembaran ini sebagai medan perjuangan. Sudikah mereka mendengar suara anak muda ini, yang jalannya masih berliku, fikirannya masih bercelaru, dan kata-katanya masih terbelenggu. Bukan mahu terburu-buru, tetapi mahu mengenal erti dewasa dan memburu impian yang satu—ingin melihat ukiran senyuman setiap mereka apabila beradu, kerana keadilan itu.

Kau memperlakukan anakku. Kau hina kakakku. Kau hancurkan

masa silam ibuku. Ayahku, abangku dan saudaraku — kau biarkan mereka mengemis di tepi jalan sehingga mereka diam membisu. Apabila dia datang menangis teresak-esak meminta bantuan dan pembelaanmu, kau lontarkan hujah-hujah bongkakmu—"Mengapa kau di situ seorang diri?", "Tidakkah kau punya harga diri, mengapa berpakaian begitu?", "Bukankah aku sudah pesan padamu!", "Eh, dia itu orangnya baik. Masakan dia lakukan begitu. Pasti engkau yang menduga kalbunya." Tidak cukup dengan itu, kau lontarkan pula kata-kata keji dan kotormu kepadanya. Contengan dan noda-noda hitammu itu akan sentiasa menghantui malamnya. Apa malammu sungguh tenang sehingga kau lena diulit sengsara kami. Tubuhku dan lenggokku menjadi sehalus-halus perhatian kerakusan nafsumu, santapan pandangan dan teguran nakalmu. Kelembutan suaraku dan perhambaanku padamu diinginkanmu selalu. Aku sudah letih memeluk takdir yang kau nodai ini. Kadang-kadang aku merasakan diri ini seperti nota-nota muzik yang iramanya sudah lama tidak bernada dan harmoni — lesu lagi longlai dendangannya. Satu demi satu harapanku dikecewakan, hampa dan tiada nyawanya. Iktikadku tergugat dalam tangan-tangan kejam engkau dan mereka. Tenggelam dalam alunan bicara-bicaramu yang dikatakan 'suci'. Ada waktu aku rindukan tiupan bayu asing kerana tanah ini — isinya — menafikan terlalu banyak bahagian dan cebisan diriku. Corengan-corengan arang pada kanvas putihku — melemaskan dan mengasingkan — yang padanya aku sebenarnya dambakan panggilan pemandangan sejernih lautan biru yang menenangkan.

Sudah terlalu lama aku memekakkan telinga dan membutakan mata, kerana didendangkan dengan kata-kata bahawa aku ini masih muda. Perasaan dan pendapatku hina di matamu. Jadi, aku sering kali dipaksa hidup berlandaskan kitab yang dikarang olehmu, bukan Tuhanku dan Nabiku. Bertopengkan gelaran khalifah itu, kau dan taulanmu sering kali ingin menulis tentang aku (dan kami), ceritaku — dengan naratif berdarahmu sendiri. Kau ingin dunia melihat aku melalui lensa dan pemikiranmu yang jumud. Kau kunci mulutku dan menafikan tempatku di medan bicara itu. Kau lukiskan tanda-tanda biru dan ungu pada tubuhku. Jeritan deritaku terus kau idamkan. Ingin aku membisu dan terus sunyi dari dunia yang ingin sekali mendengarku. Dunia yang sebenarnya memerlukan aku, sama seperti mereka perlukan engkau. Apakah kau dapat bermegah-megah akan kewujudanmu dan kepentinganmu melalui tangan dan kaki itu? Itukah mahkotamu yang akan kau persembahkan padaNya nanti? Sudah-sudahlah — kau dan tarian riakmu — walhal asalmu hanya setitis air. Aku bukan abdi keegoanmu sementara kau menabur lagi janji kepada saudaraku. Tatkala kejahilan membaluti tubuh dan fikiranmu dan kau terus mendabik dada dan mendongak ke muka langit, aku dan saudara-saudaraku menyimpul ikatan untuk menongkah takdir.

Aku melihat kakak-kakakku dari jendela kecil ini. Aku terintai-intai seperti anak kecil — aku lihat semangat juang dilaungkan, poster dan kain rentang dinaikkan, tangan dihulurkan lalu dipegang erat dan mereka mengatur langkah berani seiring lagu dan irama. Perut bumi dan tanah luhur ini seakannya bergetar dengan setiap aturannya. Kau — aku pasti gerun walaupun masih tersenyum sinis dan masih lagi mengukir cita-cita untuk memuaskan halobamu yang tiada hujungnya. Aku belajar perkataan baharu dan catatkan kata nama itu dalam kamus batinku —solidariti.

Aku kagum, tetapi buat aku termenung seketika — bisakah aku jadi seperti kakakku itu? Layakkah aku menyandang gelaran srikandi? Apa yang aku ada? Hanya suara kecil dan beberapa untai kata-kata. Puisi dan cerpenku juga masih haru. Jikalau aku komposer lagu, muzik dan iramaku pastinya terisi dengan sesalan dan ratapan, yang mekar seperti bunga-bunga di padang hijau yang luas itu. Aku akan dikenali dunia sebagai penyanyi sesalan. Tetapi demi semangat itu, aku cuba mencari sedikit kekuatan dan segenggam semangat. Aku ingin bertatih membantu aku, kami dan kita. Aku ingin menjaga saudaraku dengan kudrat zahir dan batin ini. Walaupun fana, aku ingin terus mencuba. Aku ingin berpisah dengan erti jemu. Tanganku ini bukan hanya bisa menghayun buaian itu, tetapi kurniaanNya ini akan aku pertaruhkan untuk menggoncang duniamu yang gelap.

Apatah lagi aku selalu diajar tentang kasih dan cinta oleh mama dan ustadhah. Aku ingin menjadi suara buat mereka — saudaraku, anak-anak muda dan kecil itu. Aku dambakan darussalam buat kita. Ini cara aku mencurahkan bakti dan melukiskan potret kasih. Lembaran-lembaran yang penuh dengan seru-seruku menjadi medan pertempuran pena dan kata.

Aku ingin memimpin tangan mereka. Aku ingin selami jiwa luhur mereka, dan ingin mendaki bersama gunung harapan. Jerih perih dan penat lelah — aku menadah cerita-cerita derita dalam urat biruku untuk aku curahkan kemudian hari dalam puisi dan pada muka buku. Tiada siapa perlu diusir dan dihukum bila berbicara tentang kebenaran. Berpautkan empati, aku gapai tangan mereka menangkis seribu tomahan. Aku ada untuk membela nasibmu. Ingin luka mereka sembuh dan mereka bebas dari penjara kekesalan. Parut dan noda dosa-dosa semalam tidak mungkin hilang tetapi aku tidak mahu melihat mereka berkalungkan rantai belenggu dan berselimutkan tangisan sunyi.

Sekarang, tiada lagi istilah meminta atau menagih darimu. Aku dan kakak-kakakku, kami sendiri akan mencipta riwayat kami. Biar jarak antara impian dan kenyataan bukan sedetik jauhnya, biar seribu tahun lamanya kami terpaksa dahaga dan meredah gurun gersang ini. Bertemankan nafas kekuatan baru, akan kami ubah sejarah. Ideologi perjuangan masih belum tandus. Mendaki bersama. Berpaut, satu tangan dengan satu tangan yang lain — bergenggaman erat, isi dan kuku berpisah tiada.

Ibu-ibu kami, mereka berkata padaku "Tidak perlulah kau bersusah-payah. Ini bukan perjuanganmu. Masa depanmu lebih berharga." Mereka sudah lama bermandikan hampa hingga merasakan tiada makna mencoret kisah-kisah hitam itu. Ada juga yang tidak dapat diungkap dengan bahasa dan tidak terucap zahirnya kerana terlalu perit. Hatinya bengkak menahan pedih. Usah bimbang ibu. Kami bijak menjaga diri. Biarpun disondol, kami tangkas bangkit. Tanah ini juga masa depan kami. Ke mana lagi kami ingin lari. Bukankah kau juga berkata hujan batu di negeri sendiri itu lebih baik. Malah kami dambakan hujan emas di bumi ini. Akan kami pikul amanah dan tanggungjawab ini — melakar keharmonian dan menempa keadilan di tanah sendiri. Wahai ibu, janganlah kau berputus asa atau berduka lara. Bersuaralah dan dendangkan ceritamu pada dunia. Kami di sini menyokong dan mendoakan setiap langkahmu.

Sepurnama kemudian, duniamu gamat melihat aku menutup perhiasanku, sedangkan bukan tujuan aku di sini untuk merealisasikan fantasimu. Aku memilih jalan ini kerana cintaku pada Yang Satu, tiada lagi yang lain. Walaupun sukar, dengan semangat yang menggarang, aku mencengkam erat pada ketulusan ini. Aku bukan hidup untuk memenuhi hawa tamak dan kejimu yang tidak pernah kenyang, Malah lilitan selendang ini juga bukan alasanmu untuk mengeji kakak dan adikku. Jangan kau mengotori kami dengan tempias mimpi-mimpi jijikmu. Kata-kata kami ini bukan untuk kau ratah sebagai seteru, tubuh-tubuh ini bukan sewenang-wenangnya untuk engkau jadikan tempat persinggahanmu dan jiwa-jiwa kami bukan untuk engkau tawani lalu engkau sesakkan. Halwa telinga kami bukan untuk menyimpan janji atau helah manismu yang tumbuh melata. Amanah saudara-suadara aku dan kami memanggil, dan roh-roh ini untuk mereka.

Inspirasi? Dia masih di situ. Berhati murni; membantu mereka mencari sesuap nasi. Meninggalkan kamar dinginnya, dia masih setia meredah terik mentari dan bermandi manik-manik keringat, memberi dan terus memberi tanpa jemu. Langsung tidak lokek dan kekok berkongsi rezekinya. Sering juga merakamkan harapan buat kami dan masih mengirim semangat dan menitipkan bicara hikmatnya. Aku pernah dengar dia berkata-kata bahawa dia ingin anak-anak muda berani melakar sejarah sendiri dan menangkis lagi menepis segala rintangan dan cemuhan. Tinggi sungguh cita-citanya. Katanya lagi, aku dan mereka ialah pemimpin dan harapan itu sendiri — yang menghiasi cerita-cerita hebat dan inspirasi hari esok. Tidak seperti kau dan mereka yang mengurung aku dan kami, dia meminta aku melebarkan sayapku. Tiada sempadan bagi cerita dan kejayaan kami; asalkan kami terus gigih membanting tulang muda ini. Pesannya, tubuh dan semangat ini jangan dibiar lesu. Usia muda jangan disia bahangnya.

Aku kagum akan dirinya. Ada waktu terasa juga hairan, lahiriahnya ikhlas. Mahu menggelarnya seorang teman, mungkin juga sahabat — menjadi tempat bimbingan dan berkongsi pandangan. Tetapi aku lupa. Mungkin dia juga lupa. Dunia penuh pancaroba kami yang asing dan sepi darinya — sejauh manakah dia mengerti? Harapan menggunung tinggi tetapi hati kecilku berkata-kata, "Apakah tulus harapan dan janjimu itu? Hiraukah engkau? Sekutu atau seteru? Adakah batinmu seindah zahirmu—benar kau menyayangi kami?" Ayah ada berpesan, realiti itu tidak seharum fantasi. Atau aku akan terus membiarkan diri terbuai dengan semangatmu itu, yang mungkin hanya manis di bibirmu dan indah halwa telingaku. Mungkin aku khilaf. Pengalaman mendidik aku menjadi sangsi. Mungkin kau memang berbeza daripada mereka — 'dalam setandan pisang takkan semuanya busuk'. Mungkin satu hari nanti aku bisa beritahu itu pada dunia dan mensyairkan budi-budimu. Biarlah aku pergi dahulu menabur bakti. Kebaikanmu dan nukilanmu, kami jadikan sakti. Tempiasnya sudah cukup mendamaikan.

AKU MANUSIA HINA DAN KERDIL. Kadangkala tidak sunyi daripada meratah emosi sendiri. Rasa lemah dan ingin berputus asa sering kali menjengah ke benak kalbu. Sama seperti aku, emosi-emosi itu menjadi tetamu yang tidak kenal juga erti jemu. Kering dan kontang jiwa ini apabila keringat dan ilham diperah sehabis-habisnya. Longlai, aku masih mencari sisa-sisa janji dan perjuangan yang masih belum terlihat garisan penamatnya. Poskad dan lembaran tinta di persisir medan yang masih belum terjawab luahannya serta pesanan dan rayuan di corong radio tuaku.

Tetapi demi sebuah janji dan seungkap cinta buat mereka, aku gagahkan diri mencari cebisan dan carik-carik kekuatan — dalam setiap bait-bait cinta dariNya, dan dari setiap butir kata-kata pedoman para saudara. Suara itu milik aku dan kami. Tulang, bicara dan darah mudaku ini adalah seni perjuangan dan harapan. Jiwa ini bukan milik aku seorang. Jiwa ini milik setiap daripada kami yang engkau tindas. Fitrah kemanusiaanmu tidak berperi. Kau palitkan warna-warna perbezaan, kebencian, keretakan dan diskriminasi. Mana mungkin aku terus menurut godaan lelahku dan berdiam diri. Aku tidak akan pernah tertunduk bungkam. Jikalau hilang suara dan kata-kata, hatiku ini pula akan terus hidup untuk meronta.

Ya, aku masih muda. Barangkali apa yang mereka gelar setahun jagung. Dimomokkan dengan kisah yang kusam — kesangsian dan keraguan pada kebolehanku dan keteguhan perisaiku. Rambutku kusut, masih disisir rapi oleh ibu. Tarian citaku pula masih bengkang. Tetapi tali kasutku — tali kasutku hitam dimamah usia dan debu-debu cabaran. Aku seakan-akan sudah tua sebelum masanya. Langkah dan jejak ini mematangkan aku.

Hargaku bukan pada fizikalku tetapi pada jiwa yang membara ingin bangkit bersama anak muda, ingin mengibarkan panji kemenangan dan keadilan sejati. Hargaku pada cintaku pada tanah airku yang semakin dimamah kerakusan duniawi, di mana harta, nafsu dan haloba bertaktha di sanubari. Semangat itu ada mengalir — jangan kau persoalkan mengapa. Kau lebih tahu jawapan teka-tekimu itu. Mana mungkin aku berdiam seribu bahasa apabila melihat anak kecil dan ibunya itu kau biarkan merempat di bahu jalan yang hanya sebatu jauhnya dari bangunan megahanmu. Mana mungkin aku membisu tatkala adikku ditarik dan dibentak hanya kerana ingin mengingati mereka yang telah berjuang demi sebuah erti kehidupan bernama keamanan. Mana mungkin, apabila aku melihat sang bapa tersedu-sedu dibasahi hujan—memikirkan di mana tempat lena si keluarga tercinta esok harinya, sementara kau berpayungkan permata dan bertilam empukkan tembaga.

Perlukah lagi aku menyenaraikan semua aib-aibmu? Tuhanku

tidak mengajar aku begitu. Bukan niat di hati mahukan simpati atau mempersoalkan rezeki: cuma mahu membela nasib sendiri. Aku juga terkenangkan anak-anak didikku. Jiwa guruku kuat ingin melindungi mereka. Kalbu ingin melihat mereka bertatih di bumi yang memeluk kembali kehadiran mereka — bumi bertuah yang menyambut mereka dengan seikhlas salam selamat datang. Biar mereka tenang dan bahagia di sini. Bila warna bukan lagi menjadi pintalan perbalahan. Beribu dan berjuta kata madah dan coretan puitis, mungkin terus mengalir tanpa henti, daripada aku dan engkau, tetapi kebenaran hanya satu — keadilan buat kami.

Aku teringat pesanmu lagi—berlegar selalu di ruangan pancainderaku, bak kata-kata pujangga. Kau kata aku perlu berani dan suaraku didambai. Aku sebenarnya tidak pernah gentar, wahai inspirasi. Mereka yang menenggelamkan aku dengan bingitnya hiruk-pikuk tikam lidah mereka, seolah seperti aku bisu. Tidakkah engkau melihat apa mereka buat pada saudaraku — sesaat teman dan juga handalanku memekikkan syair and isi hati mereka. mereka diherdik lagi dicaci dengan tutur kesat dan bicara durjana. Tetapi janganlah bimbang. Itu tidak mematahkan semangat kami. Lihatlah dengan ainmu sendiri — saban hari, kami masih di jalanan menuntut kebenaran dan pembelaan, melontar suara tegas bersama perang poster dan seni grafik kami dan kami berpuisi tentang perlakuan hina mereka. Mata penaku juga masih tajam dan dakwatku juga masih mengalir laju — selaut tinta. Ada selautan kisah ingin aku kongsi dengan dunia. Masih banyak sajak derita ingin aku deklamasikan dan masih beribu kekecewaan belum dinyanyikan.

Kami manusia — punya perasaan — marah, sedih, kecewa; kami hidup dalam pengharapan. Deria rasa kami masih tajam—maung, kelat, hambar, dan lebih pahit daripada manisnya. Sering kali disalah erti, malah dituduh penderhaka kerana menegakkan keadilan dan hak sendiri. Di mana lagi kami perlu menagih nasib dan menanam jejak diri, kalau bukan di bumi sendiri. Bagaikan pendatang di bumi yang mengasingkan.

Mengapa? Tiada lagikah keikhlasan dan kebaikan? Ibarat

meminta segunung intan yang sebenarnya hanya membutakan mata dan hati. Aku tiada harta dan tiada rupa, Hanya suara ini bekalan kudrat perjuanganku. Semangat untuk meneruskan hidup ada bersama janji dan pegangan tangan-tangan mulia itu. Cuma inginkan nasib terbela dan ingin mencari sekelumit makna kehidupan, kenangan dan bekalan untuk dibawa ke hari depan. Nanti Sang Dia bertanya, bukan cerita-cerita duka ini yang ingin aku karangkan. Aku hanya ingin mengkhabarkan yang indah pada langit. Sebuah pengharapan. Sebuah penyatuan. Sebuah azimat cinta.

Bendera ini akan kami kibarkan. Semangat dan seru keramat ini akan kami laungkan.

Kami ingin merdeka. Kami ingin bebas. Ini kisah kami. Oh dunia, dengarkanlah suara kami.

Secret Diary of an Outsider

(Diari Sepi Seorang Mudi)

Shafiqah Alliah Razman

Translated from the Malay by Ivy Ngeow

The night came again when the Sun said goodbye. Me, my old pen and paper are still looking for light in the darkness.

I was a slave to the fruit of my night's mind, which had asked me to carve on the millions of stars in the sky. It whispered to me, *the stars are shining brightly*, and later, someone must have heard. Deep in the corner of my heart, a thin feeling throbbed with a delicate touch of fingers, enticing this soul to chant about when the world was sweet and lulled into dreams.

Handwriting in black ink is my best bet. My heart's intention is to make a sheet of paper a battleground. Will they listen to the voice of a young woman, whose path is still winding, mind confused, and words shackled? She is in no hurry to know adulthood or to chase dreams. She just wants to see the shape of the people's smiles, because that's when they have justice.

You, with your power, ill-treated my children. You insulted my sister. You ruined my mother's past. My father, my brother and my sister — you let them beg by the side of the road until they are silent. When a woman comes sobbing for your help and support, you said in arrogance:

"Why are you all alone?"

"Don't you have self-esteem, why dress like that?"

"Haven't I told you so?"

"Hey, he's a good guy. He would have never done that. It must have been you who tempted him."

But more than that, you also threw your vile and dirty words at her and our people. Your scratches and black spots will always haunt the night. What a peaceful night you have while languishing in our misery. My body and my curves become as subtle as the attention of your lustful greed, the food of your gaze and your insolent rebuke.

The softness of my voice and my servitude to you in authority is what you've always wanted. I'm tired of embracing this destiny you've tarnished. Sometimes I feel like musical notes whose rhythm has long been out of tune and harmonious — more sluggish with time. One by one, my hopes were dashed, empty and lifeless. My faith is challenged in the cruel hands of you and the others in power. I immersed myself in the tune of your so-called 'religious' speeches.

There were times when I missed the foreign wind because this land — and its contents — has denied me too much. The streaks of charcoal on my white canvas, suffocating and isolating, make me crave the call of a view as clear as the soothing blue ocean.

It has been too long since I deafened my ears and blinded my eyes; they sang those dumb words when I was still young. My feelings and opinion have always been despised in your eyes. I am often forced to live based on the book written by you and your peers, not my Lord and my Prophet.

Under the guise of the title of caliph, you and your peers often want to write about me (and us), my story — in your own blood-stained narrative. You want the world to see me through the lens and your stagnant thoughts. You shut my mouth and denied me my place to speak. You painted blue and purple marks on my body. My screams of pain keep you going, because you want me to shut up and remain silent from the world that wants to hear me. The world needs me, just as they need you. Can you boast of your existence and importance through those hands and feet? Is that your crown that you will present to Him later? Enough — you and your ripple dance — even though you originate from just a drop of water.

I AM NOT a servant of your selfishness while you sow more promises to my brother. As ignorance covers your body and mind and you continue to rage your chest and look up to the sky, my brothers and I forge a bond to defy destiny.

I saw my sisters from this small window. I peeked like a child — I saw the fighting spirit being chanted, posters and banners raised, hands outstretched and held tightly, and they set bold steps to the song and rhythm. The belly of the earth and this noble land seemed to vibrate with every rule. You must be horrified even when you are smiling cynically and carving out ambitions to satisfy your endless avarice. I learned a new word and wrote the noun in my inner dictionary — solidarity.

I was amazed, but it made me think for a moment — can I be like my sister? Do I deserve the title of heroine too? But what do I have? Only a small voice and a few strings of words. My poems and short stories are heartbreakingly chaotic. If I were a composer of songs, my music and rhythms would surely be filled with remorse and lamentation, which bloom like flowers in that vast green field. I will be known to the world as a singer of remorse.

Hopeful, I try to find a little strength and a fistful of spirit. I practise helping myself and my people, to take care of my brothers and sisters with my outward yet inward nature. Although mortal, I want to keep trying, to part with a sense of boredom. Not only does my hand swing the cradle, but I will risk this gift to shake your dark world. What's more, I was always taught about love and affection by Mama and the ustadhah. I want to be a voice for them — my brothers and sisters, the young and the little ones. I long for darus-salam for us. This is how I dedicate myself and paint a portrait of love.

The sheets are full of my cries, and they become the battlefield of pen and word. I want to hold the people's hands. I want to dive into their noble souls, and to climb the mountain of hope. Tired and exhausted — I pick up stories of suffering in my blue veins for me to pour out later in poetry and books. No one needs to be expelled and punished when speaking the truth.

In empathy, I reach for the people's hands to repel a thousand afflictions. I'm here to defend their destiny. I want their wounds healed and for them to be free from the prison of regret. The scars and stains of yesterday's sins may not be gone but I don't want to see them clad in chains of shackles and shrouded in lonely tears.

Now, I beg no more of you. My sisters and I will create our own history. Let the distance between dream and reality not be a second away. We have had to thirst and roam this arid desert for a thousand years. With the breath of new strength, we will change history. Struggle will not be without success.

We climb together. Clinging, a hand holding another's, gripping tightly, flesh and nails.

Our mothers had said: "Don't bother. This is not your struggle.

Your future is more valuable than ours." But they have been vacant for so long that they feel there is no point writing down dark stories, those too agonizing to be expressed with language and are not spoken openly.

My mother's heart was swollen with pain. "Don't worry, Mom. We will sensibly take care of ourselves. Despite being shoved, we did swiftly pick ourselves up. This land is also our future. Where else would we want to run to? Didn't you also say hail in your own country is better than abroad?"

We crave golden rain on this land. We will bear this trust and responsibility, for harmony and justice in our own land. "O mother, do not despair or grieve. Speak up and tell your story to the world. We are here to support and pray for your every step."

A moon later, your world was in chaos when you saw me covering up my adorned body, but it had never been my intention to be your fantasy.

I chose this path because of my love for my God. Although I found it difficult, I clung to my fierce and honest passion. I do not live to satisfy the greed and abomination of the authorities who in turn are never satisfied. This hijab is not a reason to despise my sisters. Don't defile us with your disgusting dreams. Our words are not for you the enemy to enjoy. Our bodies are not arbitrary for you to make your stopover and our souls are not for you to keep before you suffocate us with your creepy sweet tricks. Your sweet but false promises which burgeon are not the music to our ears, and we shall not keep them. The trust of our brothers and sisters is calling.

Inspiration? He's there. The pure heart helps find a mouthful of rice.

Leaving his cozy room, my beloved soaked up the scorching sun. Bathed in beads of sweat, he continues to give tirelessly. Neither mean nor cagey, he'd never hesitated sharing his sustenance and fortune. He frequently recorded his hopes for us. He encouraged and entrusted us with wisdom. I once heard him say that he wanted young people to dare to make their own history and fend off all obstacles and ridicule. High was his ideal. He added that we are our own leaders and hopes we'll form the great stories and inspirations for tomorrow.

Unlike you and those who imprisoned us, he asked me to spread my wings. "There are no boundaries to our stories and successes; as long as we continue to persistently slam this young bone." The message is, this body and spirit should not be let down. Youth should not be wasted. I admired him.

There were times when I felt astonished. Wanted to call him a friend, someone and somewhere I could share my views. But I forgot. Maybe he forgot too. Our world was full of temptation that was foreign to him. How well did he understand it?

My little heart said to me, "Are your hopes and promises sincere? Do you care? Friend or enemy? Is your heart as beautiful as you look?"

Dad said that reality is not as fragrant as fantasy.

Or will I continue to allow myself to be lulled by your passion, which may be just sweet on your lips and beautiful to my ears? Maybe I was wrong. Past experience had taught me doubt and to preserve my innocence. Maybe you're different from them — 'in a bunch of bananas, not everything is rotten'. Maybe one day I can tell that to the world and recite your virtues. Let me go first to sow devotion. Your kindness and sayings make magic, its sprinkle comforts me.

I am a lowly human. Sometimes I am not lonely from giving in to my irritating emotions. Feelings of weakness and a desire to give up often come to mind. Just like me, those emotions become guests who don't even know the meaning of boredom.

This soul is dry and empty when sweat and inspiration are squeezed to the fullest. Softly, I'm feebly looking for the remnants of promises and struggles that still haven't seen the finish line. Postcards and sheets of ink on the edge of the field that are still unanswered utterances as well as orders and appeals in the old radio funnel.

But for the sake of a promise and a glimmer of love for them, I dared to look for bits and pieces of strength — in every verse of His love, and in every detail of the words of the brethren's guidance. That voice belongs to me and us, the youth. These bones, speech and young blood are the art of struggle and hope. This soul does not belong to me alone. This soul belongs to each of us whom you in power oppress. Your inhumane nature does not matter. You paint the colors of difference, hatred, rift and discrimination. How could I continue to follow my weary temptations and remain silent? I will never bow in silence. If I lose my voice and words, my heart will continue to live to struggle. Yes, I'm young.

THIS IS PROBABLY what they call the first year of corn. It's haunted by a dull story — doubts about my abilities and the strength of my armor. My hair is tangled, yet neatly combed by my mother. I dance a wobbly dance of ambition, but my black shoelaces are chewed by age and the dust of challenge. I feel like I'm old before my time. These steps and trails have aged me.

My value lies not in my physical state but in my soul that wants to rise with young people and fly the banner of victory and true justice. My price is on my love for my homeland which is increasingly chewed by worldly greed, where wealth, lust and avarice reign in the heart. That spirit is flowing — don't ask why. You know the answer to your riddle.

How could I be silent in a thousand languages when I see a little boy and his mother that you let sit on the shoulder of the road that is only a short distance from your magnificent building? How could I be silent when my sister was pulled away and reprimanded just for wanting to remember those who have fought for a meaning of life called peace?

How could it be, when I saw the father sobbing in the rain — thinking about where his beloved family would sleep the next day, while you hold a jewel umbrella and sleep on a soft copper mattress? Do I need to list all your shames? My God did not teach me that. It is not the intention in the heart to want sympathy or to question sustenance: it is only to want to defend one's own destiny.

I ALSO REMEMBER MY STUDENTS. My strong teacherly soul wants to protect them. The heart longs to see them dance on the earth that embraces their presence again — the blessed earth that welcomes them with a sincere welcome. Let them be calm and happy here, when color is no longer a point of contention.

Thousands and millions of rhetoric and poetic snippets, may continue to flow unceasingly, from me and you, my darling, but there is only one truth — justice for us. I remembered your message again — always hovering in my senses, like the words of a poet. You said I needed to be brave and my voice was coveted. I've never really been scared, O inspiration.

Those who drowned me with the tumult of their tongues stabbed me, as if I were dumb. Don't you see what they did to my brothers and sisters? For a moment my friend and also my confidant shouted poetry from their hearts. They were rebuked and reviled with abusive and evil speech. Don't worry. That didn't break our spirits. Sec for yourself — every day, we are still on the streets demanding truth and defense, casting a firm voice with our poster wars and graphic art about their despicable treatment.

My pen eyes are still sharp and my ink is still flowing fast — a sea of ink, a sea of stories I want to share with the world. There are still many poems of suffering I want to recite and still thousands of disappointments which have not been sung.

We humans have feelings — angry, sad, disappointed; but we live in hope. Our senses are still sharp — chelated, bland and more bitter than sweet. We are often misunderstood, and even accused of being a traitor for upholding justice and our rights. Where else do we have to take our fortunes and plant our footprints, if not on our own earth? We seem to be immigrants on an isolated earth. Why? Is there no more sincerity and kindness? It's like asking for a mountain of diamonds which blinds the eyes and the heart.

I have no possessions or beauty. Only my voice expresses the nature of my struggle and the spirit to get on with life is with the promise and the holding of those noble hands. I just want to defend myself and find a little bit of meaning and some mementoes to carry into the future. My God will ask me later, but it is not these sad stories that I want to write. I long to chant words of perfection while looking skywards. For an expectation, a unification, a love, we will fly this flag. We will shout about our excitement. We want independence. We want to be free. This is our story.

O world, listen to our voices.

Top 5 winner in the 2021 short story category of the "Youth of Tomorrow Writing Competition" by Persatuan Kesedaran Komuniti Selangor (EMPOWER, Malaysia)

Before you go

The book you are holding in your hand is the result of our dreams to be authors. We hope you enjoyed our stories as much as we enjoyed writing them. They exist through dedication, passion and love. Reviews help persuade readers to give this book a shot. You are helping the community discover and support new writing. It will take *less than a minute* and can be *just a line* to say what you liked or didn't. Please leave us a review wherever you bought this book from. A big thank you. On behalf of all our authors, *Leopard Print.*

About the Authors

Rumaizah Abu Bakar set sail in accountancy, detoured to public relations, and floated towards anthropology. During her free time, she works on the manuscripts for her fourth and fifth books. She hopes to return to her dream job of saving the planet one day.

Patrick Burns' international business career included eighteen years in Hong Kong and Singapore. He has written extensively about Asia, including a travel memoir, *Far Away and Further Back*, from which his story is taken. Patrick is British, married with four children and lives in California.

Cheung Louie grew up in Hong Kong, where she studied journalism and worked in project management. Currently based in London and rediscovering creative writing, *Winter Solstice* is her first fictional short story written in 15 years. Some of her favourite things are spring flowers, autumn leaves, slow-cooked soup, and fish balls.

E.P. Chiew is the author of *The Heartsick Diaspora* and editor/compiler of *Cooked Up: Food Fiction From Around the World*. A two-time winner of the Bridport Short Story Prize, her stories have been anthologised in the UK, U.S. and Singapore, and variously shortlisted, long listed, or nominated for prizes, including the Manchester Short Story Prize, Fish, BBC Opening Lines, the Pushcart and Glimmer Train. A visual arts researcher, she has had a previous career as a U.S. corporate securities lawyer.

Mason Croft was born in Vancouver, Canada. He holds a degree in Theatre from the University of British Columbia. His writing has appeared in several journals, mostly American. He lives in Singapore.

MK Eidson (Mike) worked for 15 years at the US Department of Defense as a civilian employee. Now balding, he lives with his wife and their Jack Russell girl dog in Central Florida, where he owns and operates Eposic (https://eposic.com), his publishing imprint for games, puzzles, music, and fiction. His wife braided his hair back in the 90s and snipped the braid. She still has it.

Born in Dublin, **Marc de Faoite** is a freelance writer and editor. Having spent 15 years in Malaysia he now lives at the foot of the French Alps. His short stories, articles, and book reviews have been published both in print and online. *Tropical Madness*, a collection of his short stories, was longlisted for the 2014 Frank O'Connor International Short Story Prize.

Jenny Hor, a Chinese Malaysian writer, hails from a small town called Butterworth. She writes stories about human life and the everyday scene. Jenny is also a traveller and food enthusiast. You might find traces of local delicacies in her writings.

Nenad Jovancic was born in a country that no longer exists, Yugoslavia, and grew up in Sweden. After years of working and living around the globe pretending to be a management consultant and adult, he moved to Malaysia to pursue his passion for writing and love of South-East Asia. He is currently busy with two novels and occasionally crafts the odd poem or short story.

Lynett Khoh holds a BFA in creative writing from the University of Nottingham Malaysia and is currently an editor at Linguo Go. When she's not busy wrestling with grammar or punctuation mistakes, she experiments with weaving bits of reality into short stories and poetry.

Doc Krinberg was raised in California where he experienced a significant amount of surfing and dead end jobs to include hot pretzel salesman, strip club barker, bouncer, Teamster and junkyard truck driver before a career as a Diver in the U.S.N. Post-navy, he earned degrees in education, enabling teaching abroad in Japan and mainland USA. Publications include numerous poetry anthologies and three novels. He has edited two anthologies. He resides in Virginia.

V.S. Lai is a Malaysian writer based in Kuala Lumpur, Malaysia. She has a BEng in Chemical Engineering from University College London and an MBA from Bayes Business School (City University of London). Her first short fiction was published in Endings and Beginnings, an anthology of short stories in 2018.

Ewan Lawrie is the author of two novels featuring the villainous Alasdair Moffat; *Gibbous House*, and *No Good Deed*. He has had poetry and short stories published in various anthologies. His poetry collection *Last Night I Met John Adcock* was shortlisted for the Welsh Poetry Prize. He spent some teenage years in Singapore.

Winston Lim is a Penang author of *Tan Sri Loh Boon Siew: The Life And Times Of A Fire Dragon*, the biography of Raymond Flower who wrote *Raffles, The Story Of Singapore*, and the Young Adult fantasy, *Billy and The Cloud Fife*.

Y.K. Lim is an English teacher, e-learning writer and self-publisher. When he is not writing e-books or online courses, he dabbles in some creative writing. In 2018, he self-published an ESL book for young learners, 61 Mostly Nonsense Rhymes for Malaysian Students. He rides his Brixton bike for inspiration.

Yvonne Lyon writes mainly historical fiction set in Lancashire where she was born and recently completed a novel inspired by her grand-parents' relationship. Her short stories have been published in a Historical Novel Society Anthology: Distant Echoes, and Vintage Script. In 2009 she released a YA novel, *Edgeburn*.

Sandeep Kumar Mishra is a bestselling author of *One Heart Many Breaks*, 2020. An outsider artist, a poet and a lecturer, he is a guest poetry editor at *Indian Poetry Review*. He has received Readers' Favorite Silver Award 2021, Indian Achievers Award 2021, IPR Annual Poetry Award 2020 and Literary Titan Book Award 2020. He was shortlisted for 2021 International Book Awards, Indies Today Book of the Year Award 2020, Joy Bale Boone Poetry Prize 2021 and Oprelle Rise up Poetry Prize 2021. He was also *The Story Mirror* Author of the Year nominee in 2019.

Ivy Ngeow was born and raised in Johor Bahru, Malaysia. She holds an MA in Writing from Middlesex University, where she won the 2005 Middlesex University Literary Press Prize out of almost 1500 entrants worldwide. Her debut, *Cry of the Flying Rhino* (2017), was awarded the International Proverse Prize in Hong Kong. Her novels include *Overboard* (2020) and *Heart of Glass* (2018). She lives in London.

A retired clinic nurse, **Krishnaveni Panikker**'s hobbies are reading, writing and people watching. She loves helping the homeless and writing about the underprivileged. It has made her see life very differ-ently. Their names are not used in her writings as she feels they deserve their dignity and privacy.

Sylvia Petter, an Australian based in Vienna, Austria, writes short, long, serious, sexy, and fun. Her stories appear online and in print, and in her collections. She holds a PhD in Creative Writing (UNSW,

2009). Her debut novel, *All the Beautiful Liars*, was published in 2021 by Lightning Books, UK.

Shafiqah Alliah Razman is a passionate Malaysian traveller in the world of literature who read English Language and Literature at the University of Nottingham Malaysia. Shaf has published poems, fiction and creative non-fiction, won several writing competitions and been a part of a literary magazine. As a shy coffee-lover and language enthusiast, she finds refuge in the art of writing and plans to be in a very long-term relationship with English. Feel free to say hi via shafiqahrazman@yahoo.com or https://shafiqahrazman5.wixsite.com/shafrazmancreative

San Lin Tun, guest editor at *Open Leaf Press Review* has authored over ten English books and several anthologies and literary magazines have showcased his writings. His novel *An English Writer* is available at Goodnovel. He is currently working on his second novel *A Classroom for Mr KT*. He lives in Yangon, Myanmar.

Yang Ming is a Singaporean writer. Her recent short play, *The Exit* was shortlisted for the Fizzy Sherbet podcast, an international platform for women writers and directors. Her writing explores women's themes and cultural identity. Now based in Singapore, Yang Ming graduated from Swansea University with a MA in Creative Writing.

Printed in Great Britain
by Amazon